T0307893

More praise for

The Pale Light of Sunset

"That old outlaw author Lee Maynard has really gone and done it this time. His new Tall Tale of a memoir/novel, *The Pale Light of Sunset*, is jam-packed with more action and adventure, more outlandish characters and bizarre events, more outrageous behavior, more laughs and tears, not to mention more pure poetry and heartfelt emotion than any book I have read in recent memory. And it is all rendered in language often so luminous that whole paragraphs seem to simply lift up off the page. Maynard says somewhere in here that we search all of our lives, some of us, for that one great thing that makes us who we are. Let me tell you folks, for Maynard that great thing is this deeply spiritual journey of a book, which is basically a roadmap of his never-ending quest for that elusive place in the heart we call home."

— Chuck Kinder, author of *Honeymooners: A Cautionary Tale* and *Last Mountain Dancer: Hard-Earned Lessons in Love, Loss, and Honky-Tonk Outlaw Life*

"Lee Maynard writes better than anyone I know about how a boy is infused with the rules of American manhood. . . .The persona Maynard creates, the experiences he offers us, make for a truly gripping book that you find yourself halfway through when you only meant to read a few pages."

— Meredith Sue Willis, author of *Oradell at Sea*

"A superb book. These stories of a lifetime are infused with a wanderer's soul, a seeker no less spiritual than what we see in the accounts of itinerant Zen monks from medieval Japan. Indeed, The Pale Light of Sunset is just such a narrative of the mind and spirit for our own time. If rural West Virginia is the point of departure and emotional keystone throughout the book, Maynard's internal and external geography is the Great Wide Open of both the planet and the human heart. This book is filled with surprise, humor (sometimes riotous, at other times wry and sly), full-bore old fashioned adventure, violence, mystery, and, finally, tenderness. Lee Maynard is teaching us to pay attention, to live the moments when they come, and savor them forever as the reasons that we are here."

— Richard Currey, author of *Fatal Light* and *Lost Highway*

"This memoir is earthy in the best sense. It's haunting. It has miracles. It also has earnest and honest questions and moments of grace."

— Marie Manilla, author of *Shrapnel*

The Pale Light of Sunset

The Pale Light of Sunset

Scattershots and Hallucinations in an Imagined Life

by Lee Maynard

Vandalia Press

Morgantown 2009

Vandalia Press, Morgantown 26506

First edition published 2009 by West Virginia University Press

Printed in the United States of America

16 15 14 13 12 11 10 09 1 2 3 4 5 6 7 8 9

ISBN-10: 1-933202-42-4

ISBN-13: 978-1-933202-42-6

(alk. paper)

Library of Congress Cataloging in Publication Data

Maynard, Lee, 1936-

The pale light of sunset : scattershots and hallucinations in an imagined life / Lee Maynard. -- 1st ed.

p. cm.

ISBN 978-1-933202-43-3 (pbk. : alk. paper)

1. Maynard, Lee, 1936---Childhood and youth. 2. Authors, American--Homes and haunts--West Virginia. I. Title.

PS3563.A96384Z46 2009

813'.54--dc22

Library of Congress Control Number: 2009013322

An edited version of "1948: My Mother's Coat" appeared in *Reader's Digest*, May 2002. (Runaway, Turning Pt. 980). An edited version of "1981: The Prayer Horse" appeared in *Reader's Digest*, April 1998. (My Only Prayer 1256)

To Darci & Toran

who light the pathways, real or imagined, of all my life

All stories are true, if they are well written.
The question is what they are telling the truth *about*.
—*Chuck Kinder*

The end is nothing. The road is all.
—*Willa Cather*

Contents

The Pale Light of Sunset

Foreword

I'm still here, Lowenstein, you son of a bitch.

1936

The Parlor

I am born in the parlor of my grandmother's house.

I come screaming into the world among the only valuable things my grandmother owns. There is a small settee on which no one is allowed to sit; a tiny table of unknown origin; a pump organ, which no one plays. A strange polka-dot vase with a string of white glass coiling around it. Doilies on everything.

And me, pulled into the world by a midwife I would never know and would never meet again.

I am born in West Virginia. I am a West Virginian. And, as are all of us, I am a child only of West Virginia. And of no where, of no one, else.

As I grow older and my mother brings me in from the mountains to visit my grandmother, I realize in my child-mind that my grandmother's house is the only place in my world where I feel safe, where I feel comfortable.

Each time, before I even go inside, I can smell the biscuits my grandmother bakes, larger than any biscuits I have ever seen, larger than my hand. My grandmother feeds me biscuits and homemade jelly and then I go back outside to play.

There is a cherry tree in the front yard and a small grape arbor stands sagging in the sunlight at the side of the house. There is a small garage, a shed, and a chicken house. And a vegetable garden, where my grandmother grows what her family eats. I love to play in the tall grass just beyond the garden, spending hours scratching in the dirt, digging trenches, building forts of sticks and twine, moving imaginary cowboys, Indians and soldiers through cataclysmic battles.

Fifty years go by before I learn that one of my mother's sisters, a twin, had been stillborn in the same parlor. A stillborn twin, a sure sign of a curse on my grandmother's family. It was too much for my grandmother, and her family, to bear. No one must know.

And there was another reason. There was no money for tiny burials.

In the stillness and quiet of a black summer night, with waves of heat pouring down the valley and out across the rivers in the distance, with the heavy scent of honeysuckle hanging in the night air, the tiny body was named, wrapped in my grandmother's prized quilt, and buried in a hand-dug grave beneath the tall grass just beyond the vegetable garden. Beneath the tall grass where I played.

But I do not grow up in my grandmother's house. I only visit there.

And then I do not visit at all.

And far away on the down side of my life, my grandmother a long time gone, I find the house gone, too. There is nothing but a shallow imprint upon the earth, faintly marking were the house once stood. There is no garage, no shed, no chicken coop, no vegetable garden.

But the grass beyond the old garden stands knee high.

I lie down in the grass and stare upward into a pale steel sky. And I realize that, had I, too, been stillborn, I would lie here, too, forever, next to an aunt whose name I never knew. Under the grass.

I close my eyes, and smell the faint aroma of biscuits baking in a wood burning stove.

1941

The Shotgun

It is the first memory I have.

I hear the old shotgun go off and I fall over backwards and roll down the side of a steep ridge through layers of leaves autumn-dropped from the hardwood trees. The gun makes a noise beyond all imagination, beyond all reason. When the gun goes off, time stops, the breeze does not blow, birds freeze in mid-flight. Bits of leaves are in my eyes and mouth and my ears ring from the terrible thunder of the 12-gauge. I try to cover my ears with my hands as I slide to a stop somewhere down the hill, my shirt full of dirt and twigs, my mind spinning. As the booming fades into the woods and across the far ridges, I can hear only the small crashing of something plowing through the leaves.

Me.

I am five years old.

I have been following my father through the dense West Virginia forest, early sunlight dripping through the gnarled trees in broken blobs of gold and yellow. Trees, the smell of leaves on the forest floor, warm sunlight, the huge gun, hunting with my father.

It is terribly hard to move quietly when you are five years old, and my father constantly glances over his shoulder at me, both, I know, to make sure I am there and as admonishment to hunt as he has told me—quietly, trying to move only when he moves, trying to stay behind him and not too close, scanning the ground and the trees in front of us. Looking, always looking.

I try to keep looking but, usually, my eyes are glued to my father, especially to his right arm, where I can see the worn and shiny stock of the gun pressed lightly between his elbow and his body. I walk in fear of the gun going off, of the noise it will make. Surely, I think, I will see his arm move and have plenty of time to put my hands over my ears.

We are squirrel hunting, and it is the first time he has allowed me to go with him. We do not hunt for sport. If he kills a squirrel, we will take it home to the tiny cabin on the side of the hill, and we will eat it.

There is a flicker of motion high on a tree limb, a gray instant of fur.

And then, for the first time, I am with him when he fires the gun.

His arms come up in a liquid, flowing movement and the barrel of the gun washes a thin blue arc against the gray of the tree trunks, a blur, a painted still life of frozen motion before my eyes. Before the blur can fade there is an explosion that shakes the limbs of the trees and makes the ground shudder and sends me over backwards and down the hill.

The shotgun is a pump-action with an outside hammer. Strangely, as I am falling over backwards, I hear him work the slide and I know there is another shell in the chamber of the gun, even before I, or the squirrel, hit the ground.

In all the times I hunt with him, I am never able to anticipate the shooting of the gun, the blur across my eyes always there before I am ready. As a child, I think it is because I am a child, and children are slow.

Later, I know it is because my father is fast, faster with his hands, and with a shotgun, than any man I will ever know. And, finally, I know it is because the old shotgun fits my father as the hands of two good friends fit together in warm greeting.

1942

Hornets 1

My uncle Stumpy's tiny general store sits almost at the foot of the hill, just off the dirt road that leads further into the mountains and to our cabin on Black Hawk Ridge.

I love my uncle, and I love his store. There are strange and magnificent things inside.

Whenever no one is looking, I run away from our cabin and down the road to the store, where my uncle pretends to hide me from my mother. I curl up under the counter where I can see the legs of my uncle's overalls and his heavy, worn brogans and where my mother pretends not to see me. My uncle takes a heavy folding knife from his pocket, punches holes in a can of tomato juice and hands it down to me. And that's how I know my mother is gone. I will stay at the store all day, and sometimes all night in my uncle's house.

Below the store, a tiny stream flows out of the holler and through a culvert installed under the dirt road by the men of the Civilian Conservation Corps, the CCC. I don't know what the name means, but I know the men. I don't remember any big machines; the hard, lean men of the CCC used picks and shovels to dig the huge ditch they put the culvert in.

The stream crosses a narrow strip of river bottom where my uncle raises corn, making the furrows with a hand plow dragged by a huge mule. Then, if there is any water left when it gets there, the stream slips into Twelvepole Creek and disappears.

Sometimes I play by the stream where it enters the culvert, right next to the road, and where I can see the front porch of the general store. Men wearing overalls and women in long dresses materialize from out of the hollers and down off the ridges and appear on the porch of the general store and they look at me and sometimes the men say teasing things and some of those things I do not understand. But I love watching the porch.

When I play by the stream I make rafts by tying twigs together with string I find behind the counter of the store. I put the rafts in the stream and then run to the other side of the road to watch them come out of the culvert. Sometimes, they don't come out. But, once, I followed a raft all the way to Twelvepole Creek and watched it slide onto the slow green water and ease through the dappled sunlight on the surface until I could not see it anymore. If I could ride that raft, I think, I could go away from here.

I do not know why I want to go away.

Across the stream from the store is my uncle's house, tucked further back into the holler. The store is my uncle's kingdom—what he says, goes. But the house is the province of my aunt and her three daughters. I try not to be inside the house, except late at night, and when they are feeding me.

In the yard, next to the dirt road, is a weeping willow tree, its delicate branches dragging to the ground, shuddering gracefully in the slightest movement of air, so different from the other trees that cover everything, except where my uncle has plowed. I am fascinated by the tree and sometimes lie under the drooping branches and pretend that no one can see me. But they always do.

And then I hear the paper hornets. I do not see them, not at first, but as I lie at the base of the tree there is a faint, angry buzz from somewhere up in the branches, a sound so delicate that I have to listen hard. I search the branches with my eyes but find nothing. The sound will go away, I think. But it does not.

The hornets build a nest as big as a football. I watch it grow as the sound grows and I realize that the very weight of the thing is pulling down the thin branch it is stuck to, until, when the nest is finished, it is only a foot or so above my reach. More hornets than I have ever seen guard the nest fiercely during the day, only to disappear inside, through a nickel-size hole, during the night. I come to hate their noise, hate them because I can no longer lie inside the branches of the willow tree, hate them because their sentries constantly buzz around me when I am playing by the stream.

Being by the stream isn't fun anymore.

I come out of my uncle's house early one hot morning, even before the general store is open. Before he opens the store, my uncle has farm work to do, and I can hear him up in the holler, at the barn, yelling cuss words at the mule.

I will go to the store and wait on the porch. For my tomato juice.

I trudge toward the store, my bare feet dragging in road dust still dew-heavy and near-mud. I am already sweating, even though I'm wearing only a pair of cut-off pants. I hear the noise from the willow tree, louder now, even more angry. But I do not see any hornets. I edge toward the tree and around to the side until I can see the nest. It is the most wondrous thing I have ever seen—someone has stuck a daub of mud into the hole of the nest. All the hornets are trapped inside.

Carefully, I grab the branch and slowly pull it down to me, so I can look, for the first time, directly at the huge, gray paper-mass of the nest, now only inches from my face, the buzzing from inside so loud I am sure that someone could hear it from the porch of the store. Except no one is on the porch.

I think about my uncle's pocketknife, about the hatchet in the tool shed, the saw in the barn. I think that, if I am very careful, I can cut down the limb and run across the narrow field and fling the stinging mass of hornets into Twelvepole Creek. And once again be able to lie under the willow tree.

While I am thinking this, while I am making my plan, the hornets tear the daub of mud out of the hole.

I am standing in the center of hell.

Hornets surround me in a cloud and for an instant I am dumbstruck, frozen in place. Then I squeeze my eyes shut and flail out with my arms, my feet finally stumbling away from the tree and I feel myself falling down the bank toward the stream. I never reach the water. I thrash violently in the tall grass, feeling the hornets on my skin. They have stung all around my eyes and I know if I try to open them the hornets may sting my eyeballs. I feel stings on my arms and back, down inside my pants, between my fingers, on my scalp, on the bottoms of my feet.

And then I am in the water and I don't feel much of anything at all.

My uncle holds my head out of the water with one hand and waves the flaming shirt with the other. He heard me scream—I do not remember screaming—and as he ran toward the willow tree, he stripped off his shirt and set fire to it with the matches he always has in his overalls. He waves the shirt violently and the flames and smoke drive off most of the hornets. When he thinks it is safe, he throws the burning shirt onto the grass, grabs me and runs for the house.

My aunt brings the big zinc washtub in from the back porch and clangs it down in the kitchen, in front of the wood-burning cook stove. The daughters, my cousins, strip off my pants and stand me in the tub, the pain from my swollen feet shooting up into my legs, to be met by the pain screaming down from the rest of my body. I am swelling everywhere, my arms sticking almost straight out—I am afraid to let them drop against my sides. With an effort beyond any that I know, I force my eyes open into slits. And when I do, I can see my girl cousins staring at my naked, deformed body.

My uncle appears in the doorway, a cardboard carton in his arms. He puts the carton on the kitchen table, rips open the top, takes out a bottle of some clear liquid, violently twists open the top and hands the bottle to my aunt. My aunt pours it over my head, letting it run from my scalp down over my face and body.

It is a bottle of rubbing alcohol.

This time, I remember screaming.

I try to escape the tub but my uncle holds me there, his strong hands grinding into the stings that are beneath them. I am not sure, but I think I can see tears in his eyes. The daughters open more bottles and my aunt pours them over me, again and again, until the carton is empty, the alcohol collecting in a shallow pool around my feet. My aunt grabs a tin dipper and scoops up the alcohol, dumping it again over my head, splashing it under my arms, using her fingers to dab it around my eyes.

Eventually, the pain becomes separated from me. It belongs to someone else, to someone who is not here in this steaming kitchen in a holler in West Virginia, maybe to someone who can walk out the back door and down the steps and off into the woods and never look back. And when I realize that someone else has the pain, that I can move outside the tub and look at the pudgy boy standing there in a pool of alcohol, when I know that the pain is his and not mine, I do not scream anymore.

They try to count the stings but cannot finish. My mother counts sixty, then gets to seventy, then tears form in her eyes and she loses count. My father thinks there are more than a hundred.

I don't care how many stings there are. I only care about being able to sit, or lie down, or stand up . . . or breathe, without pain. No one knows what to do.

Finally, my uncle carries me down to Twelvepole Creek. He wades into the creek and eases me into the water where I hold onto an overhanging branch and float motionless for hours. They all take turns coming down to the creek and sitting on the bank, watching over me. When the daughters come down, they stare constantly at my dick. There are stings on my dick, which is gorged into an oblong, red lump, so tightly swollen that I can hardly pee. It sticks up out of the water. I try to turn over, but then I can't hold onto the branch. Finally, I quit trying. They can look at my dick all they want.

Days later, my swollen body sucks back to its original size and I am able to walk again without swinging my legs out to the side. But not everything is normal. Even after the swelling goes down, I don't know if I have a normal dick. But it doesn't matter. I don't know what a normal dick is.

1943

Thanksgiving

The cabin has only two rooms. We sleep, sit and "visit" in one, cook and eat in the other. A good cabin does not need any more rooms.

My father built the cabin. He stuck the tiny shack on the side of a hill, tucked it in behind an enormous oak, one corner of the cabin firmly attached to the tree. Hug that tree, boy, my father says, because if it ever disappears this cabin will surely slide off the hill. A narrow porch runs along the front of the cabin, hanging out over the hillside, a long drop to the ground. Creaking wooden steps lead down off the end of the porch to where the hill flattens out and a small field catches the acorns and hickory nuts that came down from the hill in the autumn. Beyond the field, a creek cuts along the base of the next ridge, a creek that will flood the field at least once each year.

The shotgun, always unloaded, hangs on pegs over the front door, where my father can reach up and grab it as he goes out onto the small porch.

It is almost Thanksgiving. There is no money to buy the things that are bought at Thanksgiving. Even if there were money, the nearest town where such things can be bought is forty miles away, half of it over an unpaved road. And there is seldom gas for the old car.

But it is not my job to think about these things, not my job to wonder why there is no money, here in the dark heart of Appalachia. Whatever is, is. It is all natural, the way we live; the way things are supposed to be.

It is my job to watch my father, and watch the gun.

I cannot reach it, up there on the pegs. But I can watch it in the glow of the kerosene lamps and see the soft shine of the stock and marvel at how the wood meets the steel in a seamless blending of power and beauty. I know the slide works like silk and I swear the fore-grip has grooves in it that exactly match my father's fingers.

On cold mornings when my father takes the gun down, he will sometimes put his hand in the pocket of his tattered hunting coat, finger the heavy red shells that bulge there, and cock his head at me. It is the signal that I can go along.

But not this day.

It is now the day before Thanksgiving and my father knows there are wild turkeys in the hills. Hunting turkeys is not the same as hunting squirrels; there is little room for error, no tolerance for the clumsy steps of a seven-year-old. I am sad, but I understand.

The early cold clamps the hills, stiffening the tree branches and sometimes snapping them in the frigid breeze. I know my father does not really want to go hunting. I know that, for once, he would rather sit beside the pot-bellied stove and read his books, or talk to my mother. For once, he does not want to go out and freeze, looking for food.

But I know he will go.

He hugs my mother and runs his fingers through my hair. When he does that, I know it is now my job to stay at home, the man of the house until he comes back.

He reaches up and takes down the shotgun and slings it in the crook of his arm, his other hand in his coat pocket. He fingers the heavy shells. And then he loads the shotgun.

I have never seen him do that before, load the shotgun before he goes out the door. And why he does it on this day, I will never understand. He just does it.

My father is the sort of hunter who starts hunting when he picks up the gun, even if he is inside the house. His voice becomes lower, his step careful and silent, his whole attitude switching to one of constant alertness. If he is going to hunt, he wants to succeed. It isn't a game. It isn't a sport.

But he never loads the shotgun before he goes outside.

He eases the door open, feels the cold against his chest and squeezes through quickly, slipping the door shut behind him. And then he is gone, not a noise on the porch, not a sound from the wooden steps at the end of the cabin.

My mother and I are alone. We do not know when my father will return. We stand mute behind the closed door, listening to the flare of crackling in the pot-bellied stove that always happens when the door opens and closes and the fire gasps at the swirl of cold air that pushes into the room.

The shotgun goes off.

The door has hardly closed, we have not moved, the room has just started to seem empty without my father when the shotgun goes off, rattling the one tiny window at the end of the room and making small ripples on the kerosene in the lamps. The shotgun goes off on the porch, and the small porch roof has trapped the sound, pounding it back into the cabin, seeming to bend the walls as the rolling thunder of the blast explodes into every corner of the tiny rooms.

On the porch. The gun has gone off on the porch.

My mother's face contorts and she grabs the door latch with both hands, wrenching it open and slamming it back against the wall. I don't see her feet move but there is a flash of light against her red hair as she suddenly bursts through the door and out on the porch, looking for my father.

. . . who is standing just to the right of the door, looking sheepish.

He had stepped through the door, pulled it silently closed behind him, and looked out into the small field below our cabin.

Looked out at two tom turkeys feeding there, fat from the food that lay everywhere. Standing within range.

My father has shot a turkey, without ever getting off the porch.

It is Thanksgiving.

1944

Delivery Boy 1

There is a war and our soldiers are fighting some people, only I'm not sure who they are. I only know that they are bad people, and they live very far away from the mountains where we live. I feel safe here, in our cabin, deep in the thick shadows and dapples of sunlight that cover the hills and hollers.

But then, for some reason, the war makes us move to Baltimore, a town that I have never heard of until we arrive there in our ancient Chevrolet.

There are no cabins in Baltimore. We live in an apartment in a basement and I feel buried under a building larger than I have ever seen. There are floors above us with apartments that have windows that look out onto a wide street. But our apartment is in the back and has only one window. It looks out into an alley, into a cubicle where people throw their garbage and bags of trash. The bags are made of paper and when the late winter rains come, the bags split and spill and I sit inside the window and watch sleek wet rats creep and dart among the bags, picking and choosing as they go. One rat is larger than the others, a splotch of gray-white on his side. I see him often. I have never had a pet and I think I will give the rat a name, even though he is outside and I am not. But I do not name him. I am embarrassed to think that I would name a rat.

But the cubicle is a safe place and sometimes I go out there and hide among the bags of garbage, digging down deeply until I am warm. There is a cubicle behind every building on the alley and now and then wondrous things are thrown into them. Once I found a dress lying on top of one of the bags in a cubicle down the alley and I proudly took it home and gave it to my mother. She cried and made me scrub my hands and stand against the wall. She held the dress away from her, as though it were hot, and went into the hallway and out the back door. When she came back she didn't have the dress and she was still crying. I stood against the wall for an hour before she let me go. When I went out to the garbage cubicle, the dress was thrown on top of the pile. It was a perfectly good dress.

When I go out in front of the apartment building there is only the cracked concrete of the sidewalk, the mottled pavement of the streets and the hard faces of drab buildings that, for some reason, have shiny marble steps. There is nothing soft, nothing green. But I have no choice. There is the alley and the cubicles, or there is the street. There are no other places for me to go.

There are other kids in the neighborhood but none of them talk like me. They make fun of the way I talk and they chase me and I am dumbfounded to learn that I cannot outrun them. I have never known kids who could run so fast.

And when they catch me, we fight. There is nothing else for us to do.

Their mothers are just inside the windows in the apartment buildings, looking out into the street. When they see us fighting they come running out and drag their kids away, up the marble steps and into the cool insides of the buildings. But my mother never comes running out. She is in the basement, in two tiny rooms at the far back of the building, by the cubicle with rats, and she never hears me when the fight is on and I am screaming.

Gradually, I learn to fight, to play in the streets, and to stay alive there.

I sit on the cold marble steps of the apartment building and wonder why we are here. And how long we must stay. Once, I ask my mother that question and she says, “For the duration,” and there are tears in her eyes. I don’t know what a duration is, and I’m afraid to ask, afraid that my mother will cry again.

I still don’t know about the war. But somehow we seem closer to it, here in Baltimore. There are sometimes men in the streets at night wearing hard hats and carrying flashlights and warning us to keep our windows dark. We only have one window and it is always dark. No light escapes beyond the cubicle with the trash.

There is a small drugstore next door and on its shelves are glass ashtrays with a picture on the bottom of a man with funny hair and a tiny moustache. People are supposed to crush their cigarettes against his face. I ask the man in the drugstore who he is, this man with the tiny moustache. The drugstore man is surprised I do not know.

“Where are you from, boy?” he asks, his words slipping out in some musical cadence I have not heard before.

“Wes’ Vurgin’yuh,” I answer.

There is another man in the drugstore. “Hill nigger,” he says, looking at me.

Both of the men laugh and I know they are laughing at me.

I don’t know what a hill nigger is but somehow it is bad, and I am bad. It scares me.

I am always afraid, here in the city of Baltimore.

I sit on the white marble steps of our apartment building and watch the students come and go from the school across the street. It is Saturday, but, still, there are students there and I marvel that young people would go to school on a Saturday. The school is called a "polytechnic institute" and I would like to go over there and learn what they do, but I am too young. And I am a hill nigger. That's what some of the students call me, those students across the street, older and knowing much more than I. But now I know what a nigger is and I wonder why they call me that. I am not black.

The drugstore man comes out of his little store and stands in the morning light. He looks at me and I look away, and when I look back he is walking toward me.

"Know how to ride a bicycle?"

"Yes." I lie. I have never had a bicycle, never been on one.

"There's a bike out behind the store. Back there where the trash is. I keep it back there in case I need a delivery. You want to make some deliveries for me? I'll pay you, and you can ride the bike."

I go through the apartment building and out the back door and into the cubicle behind the drugstore. The bike is there, leaning against the wall. It is tall and heavy, has no fenders, and there is a wide crack in the worn seat. It is beautiful.

I take the bike out into the alley and try to ride it. I have seen other kids in the neighborhood ride bikes and there seems to be nothing to it. I climb on and push off but before my feet can find the pedals the bike hits the cold brick wall across the alley and I am popped forward off the saddle and my stomach is crushed against the handlebars. I slump against the bike and cannot stop the groans from escaping my throat.

I point the bike down the alley and try again. This time the handlebar catches on a trash can and the bike spins crazily into a cubicle and I am thrown hard into some bags of garbage. I feel something tear in my side, but the pain is not too bad and I climb back on the bike. By the end of the day, I can stay upright to the end of the alley, where the real street begins.

And then I realize that I will have to ride the bike in that street.

I do not tell my mother about my new job.

A few days later the drugstore man asks me to make a delivery. He gives me a brown paper bag and shows me a piece of white paper with the address written on it and explains to me how to get there. He says that I must remember the address, that I must never carry the piece of white paper, that I must never write the address on the bag. The address is not too far away and the bike flies over the streets and it is magic. For the first time in my life I have a sense of freedom. I am on a machine that can fly and all I have to do is point it where I want to go and I can go there. Fast.

I find the address and go into the building and find the name on the mailboxes in the vestibule. The building seems nicer than the one I live in and I wonder what the apartments look like, how people live who didn't come here from West Virginia. I decide I will try to look into the apartment when I hand over the bag.

I drag the bike into the vestibule. I ring the bell. In a few seconds there is a buzzing sound and I pull open the door and go inside.

I tap lightly at the door of the apartment. The door opens immediately, but only a crack, just enough to push the bag inside, and that's what I do. Someone takes the bag and the door closes immediately. I never see them.

I stand in the hallway for a moment, not realizing that my delivery is over. It is my first delivery, my first job, and somehow I think that there is supposed to be something more to it. I have done it. It is important. And no one cares.

Downstairs, I take the magic bicycle and ride into the street, but do not go straight back to the drugstore. I ride around the block and then down an alley and then around another block. I see some other kids playing and I ride near them, but one of them yells something I do not understand and makes a fist.

I ride out of there.

Back at the drugstore I park the bike in the cubicle. The drugstore man asks if I had any trouble, if I had seen anyone. I don't know why I should have trouble; I tell him that I have seen no one. I do not tell him about the kid who yelled and made the fist.

"Good," he says. "You check with me every day." He gives me a dime.

I will check with him every day. I want to ride the magic bicycle.

But he doesn't even know my name.

It is late summer and the bike is not magic anymore. It is just a bike.

I make deliveries for the drugstore man and the sun cuts down into the hard streets of Baltimore and bakes my neck and forehead. Sweat soaks my shirt and runs in streams down into the tops of my pants and once, when I get off the bike, the drugstore man thinks I have wet my pants and he wants to know why I did that. He doesn't believe me when I tell him it is sweat, but he gives me my dime anyway.

It is a Saturday morning. The heat is already making the tiny patches of street tar bubble and the kids are poking them with their fingers, yelling when the tar sticks and burns.

The ice man parks his truck in front of our building and uses fierce metal tongs to lift a square block of ice from the back of the truck and carry it into the dark, cool hallway. I hear his feet climbing the stairs. I hear him stumble once from the weight of the ice.

Ice water drips through the floor of the truck. It is like a magnet. One of the neighborhood kids climbs on the back of the truck and opens the door. The inside of the truck is dark and cool. The walls are lined with wood long since saturated with the wetness of melting ice, softening into a velvet surface that smells of something that I can only remember as . . . something melting. And I know that I will remember that smell for the rest of my life.

There are several ice picks stuck into one of the walls and the kid grabs one of them and jumps out into the street. He waves the pick around, pointing it at us, jabbing, laughing. I think he is afraid to get too close, knowing that we might fight him for the pick. And we are afraid to run, knowing he will chase us. We stare at the pick, and we know that something on the street has changed.

The ice man comes out of the building and chases all of us, his huge feet slapping on the hot sidewalk. We run to the corner and split up, some of us running down the alley. The kid with the pick drops it but the ice man doesn't notice and when the chase finally ends, the ice man has caught no one and each of us is hiding in whatever his favorite hiding place is. I am in the cubicle outside our apartment.

The next day I find the pick lying in the gutter. I pick it up. After that, I have it with me all the time.

It is raining and I am bored and I go to the drugstore to see if there are any deliveries. A policeman is coming out of the door, and he turns and locks it. I do not know why a policeman would have a key to the drugstore.

"Tell your Ma the drugstore is closed, kid," he says, not even looking at me. Rains drips from the shiny bill of his hat. I know he thinks I am there on an errand for my mother.

"We got this guy, and we'll get the rest of 'em. We'll get 'em, you can bet yer arse on that. Put ever one of 'em in the big house. Won't be long before there ain't gonna be no more drugs in this city, nossir."

I do not tell him about my job as a delivery boy. I do not tell him about the bicycle and the brown paper bags and the apartment doors that only open wide enough for a hand to reach out. Instead, I run down the street and back to the alley, back to the cubicle outside our apartment. I crawl over the garbage bags and hide against the back wall. I pull out the ice pick and hold it out in front of me. And I wait. They'll get 'em all, he said. I wonder how long it will take.

And I hear a rat sliding through the garbage below me.

1945

Delivery Boy 2

The war is over.

The people of Baltimore walk hand-in-hand in the streets, some of them hugging and kissing. Traffic stops for no reason at all, everybody waves flags, musicians stand on corners and play clangy music, saloons block their doors open and hand free beer to men who go by on the sidewalks.

I want to celebrate, too, but I don't know how. Or why. Yes, I know about the war, now. About the huge Germans and the tiny Japanese who wear funny glasses. I have been told about how they might have landed just over there, on the shores of Maryland, marched down the street and taken over the school on North Avenue, just across from our apartment building. I never understand why they would want the school, but I am sure it is important.

And then my father gives me reason to celebrate.

We are going back to West Virginia, my father says. We are leaving the city of Baltimore. My mother is crying.

I never think about going back to West Virginia, or whether or not I like it there. I only know that I don't belong in the city of Baltimore. I only know that I want to leave before the policeman comes back.

And so I am happy. We are leaving, going someplace. We will pack some stuff in the Chevrolet and drive away, back down and through the mountains to a place where trees grow anywhere, not just in the tiny patches of dog-pissed dirt between sidewalks and streets. Where water runs in creeks, and there are no gutters.

I think about leaving the city of Baltimore and I am happy, very happy.

I go out the back door of our building, into the alley. I climb over the wooden wall that covers the back of the drugstore, open the gate from the inside and push the old magic bicycle out into the alley. I have been stealing the bicycle and riding it ever since they put the For Rent sign on the front of the drugstore. I think that no one will notice until they take the sign down. I always put the bicycle back, so I am only a thief while I am riding it.

I ride the bicycle down the alley, out into the side street and around onto North Avenue. It is like a party. People have not gone to work, or they have left work and are just walking around, like in some sort of dream. Across the street, at the school, the doors are open and students lie on the grass, books thrown down all around them.

I am trying to celebrate, but I don't know how. I don't remember ever "celebrating" anything. What am I supposed to do? I ride the bicycle around in circles in the middle of the street. Most of the traffic doesn't move and I ride on and off the sidewalk, waiting to learn how to celebrate.

A man is walking down the street handing tiny American flags to everyone. His pockets are full of flags, and if he can't find anyone to give one to, he tapes them onto cars and the fronts of buildings. He sees me riding the bicycle and he walks out into the street and stops me.

"Here, kid, everybody got to have a flag," he says. "Greatest flag in the world," he says. As he hands one to me I can smell a sourness on him, the same smell that comes out of the doors of saloons when I sneak past them in the late afternoon. I take the flag, but now I only have one hand free. Can I ride a bicycle with one hand? He takes the flag back and tapes it to the handlebars. Right in the middle.

"Hell," he says, "looks pretty good there, don't it?" And then he tapes another flag on the handlebars.

"Where you from, kid?" I almost say Wes' Vurgin'yuh but then I catch myself and just nod toward my apartment building.

When he walks away, there are flags taped all over the bicycle. There are flags all across the handlebars, on the bent and rusty frame, on the metal bars that hold the wheels. I have more flags than anyone. I have learned how to celebrate.

I ride up and down the block, showing off my flags. I decide to show them to people on the next block, and then the next, and then . . . and then I am riding down a street I've never ridden on before and there are people sitting on steps in front of apartment buildings and they sit there almost quietly and seem nervous and they watch me as I ride by, my tiny flags flapping, a huge idiot smile on my face.

Far down the block some bigger kids, maybe a couple of grades older than me, see me coming and they stroll out into the middle of the street. I ride toward them, to show them my flags. To celebrate. Maybe I'll even tell them I am leaving the city of Baltimore.

I stop. There is a silent and unseen signal that cuts through from them to me, the same signal that I know cuts between a hawk and a rabbit, a signal as old as anger. I turn the wheel of the bicycle and start to move slowly in a circle, not really riding, just pushing the bike. I'm halfway around before I see that there are other kids behind me. I stop again. No one moves.

"What block you from?" His words sound funny, like he is trying to connect them with other letters that don't have any words. He isn't the biggest kid, but he is a step out in front of the others.

"I don't know the name of it. It's just a block." I smile.

He doesn't smile back. He turns his head to the others.

"Don't know his own fuckin'a block. Don't even know his own territory." He takes a step closer. He can almost reach me.

"Get off'a the fuckin' bike."

I hit him full in the middle of his face and I hear something crack. He goes down as I leap off the falling bike and another kid jumps over him and I hit that kid, too, only I am off balance and I don't put him on the ground. So I kick him in the balls. Somebody grabs me from behind and spins me and I am swinging as I turn but my fist never gets there. The sharpest punch I have ever been hit with drives into my ribs and I lose all my breath faster than I thought I could. And then I am crawling on the street and fists and feet are bouncing off every part of me. I reach behind my back and fumble at my belt for the ice pick that I carry there, but it is gone. I roll over and puke, and they stop hitting me. I guess they don't want the puke on their fists.

I sit up, still feeling sharp little pains inside me, as though someone is working a needle in there. I watch as the other kids rip the little flags off the bike, breaking the thin sticks that hold them in place, throwing them on the street, stomping on them. And stomping on the magic bicycle. They bend the spokes and twist the handlebars. One kid unfolds a knife and drives it into the tires.

After a while, they get tired of that. A little kid ambles over and pulls out his dick and pisses on the bike. From high up in one of the buildings, I hear someone laugh. And then they all walk away.

I sit in the middle of the silent street with the busted magic bicycle, blood seeping out of my nose, puke running down the front of my shirt. And then I think I should try to get the hell out of there before they decide they aren't through with me yet. I manage to get to my feet. I wrap my arms around my ribs and stagger down the middle of the street, back the way I came.

"You not Ee-tal-eeano, you don't come back here." I didn't look around to see who said it.

We are leaving the city of Baltimore.

I don't know why we came here in the first place.

1946

Sometimes It Will Be Harder

We have come back and we live again deep within the ancient soul of Appalachia, Black Hawk Ridge. Along the ridge and down through the hollers and up the creeks and branches and beside the rutted dirt roads relatives are strung in a web of history that traps us, where, over generations, the very soul of our family seeps into the bark of trees and rides on shafts of light that streak through the forest.

But we are related. And we survive. And that is the way of things.

Once again, I am following my father through the dense West Virginia forest, early sunlight glittering through the gnarled trees in ragged shards of gold and yellow. We leave the tiny cabin on the side of the hill before first light comes to the mountains. We leave without eating and I am hungry. I don't know why we left without eating.

We are squirrel hunting. Again.

We did not squirrel hunt in the city of Baltimore.

Trees. The smell of leaves on the forest floor. Warm sunlight. The huge old shotgun my father is carrying. It is all part of hunting, and I love it all. But I am hungry.

We do not hunt for sport. We hunt for something to eat.

I wonder why we don't just walk out of the holler and down the dirt road to the tiny general store and buy something to eat. It seems much simpler than hunting.

I explain this to my father. Why don't we just do that? I ask. He looks at me for a long moment and there is a veil across his eyes that I have never seen before and for some reason he seems angry with me.

There is a flicker of motion high on a tree limb, a gray instant of fur.

And then, once again I am with him when he fires the gun.

His arms come up in a liquid, flowing movement and the barrel of the gun washes a thin blue arc . . .

But I have told you that before.

My father, and the shotgun, never change.

And I fall down. Again.

The thunder happens twice more, and only on the last time do I not fall down.

We start back across the ridge toward the cabin.

I venture that there are still more squirrels, still more shooting that could be done. He looks at me calmly. If we kill them now, he explains, we will have to eat them now. And we already have what we need. That is enough.

At the cabin my father cleans the tiny animals, one each for my mother, him, and me. It is now nearly noon and I am very hungry.

When can we eat? I ask my mother. My mother is beautiful and her red hair glistens in the soft light that filters into the cabin.

When the cooking is done, she says. And while you are waiting, wash the greens.

I take the bowl of green leaves outside and pour cold water on them from a dented metal bucket, the bail long since lost or used to repair something broken. I do not know what the green things are, but I know she has picked them wild from the side of the hill.

I put the bowl on the table. I hear the lids clank on the stove as my mother adds wood and I smell the meat beginning to fry in the large iron skillet.

I fold myself back into a corner by the stove where I can feel the heat against my face. I am happy. I have gone hunting with my father. We will eat.

I do not know that we are poor.

Later, I ask my mother, Will it always be this way?

For a moment she is still, looking at me with eyes so shiny that I don't know what color they are.

What way, she asks.

I have no answer. I don't really know what I want to know.

She bends and hugs me. No, she says, sometimes it will be harder. But you must always find a way.

Older, now. I went out and beyond. I went into a world that was sometimes light and sometimes dark and during the dark times I would lie frozen in the darkness and listen for the faint echo of the old shotgun through woods that were forever beyond my reach.

I learned the darker definitions of rich, and poor, and hunger.

And my father was right. Having what you need is enough.

And my mother was right. Sometimes it is harder.

Desperately harder.

1947

Hornets 2

The old green Chevrolet climbs Bull Mountain slowly, grinding its way over the top in the heat of mid-summer, slowly picking up speed as we lumber down into Bull Creek.

We are going to Huntington.

My father drives, my mother in the passenger seat. I sit in the rear, where I am always made to sit, looking straight ahead, trying to keep my stomach calm enough so I do not throw up. My father hates it when I get sick, hates stopping the car, hates waiting for me to bend over at the side of the road and puke, sometimes puking so hard that I nearly pass out, losing my balance and lurching against a tree or a rusty guardrail. Once, head spinning, I fell forward into my own puke and then skidded down a small bank, leaves and dirt sticking to the puke, ruining the shirt my mother had ironed for this trip. My father would not let me back in the car until I had climbed farther down the bank to a small creek and washed out my clothes, standing naked in the cool water, glad that the water was mingling with my tears so that no one would notice. So that I would not notice.

We were going to Huntington that time, too, and I rode the rest of the way in my wet underwear, my pants and shirt flapping outside the rear window.

I stare straight ahead, the hot air streaming in through the open windows and pushing against my face. I breathe deeply, trying not to think about my stomach.

And then a hornet flies in through the window and hits me in the center of my forehead. I catch a glimpse of it just before it hits and I think it is huge, the size of a hummingbird. Yes, the size of a hummingbird. I am positive.

The hornet whacks into my forehead and bounces off into that space behind the rear seat where it buzzes angrily against glass of the window.

I am trapped in the back seat with a hornet.

I feel the terror in my throat.

I twist in the seat and dive to the floor, a space so tight that I barely fit. I know I am pushing against the back of my father's seat, but I do not care. I raise my head slightly so I can see the hornet . . . and I am back standing under my uncle's willow tree, the paper hornets swarming over my body, the stings coming so rapidly that I do not know where I am being stung, only that my skin is a sheet of pain, my eyelids are stung shut, and my mind is shutting down. And all I can hear is the buzzing.

And I hear the buzzing now, here, in the back seat.

I scream. I had not known, until that moment, that a mortal fear of hornets lurked in some dark recess of my heart.

My father pretends not to hear. He has seen the whole thing in the mirror. He drives carefully, still easing the old car down the mountainside.

The hornet makes a sweeping arc out of the rear window and down past my face. I scream again.

My father slams on the brakes. The old car sits on the highway, engine running, my mother with her arms braced against the dash. She looks at my father. My father reaches down and grabs the handle of the parking brake and jerks it toward him. I hear the ratchet sound of the brake locking and then a car door opening and then my father is ripping open the door to the back seat. He reaches in, grabs me and jerks me from the car. I hit the hot blacktop and slide, skin coming off my elbows. But I'm still focused on the hornet and I do not seem to notice any other pain. I sit up on the hot pavement and watch as my father flails his arms against the back window, trying to crush the hornet. He hits it a glancing blow, knocking it out of the car and onto the road. My father, moving slowly now, steps carefully away from the car and, with one dramatic stomp, mashes the hornet into the hot tar.

My breath catches in my throat and I realize I have been sobbing. I look up at my father. I am so grateful that he has killed the hornet. I want to tell him how grateful I am but I don't know how, so I just stare at him, my face wet with tears.

My father doesn't look at me. He closes the rear door and then gets back behind the steering wheel.

Why has he closed the rear door? I wonder. I stand up and reach for the handle.

The car moves forward, just out of my reach.

"Walk," my father says.

I am stunned. There is nowhere to walk to, just the road, baking in the hot light of summer, leading on and on into the mountains. I don't move.

"Walk," my father says again. "I don't want a coward in my car. Cowards walk."

A recognition settles into my mind and into my heart, a recognition of what I am and what my father thinks of me, maybe has always thought of me. I begin to walk, moving past the car and down the mountain, my heavy shoes almost silent on the hot tar at the edge of the road. Tears form in my eyes and I can hardly see, but I won't raise my arms to wipe them away because I know my father will see that I am crying again. I walk around a curve and out of sight of the car. I am far enough away that I can hear nothing but the buzz of insects in the weeds.

And then I hear the car coming.

I hear the engine roaring, my father driving fast. The car rounds the curve and flashes by me. Out of the corner of my eye I can see my mother looking out the window at me but I cannot really see her face, cannot really see what she is feeling.

And as the car goes by, I scream. Again.

I can't help it. The scream just comes up out of me and is into the world before I can stop it. I know my mother has heard the scream. And I know my father has heard.

Down the road, almost to another curve, I see the brake lights of the car come on and the old Chevy slowly rolls to a stop. It does not back up. It sits there, waiting, as I stumble toward it.

And as I stumble, I form a pledge in my mind, a promise, I swear an oath to some power that I don't even know . . .

I will never scream for my father again.

1948

My Mother's Coat

We are a small family surviving within a tiny existence. My father works two jobs and has to travel into the next county. He goes to work early and comes home late and sometimes, when he has not been paid and there is no gas for his crippled car, he does not come home at all. I sometimes wonder why he does not come home.

I am a child filled with no knowledge and a vivid imagination and I feel that I do not belong here. At every opportunity I run away. But there is no place to run to. We no longer live on Black Hawk Ridge or near any of our relatives. I can only run into the brooding hills or down along the muddy river. But that does not stop me. I run away. It is what I do.

And I have done it again.

This time, I have run to the woods because I imagine I have suffered some slight. My imagination, and my fearful, rigid sense of little-boy-right-and-wrong. I would show *her.* I'd make her sorry. I ran to the woods.

But now I am cold and hungry and I know that it is time to leave the hills. But when I come crashing down out of the woods and stumble through the chill of weak evening light to the ramshackle clapboard house on the riverbank, she is gone.

My mother.

Mothers are not supposed to be gone.

I charge through the small rooms, breathing in the scent of her, knowing that she has been here, waiting for me.

There is no fire in the stove and the house is chilled. She is gone. Without her, the house has no meaning.

I run outside and circle the house, my feet thumping on the hard-packed clay. A dog I have never seen before slinks under the porch, but I am not interested in dogs.

I run to the small shed where I keep treasure, flotsam I have pulled from the river, iron things found on the railroad tracks, things I will never part with. Maybe my mother is waiting for me here, knowing that each day I check to see that my treasure is safe. I pull open the sagging door, the rusty hinges squealing. Nothing alive is in the shed.

I run hard along the riverbank, stiff little tines of river brush whipping across my face. I come to a neighbor's house, a quarter-mile down the river.

No, boy, yer ma ain't here. Come by when hit was full light. Jist went on by. Said . . . well, didn't say much thet I can re-call. Jist run off in a right hurry, like.

Run off.

Why?

Maybe she has wanted to run off for a long time. What is she doing in our clan, anyway? What is she doing out here in this place, where there is no piano to play, where no one sings, where no one can hear the lilt of her voice?

And why did she leave me here?

Mothers are not supposed to run away. Only I can run away.

I run back to the house, dark now, dead with the absence of my mother.

I sit on the rocks that form the steps to the back porch and wrap my arms around myself against the chill; I listen to the river and try to control my imagination.

Finally, I wander to the edge of the riverbank and throw clods of dirt out into the weak light, watching them burst below me in a narrow cane field that has just been cut. On the far side of the field, river willows guard the water and I try to throw the clods into the willows. And then I see, dangling from one of the willows, my mother's ragged coat.

I crash down the riverbank and across the cane stubble to the coat. I can't see any tracks in the dim light but—my imagination explodes—I know where she has gone. She has run away to a dark and foreign land. She has crossed the river into Kentucky.

I storm my way down through the willows and crash into the water and flail out into the river yelling for my mother and yelling and yelling until my voice finally stops and the only sound I hear is my own fractured breathing in the early night as I float downstream.

And then silence.

I climb up the slimy bank and find the coat again. I hate it, that ragged sign of my mother's running away. I'll tear it to shreds. I grab it and pull at it, whirling it against the black sky, ripping it against the brush, stomping it into the soft earth. A large, flat, brown button rips off in my hand, and that is the only real damage I do to the coat before I fling it over the willows and into the river.

I don't want to go inside the house. In the shed I find a tattered horse blanket and I sit there, wrapped against the chill and the wet and the ice that plugs my heart. I am still sitting there in the morning when the cold light seeps over the high ridge and down into the valley and my mother comes down the dirt lane that bends toward the house, walking with that grace that none of us will ever have, the light glistening in her red hair, a shawl wrapped around her shoulders.

I do not move, terrified that what I am seeing will vanish even as tears form in my eyes. She sees me, but says nothing. I can tell she is angry with me. After all, yesterday I ran away.

When the stove is fired and the house is warming, I slink into the kitchen and sit on the woodbox in the corner. She is talking, as though to herself, but I know she is really talking to me. A downriver neighbor lady was ill, and my mother went to help.

But I seed yer coat down on the riverbank.

Saw. You *saw* my coat. I gave it to the downriver neighbor girl. I have a shawl, and she didn't have a coat. I expect she never even got home with it. You know she isn't quite . . . right.

She looks at me and I see a face that I have not seen before. She knows what I have been thinking, that she had run away.

Real people don't run away *from*, she says. That isn't the way to live your life. But real people can run away *to*, if there's something there that's better.

And that is all she says. And it is my way out.

She feeds me breakfast, biscuits and bacon and hand-churned butter, and I know that I am forgiven.

When the late evening light slips up and away from the roof of the house, I go to the shed and look at my treasure. And suddenly it isn't treasure anymore. In the growing dark I carry the worthless stuff to the edge of the riverbank and throw it over, piece by piece.

I never tell her about the coat.

1949

Mean Rafe

He has hands that can wrap around a beer bottle like my hands wrap around a broomstick. And he wraps his hands around a lot of beer bottles.

His name is Rafe Hensley but we call him Mean Rafe. But not to his face. And only when he is drunk. And only when we are not within his reach. He is the meanest man in town. Mean Rafe has a brother, Cobb, who does not live here. If Cobb lived here, Cobb would be the meanest man in town. But we seldom see Cobb in town, or anywhere else.

It is a summer Saturday in Crum, West Virginia, and Mean Rafe is painting his house. Mean Rafe hates to paint. But each summer, like some sort of religious thing, Mean Rafe paints his house without ever scraping off any of the old paint, layer after layer of new paint going on over the old, cracked layers, the slab-sided house seeming to groan under the weight of countless brush-strokes of thick heavy gunk bought on sale at the general store.

Before any of the paint is dry, a coal train rumbles down the tracks that are so close to Rafe's house that he could throw paint on them if he wanted to. And, now and then, he wanted to. But not now. Now, Rafe simply watches the black monster engine go by, its smoke billowing, a cloud of tiny, hateful cinders raining down on the dirt lane, on Rafe's rusted pickup truck, drifting into the drinking water in the bucket on the porch of Rafe's house.

And onto the wet paint that Rafe has just slapped onto his house.

Mean Rafe hates to paint.

He stands silently, hating the paint, hating the train, hating everything in sight.

To ease his hate, Mean Rafe has been drinking while he has been painting. There is a washtub under the edge of the porch with a handwidth of cool well water in the bottom. Beer bottles and at least one Mason jar of moonshine lie in the water. Mean Rafe paints with one hand and holds a beer bottle, or the Mason jar, in the other, sipping, constantly sipping. The more he paints the more he drinks, and the more he drinks the slower he paints until he isn't painting at all.

Mean Rafe sits on the ground, leaning back against the trunk of a scraggly tree, quietly staring at the half-painted side of the house, sipping, constantly sipping.

The three of us—Nip, Mule and me—watch from across the railroad track. It is Saturday, and Mean Rafe is drunk. And we know that, like many Saturdays, this may be another Saturday to remember.

Mean Rafe's wife sticks her head around the corner of the house. She sees Rafe sitting there, under the scraggly tree, moving only the arm that raises the beer bottle to his mouth. Her expression does not change. She says nothing. Nothing here is new to her.

It is late. The bottle is empty. Mean Rafe struggles to his feet, stands staring at the tub beneath the porch, then moves off slowly toward his rusted pickup truck.

We pray that the engine will start.

And it does.

Mean Rafe drives away down the cinder-covered lane, heading down-river to the railroad crossing and the pitted two-lane highway on the other side, driving slowly and carefully through the shadows.

Mean Rafe is going to the Mountaintop Beer Garden. There, he will find someone to fight. It is what he does.

We race down the track to where we have left our bicycles.

It is a long way to the Mountaintop Beer Garden, and all uphill. The sad old bar sits on the ridge at the top of Bull Mountain where the highway leaves the Tug River valley and snakes down into the twisted land that leads away to . . . God knows where. We have never ridden our bicycles down the other side of Bull Mountain, fearing that the people who live over there would never let us come back. We actually believe that sort of thing in Crum.

By the time we get to the top of the mountain it is almost full dark. The old wooden building looks as though it is preparing to slip off the mountain, its collection of beer-swilling drunks the only thing holding it in place. We see Rafe's truck parked at an odd angle up against the side of the hill, as though he just let it come to rest wherever it wanted. The driver's door is hanging open. There are a bunch of other old cars and trucks strewn randomly about the dirt parking area.

We walk around in the circle of yellow light thrown by the one naked light bulb hanging above the door of the beer joint. We stretch our legs and breathe heavily, all the time watching that no one sees us.

We sneak around the side of the building, push through some brush and garbage, find some beer crates to stand on, and put our faces close to a window filthy with substances of unknown origin. Although most of the filth is on the inside, we try not to touch the glass.

We squint our eyes, as though that will make the glass cleaner. We peer carefully into the saloon. We are worried that Rafe will already have found his fight and that it will all be over, worried that all we will get to see is some other drunk lying on the beer- and piss-stained wooden floor.

But everything is quiet inside the Mountaintop Beer Garden.

Rafe is standing at the bar, his back to the door, a bar stool lying on its side on the floor behind him.

The only other guy at the bar is thin, youngish-looking, maybe in his twenties, but we do not really know. His straight blond hair comes down over his forehead and a light tan jacket covers his slight shoulders. There are some odd-looking colored patches sewn on his jacket, but we cannot see what they are. He leans against the far end of the bar, sips beer, a half-empty pint jar of moonshine on the bar in front of him. He does not look at Rafe. He does not look at anyone. His eyes just stare at nothing. We have never seen him before.

There are a bunch of others in the room, maybe eight or ten, but they are sitting at tables near the door and at the side of the room, not looking at Rafe, not looking at anyone, not even talking with each other. They are being very careful. None of them want to attract Rafe's attention.

The only other guy in the place is Woody, the owner, who is behind the bar. None of us have ever seen Woody anywhere else. We think he sleeps there, behind the bar.

Rafe is grumbling to himself. We can hear his grumbling coming through a crack in one of the window panes, the gravel sound of his voice seeming to widen the space in the broken glass.

We wait. Sooner or later we will see the show we came for.

Rafe is getting restless. He turns and roars something toward the back of the room, the sound of a drunken man trying to make some sense out of his world and failing.

No one responds.

We wait.

All the time we wait and watch, Rafe has not looked directly at the young guy at the end of the bar. It is as though the kid isn't there, as though he is nothing more than another fly speck in a room where fly specks do not even register. The fact that Rafe is ignoring him makes the kid's presence all the more prominent. But if the kid is aware of it, he gives no sign.

A pickup truck turns off the road and into the dirt lot, its lights sweeping the building. We duck down behind the brush and trash. The driver goes inside and we go back to our window. The driver has just come into the light.

It's Cobb.

Somehow, in the tiny bit of time we ducked down out of the lights of the truck, things inside the beer garden changed.

Rafe is standing with his back to the bar and the blond kid is standing directly in front of him. We will never know, when we tell this story over and over again, how the kid got there, in front of Rafe. But there he is. Maybe Rafe's big mouth just got to the kid and he thought he had to do something. That is the problem with people with guts, they end up thinking they have to do something.

We can see that Rafe is mad, his mouth open and working, but no sound coming out, cords standing out in his neck, his fists clenched.

The kid just stands there, looking right into Rafe's face, his arms dangling at his sides. He doesn't turn his head when Cobb comes in. Maybe he saw him in the cloudy mirror behind the bar. Maybe he didn't.

Cobb eases over to a table and sits down. He does not take his eyes from the kid.

Rafe is saying things to the kid more quietly now, making sure the kid knows Rafe is talking only to him.

The kid says nothing; does not move.

Rafe's big fist shoots out, a massive hammer flying straight at the kid's face. The kid sees it coming and rolls a little, just enough to keep his head from being split but not enough to get away entirely. The huge wad of knuckles catches the kid a glancing blow on the jaw, staggers him backward. He hits a chair, falls, rolls over backward and is up again in a split second.

Rafe walks away from the bar, not expecting the kid to get up—or, if he does get up, to run for the door, because he is, after all, Mean Rafe.

We think the fight is over. And we are disappointed in how little time it took.

But the kid is on his feet and sliding toward Rafe, never quite taking his feet off the floor. Rafe turns. As the kid gets within range, his left fist snaps back almost into his own armpit as his right fist shoots out in an absolutely straight line and into the center of Rafe's chest. There is a thumping sound as the fist drives into muscle and bone. We can hear it.

Rafe's breath whistles out in a long gasp and his knees sag, just enough to let the others in the room know that Mean Rafe has been hit as hard as he has ever been hit.

Rafe recovers enough to throw more punches, and he and the kid seem to fly around the room, Rafe throwing his big fists and the kid throwing nothing—he spears, his fists shooting out from back against his body like sharp pistons, slamming into Rafe's body and head, all the kid's weight behind them.

The other men back away from the tables and spread themselves along the walls, trying to stay out of the way.

Then the kid steps into Rafe, pulling the big man's body into him, bending at the same time. Rafe comes off his feet as lightly as a bouncing ball, flies over the kid's shoulder and is driven into the floor in a thundering crash that shakes the window we are looking through.

Rafe is on the floor, his face a mass of pulp, his eyes open, but not seeing.

The kid is bleeding from somewhere, blood on his face and hands. But he is standing up.

Until Cobb hits him with a chair.

He does not catch the kid solidly with it, but solid enough that the chair breaks and the kid flies across the room, rolls over a table and slams into a wall. He slams hard, seems to actually stick to the wood, then slides slowly to the floor. He ends up sitting there, facing Cobb, his eyes glazed but wide open in surprise. His left arm is twisted at an odd angle and he holds it with his right hand, trying to ease it back into place.

Behind Cobb, we see Rafe slowly getting to his feet, wobbling, looking at the kid. He picks up another chair and half-staggers toward the kid, raising the chair as he comes.

The kid watches him come, almost as though waiting for Rafe to give it up, to drop the chair.

Rafe does not.

The kid, still sitting on the floor, reaches under his jacket and comes out with a pistol that we later learn is an army issue Colt .45. He points it at Rafe and Rafe stops in his tracks, the chair still raised above his head. Their eyes hold each other and neither moves, the kid holding the pistol steady and Rafe unsure what to do with the chair.

Cobb has already decided. Half hidden behind Rafe, Cobb reaches into his back pocket and pulls out a short, snubby little pistol. He steps out from behind Rafe and raises the gun toward the kid.

And the kid shoots him through his big truck driver's belt buckle.

The bullet lifts Cobb, drives him back on his heels and slams him backward onto the floor. The noise of the huge pistol is so loud that we think the glass in our window will break and we fall over backwards, scared of the glass, scared of the noise, scared of what we are seeing.

When we scramble back to the window, Rafe is still standing there, the chair still dangling in his hands, his head turning from the kid and then to Cobb, and then back again, Rafe not getting it, not understanding.

He turns back to the kid. He raises the chair slightly. The kid carefully, deliberately, shoots Mean Rafe through the back of his big right hand.

The chair flies across the room as the bullet takes Rafe's hand and then spins his whole body around, whipping Rafe down onto the floor in a grinding of bone, meat and blood.

Men knock each other down in their panic to get out the door. They scramble to their old cars and trucks, the parking lot suddenly seeming like the start of a stock car race, drivers running, engines racing, wheels spinning.

Rafe, Cobb and the kid are still on the floor, Cobb lying motionless, Rafe rolling around with his hand clamped to his chest, the kid just sitting there, bracing his left arm again, waiting for whatever would come.

Woody is gone.

We figure Cobb is going to die. It is a pitiful way to die, lying there on a floor that stinks of beer, sweat, piss and vomit, lying there with your life oozing out through a hole in your big, chrome plated belt buckle, lying there because you were born in the wrong place at the wrong time, lying there because you were really too dumb to figure out what it is all about anyway. It is Saturday night in a beer garden on the top of a mountain near a place that no one cares about and you are dying because you pulled a gun and tried to shoot a kid who doesn't even know you.

Just before Cobb dies, he vomits.

1950

The Constable

They send me to the upriver end of Crum, to Benny's house, to get a chicken for Sunday dinner.

Benny lives on the high riverbank next to a cornfield and his mother keeps the largest chicken coop on the river. I don't like to go there and get chickens. I don't like to get chickens anywhere, don't like watching them hunt and peck their way across the bare dirt yards in front of the tiny houses, don't like the chicken shit that ends up on my shoes, don't like the sight and smell of them crammed together in a coop, rushing in a hysterical pack at some sick and fallen bug that pings through the wire and plunks onto the hard-pack. The only way I like chickens is dead, blood-squeezed, dipped, fried hard and dry and piled on a plate beside a football-sized glob of mashed potatoes.

But getting the chicken for Sunday dinner is my job and I go down early to Benny's house to get it over with.

It's hardly light enough to see. The chicken coop is right next to Benny's house and the damned chickens have just started coming out, their little flat heads bobbing and turning as though they are surprised at living another day.

If I have my way, one of them won't.

Constable Clyde Prince comes out on the porch and leans against the railing, a cup and saucer in his hand, the coffee steaming above the rim.

Constable Clyde Prince. The law of the town, such as it is. Such as Clyde is. He is a man who was born with a pissed-off attitude and when he grew up someone gave him a gun and made him a lawman and said, "Clyde, boy, don't you ever lose that attitude." And he never did.

And the son of a bitch hates me.

I have never seen him at Benny's house before. He isn't Benny's father, and it is too early for him to go a-visitin' on Sunday morning. I wonder where Benny is, then remember that he usually sleeps in the barn out behind the house. Now I know why.

Clyde stares silently at me, his eyes like little chunks of coal stuck into a hard, pasty face. He raises the cup, tips it, and lets the searing black coffee run down the side and into the saucer. He blows gently across the saucer then sips from its edge, slurping the coffee in shallow draughts. He never takes his eyes from me, squinting in the early light.

I decide to ignore Clyde. I'll just go into the coop and get the goddamn chicken.

The chickens move warily as I ease inside the coop. I always want it to be easier, but it never is. Selecting the target, edging up cautiously, and then the final lunge, trying to trap the chicken between me and the fence. Always takes two or three tries to make it work. Always get covered with chicken shit. Always feel like a goddamn fool. But, finally, I catch one.

I stand outside the coop, holding the chicken in both hands. Clyde is standing there when I turn around, right in front of me, no coffee cup, his arms hanging loosely, his face a flat mask of mean.

"Goin' to wring hits neck, boy?"

"No, sir, constable. Guess I'll just take it back to Mattie and let her do with it. She likes to tend to all that stuff herself."

I hate wringing the necks of chickens, even more than I hate chickens. And Clyde knows that.

"Well, boy, I think you ought to wring out that chicken. Mattie would probably 'preciate the help."

I ease to the side, still holding tightly to the chicken. There is no way I am going to wring that damned chicken's neck, not now, not ever. I am getting ready to run.

"Wait a minute there, boy." His voice drops a notch, down to some level of evil I haven't heard before. "How I know you ain't jist stole that chicken?"

"Wha . . ."

"That's right. Stole. That chicken, there. I jist come out on the porch to sip my coffee, and there's you, a-sneakin' into the chicken coop, right in broad daylight. How do I know that's what you was supposed to be a-doin'?"

"Listen here, c-c-constable," I stutter. I have never stuttered before and it surprises me. "Mattie sent . . . I come down here ever Sunday . . . she always buy these Sunday dinner chickens . . ." The son of a bitch. The son of a bitch. The son of a bitch.

"I jist may have to arrest that chicken, boy," he says, a kind of low chuckle down underneath the words, his hand drifting behind him, "hold it for evi-dence." Almost lazily, he pulls a huge pistol from his back pants pocket.

"Now, you jist hold out the evi-dence and let's have a look at 'er." He flicks the barrel of the pistol at the chicken.

I jerk my head to the side, looking at the house, then back at the barn, at the chicken coop, anywhere, everywhere, looking for somebody, anybody. There is no one. Clyde is going to kill me.

"I said, boy, let's see her." He motions at the chicken again, the barrel of the gun swinging slightly toward me.

The chicken is quiet, moving its head in little jerking motions, looking at Clyde in that sidelong stare that chickens have, the beady eye glaring out from the side of its head. My hands move forward slowly, shoving the chicken out toward Clyde.

"Shit, boy, I can tell this chicken's a outlaw, jist by the look of it's eye." He pulls the gun up higher.

And then he pulls the hammer back. The cylinder turns easily, smoothly, and I can see the dull leaden noses of the bullets nestled in the little holes, waiting.

Click. The hammer locks back.

"Chicken, you under arrest now. Afraid I'll have to take you down to Wayne and put you in jail for a while, jist to see if you can lay any evidence." He laughs aloud, a sound that must sound good to him but, to me, sounds like someone gargling in the bowels of hell. The chicken suddenly panics, one wing busting free from beneath my hands and flogging the air. I hold on. The chicken quiets instantly.

"What's this? A-tryin' to e-scape, as sure as I live and breathe!" And Clyde puts the pistol to the chicken's head and pulls the trigger.

The thunder of the pistol rolls across the river and balloons into the Kentucky ridges and then back across the flat river bottom and the tin roofs of the tiny houses of Crum, rushing away in a wave down the valley, rattling windows. The chicken's head explodes. I am holding the chicken out almost between Clyde and me and fragments of bone and beak and squirts of blood come back into my face, stinging. I close my eyes, squinting against the gore that runs down my face and across my lips, ears ringing, stomach churning.

"Well, reckon that one won't get away, hey boy? Now, you just hold her upside down 'til you get back to Mattie's, and she'll be all drained out proper like. Jist right for pluckin'."

He is still laughing to himself and I hear him walk away across the dirt and up the stairs to the porch. The screen door squeaks lightly open and shut and he is gone, me still standing there in the Sunday new-born sunlight with my eyes closed against the gape and maw of the pistol and chicken blood painting tiny stripes down my chin and into the top of my only Sunday shirt.

1951

Tommy Hatfield 1

The first time I see Tommy Hatfield, he is walking through the door into the stuffy classroom, his chest puffed up like a toad. He swaggers down the aisle, his hands bouncing at his sides as though wearing imaginary boxing gloves. The sides of his head are nearly bare, his black hair cut evenly all around, as though someone has put a bowl on his head and trimmed away whatever hung out beneath the rim. In spite of this, he's almost handsome. He takes a seat at the front of the class and then turns, slowly and deliberately, and looks directly at me. His fingers brush across the front of his wrinkled denim shirt as though flicking away something that is insignificant. There is not a sound in the classroom.

I try not to look back, but I can't help it. I've heard all about Tommy Hatfield, how tough he is, how he likes to bully up against the new guys. And that is me. I'm a new guy in this fucking, nowhere high school buried in the mountains of West Virginia.

When the bell rings at the end of class, I'm up and out of my seat and into the hallway as quickly as I can, melding into other kids who are milling around. I think I'm unseen, but when I turn around Tommy is there.

He doesn't look at me. But as he walks past, he bumps my shoulder, hard, hard enough to make my upper body twist. He goes on down the hallway, his engineer boots clumping on the floor, not bothering to look back or say anything. Other kids look at me and then look down, knowing that Tommy has picked out another mark. And knowing, for a while, they are relatively safe.

In the weeks that follow, Tommy Hatfield turns my life to shit. Which, all in all, I thought had already happened.

Tommy bumps me in the hallways, steps on my foot as he struts down the aisle. If I am talking to a girl out in front of the school, Tommy walks up, puts his arm around the girl and pulls her away. The girl says nothing.

I am afraid to go to school.

I am afraid of Tommy Hatfield.

I am a big kid but he is bigger, stronger, older, a kid who's been held back a couple of grades. But that isn't it; that's not why I'm afraid. He has an anger, pure and true, the type of anger that I haven't seen before, an anger that boils out of a damaged soul and steams out of his fingertips, an anger that doesn't care and Tommy Hatfield doesn't care, and if I am going to survive in this school, I will have to learn not to care. And to be angry.

I will see such anger again in my life.

Sometimes, after school, I sit on the riverbank and watch the brown, stinking water and think about Tommy Hatfield. I long to be able to walk down the hallway without worrying about Tommy. To sit in my seat without worrying about Tommy. To talk to a girl without Tommy making a fool of me. Tommy Hatfield dominates my life. My shit life.

I am walking down the stairs. Beside me is a girl I like a lot, a redheaded girl, a girl I am trying to impress, talking about the books I've read—books she has not even heard of—smiling a lot, trying to say clever things. Mostly, I'm just mumbling like an idiot. And then I feel the hard slam in the middle of my back and suddenly I am flying down the stairs, my arms flung out in front of me. I hit the tile floor of the landing face first and my arms don't protect me and my nose splatters like an egg. I roll over and sit up, my arms covering my face, blood running down onto my shirt. I peek between my arms. There are kids on the upper floor, kids on the stairway, kids down below me, none of them moving. There is absolute silence. Tommy stands in the center of the stairs, his arms hanging loosely, a slight smirk on his face. He slowly lifts his right foot and waggles it, showing me that he has kicked me down the stairs. Showing the other kids.

I get up slowly, feeling other hurts in my body that I didn't know were there. I turn and slink down the stairs, out the door and across the field behind the school and over to the riverbank.

I stand in the hallway outside the classroom.

The door to the classroom opens and two or three kids come out. They look at me, their eyes getting larger, and then they quickly step aside. A few more kids come out, move out of the way, and then wait with the others.

Tommy Hatfield comes through the door.

I swing the tree branch will all my strength, straight at his head. I will kill Tommy Hatfield. He sees the club coming and flinches backward. I miss his head and hit him full across the chest, just below his neck. The club shatters and pieces fly down the hall and I'm left with a stub in my hands. But it's still a good hit. Tommy is smashed backward into the classroom. I grip the stub and jump in after him. Before I can hit him again a teacher is on me and wrestles me to the floor. It is over.

They load Tommy into a car and take off toward the nearest doctor, in Kermit, maybe fifteen miles away.

They kick me out of school for three days. Big fucking deal.

I walk slowly onto the school grounds, knowing that Tommy Hatfield is going to beat the living crap out of me. A doctor has looked him over, found nothing really wrong—except that Tommy will have trouble breathing for a couple of days—and has sent him back to school.

Me? I sit around for a week, mostly on the riverbank, knowing that Tommy is going to beat the living crap out of me.

I walk through the door and try to ghost down the hall toward my first class. No one speaks to me. I do not see Tommy. When the class is over I slip out the door as quickly as I can and make it to my next class and do not see Tommy. At noon I sit on the front steps of the school, at the top, with my back to the wall, waiting. But I do not see Tommy. Maybe Tommy is not in school. Just before the bell rings I go to the restroom to take a leak. When I am finished, I turn around, buttoning up my pants. I never get to the last button. Tommy's fist comes out of the sky and hooks down hard toward my face. I turn, just a little, and the fist catches me on the side of the head. I go face-down on the piss-stained floor with Tommy on top of me.

Tommy Hatfield beats the living crap out of me.

Nobody takes me to Kermit.

Nobody kicks Tommy out of school.

The door to the classroom opens and kids come out. They take one look at my crumpled face and step away, waiting.

Tommy Hatfield comes through the door.

I swing the tree branch will all my strength, a better tree branch this time, not quite so rotten. I swing straight at his head. I will kill Tommy Hatfield. There is a look of total surprise on his face and he throws up his arms to block the club. I hit him hard and I hear a cracking sound. Tommy screams and drops to his knees and then teachers and other kids pile on us and it is over. Again.

They take Tommy back to the doctor.

They kick me out of school for a week.

Big fucking deal.

I know that when Tommy's broken arm heals he will beat the living crap out of me.

Tommy Hatfield walks down the hallway, making heavy thumping sounds with his engineer boots. I look at the boots, wondering what it would be like to wear them. I have never owned engineer boots. I wear rough brogans; the kids call them "clod hoppers."

Tommy's arm is broken. He is showing the redheaded girl his arm, in a heavy plaster cast from fingertips to elbow. He seems proud of the cast, like it is some sort of badge he earned in combat. I am glad to see the cast. At least I will be safe until Tommy has two good arms again.

At noon we stand in groups out in front of the school, Tommy talking to the redheaded girl, other kids watching him. And watching me. Waiting.

I am the only one not hanging around with a group. No one wants to be around me as long as Tommy is there.

Nothing happens. The bell rings and we shuffle back toward the stone steps and start into the school. I reach for the heavy door just as I see Tommy moving slightly to the left of me. And that's all I see. Tommy slams the heavy cast into my side and I feel something tear in there and then I try to cough but I don't make it and instead I throw up there in front of the heavy doors.

Nobody takes me to Kermit.

Nobody kicks Tommy out of school.

I don't go to school for a week. I lie in the sun on the hillside above the tiny house where I stay and try not to move my left arm.

Now and then I go down to the riverbank and look for another club, but I can't find a good one that I can swing with one hand.

I stand at the corner of the old stone school building, watching the busses come in and unload. I know which bus Tommy rides. When I see it turn in on the gravel road to the school, I slip into the parking area and hide behind another bus. Tommy's bus pulls up and the door opens. Before the first kid has thumped down the metal steps, I am standing just to the side of the door, a piece of heavy, rusted chain hanging from my good hand.

The bus empties, and Tommy isn't there.

I leap up through the door and run down the aisle, sure that I will find Tommy Hatfield. But the bus is empty.

Moved away, the bus driver says. Whole family. Just packed up and left the county.

I sit on the sidewalk outside the bus, the chain on the ground in front of me. I feel a hollow place inside, something not right, something missing. It is over, but it hasn't ended.

I know I will look for Tommy Hatfield. Wherever I go, every time I wake up, any time I am in a new place, whenever the lights come up and I see faces, I will look for Tommy.

It is twenty-five years before I see him again.

1952

Tiny Rooms

When the money runs out, or when my father loses his job, we move.

We do not call "the movers." There is no telephone to call "the movers," and there is no moving company.

We are "the movers."

We drive to the far end of the county and borrow my uncle Stumpy's old Chevrolet stake-bed truck.

We pack the truck loosely; everything we own fits into a single load. We drive carefully through the mountains to the next house that we will rent until, once again, we move.

We never seem to move far; we always stay in the same county. But, still, it is a move. One that we seldom want to make.

Although I have never seen the house, I know what it will look like. It will be small, cramped, tiny rooms pounded together with no space to breathe. I know that I will feel trapped, held within. I think I will suffocate.

I think I did.

For the rest of my life, tiny rooms build a discomfort in me, a fear, that is unreasonable, uncontrollable, unacceptable.

I will explore caves, crawl through tunnels, wear a hard-hat diving helmet and spend hours underwater. None of that will bother me.

It is only tiny rooms.

Tiny rooms, the measure of our level of existence. Tiny rooms; the smaller the room, the more difficult our life.

Tiny rooms.

I spend a major part of the rest of my life in the wild outer places of the earth, places where the nearest wall is solid rock and a hundred miles away.

I spend the rest of my life trying not to remember those tiny rooms.

But they are always with me.

1953

The Train

This time I will go somewhere.

I will get the hell out of here.

The concrete culvert sticks out of the railroad bed and is big enough for me to crawl into. I hide there, curled into the dark and dampness, my breath coming in rasping gusts and echoing through the yellowing pipe. I make it into the pipe just ahead of the freight train and I can hear it coming around the bend, pounding slowly up a slight grade, the weight and power of it shaking the earth and the culvert.

And then it is there, above me. The culvert becomes a huge drum with me inside and my ears go dead, refusing to hear any more of a noise large enough to fill the Earth. The train is empty, long, the cars rattling and loose, a string of black metal boxes coming from downstream, heading up through the narrow valley, past our tiny cabin on the hillside, through Crum, and then on to the coalfields. I know most of the train is empty coal cars, but usually there are some freight cars in the string somewhere, their doors sagging open, square empty eyes staring at the passing ridges and small open fields of stunted corn and sugar cane.

The bend is a long one, the train pinned between mountains on one side and river on the other, and I know the engineer can't see me, once the engine has gotten well past. All I have to do is find an empty freight car, its door open, before the caboose comes into view. Nothing to it.

I jump from the culvert and scramble up beside the moving train. The railroad bed is wide in front of me and I wait for a freight car, knowing that I will have to time my run at the car just right. I have never done this before. The drumming in my ears gets louder and I realize it is my heart. I am going to hop a freight train and ride away from Crum, West Virginia.

The open door is directly above my head before I realize it. I start to run with the train, keeping one eye on the track and one on the open door, my old high-top basketball sneakers sliding sometimes in the loose cinders and gravel. It is easy. Almost loafing, I catch the car and pull even with the open door, then in a burst of speed I gain the middle of the door and run beside the car, trying to look inside. I see nothing. The roadbed is narrowing and seems to drop away from the car and the open door rises slowly above me, sneaking gradually out of my reach. I aim my hands at the corner of the door and jump.

My fingers lock on the edge and I swing upward, legs flailing behind me, the wind screaming past my ears and the tears coming just from the thrill of it. I am going to make it. I am going to some place I have never been. Going somewhere, anywhere.

Somehow, I have done it wrong.

I had watched some guys in Crum jump the trains and I thought I knew how to do it but this is one of those times in my life when I learn that watching and thinking do not make up for doing, and sure as hell I have done it wrong. My own speed and the movement of the train do not join in the effort and I dangle from the edge of the car, my feet dragging in the cinders of the road bed, my body flailing at the side of the car like a heavy sack being dumped in the wind.

There is no way to get into the car. I pull my legs up under me and let go, trying to turn and hit the cinders running. And that doesn't work, either. One foot hits the ground and I never know what happens to the other foot but it isn't there and then the front of my shirt is gone and cinders and railroad gravel are scraping the skin off my chest, working down to my belt buckle. My face augers down into the gravel and my mouth opens, a large mistake in the general scheme of things. Somehow, before my mouth fills completely from the forced infusion of cinders and gravel, I stop sliding.

I wasn't in pain yet, but I knew it was coming.

All my parts seem to work and I jump up, gagging and spitting, watching the freight car pull away from me. Behind me, more cars keep coming, but none of them are freight cars. I panic. If I am going to jump this train, I would have to catch the one car I have missed. I start running again, the tattered shirt flying behind me, a beaten battle flag.

In less than a hundred yards I catch the car again. I leap for the door, get my arms inside, pull hard and end up in a heap on the floor. I am in, but I don't really know how I have done it. Gasping, I roll over on my back and fold my hands across my chest, staring out the door at the moving wall of ridges across the river in Kentucky and trying to calm my breathing. My hands feel slick and I move them across my skin. Blood oozes from a thousand cuts, runs down my sides and disappears under my back. And that's when the pain starts.

When I sit up, I realize the train is picking up speed, heading through a straight stretch that will take it through Crum. We will go past the bus stop and the high school, then the old clapboard church and the tiny post office, and then slide by the general store. And that is all there is.

We will be out the other side of Crum and I will be on the way to anywhere else.

The pain is making me a little crazy, but I know I should get to the side of the freight car door, out of sight, especially when we go past the general store. The men who sit on the porch every day looking at the passing trains will see me, and I don't want that. Not that anyone will really care whether I leave town or not. I just don't want anyone to know I have actually gone, or in what direction.

As I slide toward the edge of the door my hands move through an inch-thick layer of something on the floor, something as black as coal dust, only it isn't. It is slicker and lighter, rising in the air with each movement I make, coating every inch of my body. As the train gains speed, the hot air rushes through the old car and the bumps of the wheels on the worn rails grow sharper and the stuff on the floor rises into the air all by itself and hangs there, whirling, a black and lingering fog. I peel off what is left of my shirt and wrap it around my mouth and nose, pulling the stink of my sweat deep into my lungs. The general store slides by in the white sunlight outside the car and I know I am out of Crum, bleeding, covered with blackness, with no idea where I am going. With no idea about anything.

The train stops. I don't know how long I have been riding or where we are, but the damn thing just stops. Since we left Crum I have been sitting just to the side of the door, my eyes closed, my arms wrapped around my gut. The ooze of the blood has stopped but the heat in the wounds has not and all I am trying to do is block out the fire.

The freight car is on a narrow trestle, thirty feet above a small river. I don't know what river. I scoot around and dangle my feet out the door and look down at the dark green water moving like a great flat snake off and into the coolness of shade in the near distance. In the light of the doorway I look worse than I have imagined. I am covered with a mixture of blood, black dust and sweat, a thickening plaster of darkness that clings to my body and blackens my mind. I fight for control of the pain. I can't stand it. When I realize what I have to do, I just do it. With no hesitation, without even a second's thought, I jump. And I am in the air. Free.

Seems it takes about an hour to hit the water. The rushing air softens the pain in the cuts and blows through the sweat and then the water catches my feet and shoves my legs up hard before the dimpled surface splits and swallows me in a blinding flash of light and wet. I never touch the bottom. When I know I am not sinking anymore I just hang on to my mind and let myself float up. The dark green water turns pale and I am on the surface in the warmth of a noon sun, floating gently away from the train, the trestle standing crosshatched and black against the mountains behind it.

As the thrill of the jump wears down, a thousand stinging needles come alive. The water seeps through the black covering of my wounds and makes the cuts fresh again, each nerve ending screaming from the soaking. A sandbar humps golden out of the water a few yards downstream and I stroke toward it. The water shallows and I touch the bottom. I crawl out on the sand and take off my clothes, what is left of them. Blood is oozing out of me again, and I think maybe I should get rid of as much of the black coating as I can. At the edge of the river I scrub myself, as lightly as I can, with river water, mud and sand. I only scream once.

Afterwards, I lie on the warm sand and let my pants and shoes dry until the shade edges out and covers me. I don't know what I am going to do, or where I am going to do it. All I know is I am out of Crum.

But it isn't going to work. I know that. Not this time. I have no money, no shirt, no direction, no heart. I just can't do it. As the day fades into the heavy trees I pull on my pants and shoes and start walking gingerly toward where I think the road might be. I don't know where I am going, so it doesn't matter what direction I walk.

It takes me two days to get back to Crum.

1954

Saying Goodbye

It is three o'clock in the afternoon of a stifling day in early August and I am going down to the river to say goodbye and to get my brains beat out.

It is a ritual. I don't know that it is a ritual—I would not realize it until many years later—but it is a ritual and there is no escaping it. There has been one at each stage of my life in this shit place called Crum, West Virginia, and there will be one now, just before I leave. There is no way out. But if I am going down to the river to get my ass kicked, by God at least they are going to have to work at it. This time they are going to have to pull out all the stops.

The stench of the river finds me before I find it. With the water down to only waist deep in most places, the sluggish stream simply cannot carry the load of garbage piled up along the banks. The whole river stinks.

At least six different guys have stopped by the house to ask me to come down to the river for a swim. They know it is my last day in Crum and they want to make sure I get a proper send-off. The bastards are there now. I can hear them splashing and shouting, the noises ringing sharp, loud, through the heat that layers the valley. I know they will be spread out, each waiting to be the first to see me as I top the rise of the river bank, each wanting to be the first to fall silent and to settle down in the water.

Well, screw them. I am scared and they are the reason for my fear and I have always hated things that frighten me for no good reason. I don't know about rituals, so I don't know that they don't understand what they are doing, either. I top the rise of the river bank and half-gallop down the slope. I paste a large grin across my face, wade into the water, and float and push my way out toward the middle.

Time slows down. The sun beats on the surface of the river and reflects into my face, and I can feel the heat on my shoulders and back as I move into the water. The river is hardly flowing fast enough to make noise and the others in the river are silent for a minute or so. There are no clouds in the sky. It is one of those Appalachian August days when the heat is so intense that nothing moves, and everything bakes that's caught in the narrow river valleys. It is one of those days where just opening your eyes makes your forehead sweat.

The others are nearer the Kentucky side, lounging around the large rock that is our diving platform. Four of them sit on the top, three more bob around in the slow current. The water is about chest deep at most and the shallow parts only come up to my knees.

I have spent the last week selling everything I own, everything except my old rifle. I sold the stuff quietly, trying not to stir up questions, holding off the poking and prying that I knew would come if word got around. But the word got around anyway, and so now I am going to have to beat it out of here before I had planned, just bug out without telling anybody. Slip away. Just me and an old cardboard suitcase.

I forgot about the ritual, but it didn't forget me. And here we are in the stinking Tug River, seven bodies and a victim.

Things start pleasantly enough. It actually is sort of nice. Of course, nobody says "sorry to see you go" or anything like that. But then, guys don't do that. We are just sort of loafing there, us guys who have known each other for all these years, just lollygagging around in the river, letting the sun beat down and the river wash up and talking about all those things that are usually talked about, like we'd done a thousand times.

Ott Parsons is there, his big mouth spouting cuss words and streams of river water. He is trying to climb on the rock and the others are pushing him off. It is funny to watch Ott haul his big frame out of the water, get about halfway up the rock, begin to lose his balance, and then be nudged off by Nip, the smallest guy in the bunch. Ott is enjoying it, or he wouldn't let people push him. He makes a hell of a splash when he hits the water.

I am standing clear of the action, just letting things slide by, when Ott takes a particularly spectacular fall and lands near me. His arm goes out as he comes down, grazing my shoulder and knocking me off balance. I laugh, just a little, and then wait for his next move because I feel sure there will be one. Instead, he splashes around in the pool and then makes another try on the rock. The atmosphere is getting more strained. They all know, I think, that the next time they look I am going to be gone, and it is these guys—my friends—I am leaving. They don't know what to say, and formal goodbyes are out of the question. The only thing left is to pretend that it really doesn't make any difference, that I don't really count for anything and to pick a fight with me to prove it. Of course, to *really* prove it I have to lose the fight, and since they know I won't lose on purpose, they are going to have to throw someone against me who they know can do the job. That will be Ott.

A few minutes later a game of horse starts in the river. Ott and I are the horses. We pull and shove for a few minutes, then I lose my balance and my rider, Nip, and I fall under. As we come up, Ott is shouting that the losers get another ducking and he makes a grab for me. Except maybe for Cyrus Hatfield, Ott is the strongest guy in Crum and he had the bluff on every guy there. None of us think we can lick him and, as a result, nobody tries. He pretty much gets his way and we never cross him up much, at least not so that he can figure out who did it. If you get the best of him in a wrestling match, he gets mad and starts throwing punches. Ott wins in the end, one way or another.

So Ott is the man chosen to do it, to goad me into a fight and to lick me.

When he grabs me it isn't friendly. He means to have the advantage from the very beginning and get it over with. I am really scared of Ott, but I am mad, too, and I don't really want to get licked in front of all those guys. Ott tries to shove my head under water and that scares me even more, so I begin to wrestle, to resist in earnest. I know that I won't throw a punch except as a last resort—if I throw a punch first, that meant that Ott will be free to do the same, and I am still clinging to the hope that I can get out of this without swapping punches.

I take a deep breath, gather my legs under me, shove upwards with most of my strength and then, when I feel him resist the upward thrust, I drop all my weight and sink underwater and out of his grasp, slipping his bear hug with hardly any effort. I bob to the surface and immediately face him. The others don't make a sound. The victim has been baited and the punishment has been chosen and there is nothing to do now but to sit and watch.

Ott lets out an embarrassed laugh. He hasn't counted on losing me so fast and it doesn't do much to make him look good. He makes a dive for me and gets one of my arms and I twist to the side to avoid his full weight. As he throws himself forward, he launches himself in the water and it is easy to drag his weight to the side as I twist again. His grip on my arm begins to hurt like hell and I grab his hand to try to pry it off. That is a mistake. He gets my other arm then and begins to twist it, grunting as the struggle gets a little tougher. We are both wrestling in deadly earnest now, no more tight smiles or tense laughs. And I know we were getting down to it when I twist to the side again and escape one of Ott's hands—because he balls up a fist and smashes me full in the mouth.

The blood and salt flood my mouth and nose and I spit to clear it away. Ott is standing there, lining up the next punch, and I look at him through the tears that are coming now. As he draws back his arm, I raise my foot free of the hip-deep water and kick him in the chest. It is a move I have been practicing ever since I saw a soldier do it in one of Coach Mason's war movies and it pays off. Ott is taken completely by surprise and I am able to punch him twice and kick him once more before he recovers.

It is like banging on a wall. I can't make a dent in him. We grab, gouge, kick, punch and claw each other for a full five minutes, standing and slipping there in the river, halfway between two states, blood running from wounds as scraps of cloth from our pants float away in the current. The battle stirs up great clouds of sand and muck from the bottom and makes the fight seem more dramatic than it actually is.

Ott has one major task—to force my head underwater, to actually shove it under. If he can control the situation long enough to do that, then I would have to give up and he will clearly be the winner and I will be beaten. I try to keep him from doing it and I almost succeed, but in the end he is a better fighter and stronger, and I get locked into his grasp and can't get out again. He begins to bend me toward the water. I resist with everything I have but I know I am going to lose. All I want to do at that point is to make it cost him as much as possible. As I am forced over, I manage to reach down between and through my legs and grab a solid handful of Ott's crotch. I can't tell what I really have hold of, but I'm not going to let go. I squeeze and pull, trying to rip out anything that is growing there. Amazingly, Ott does not let go of me. He knows that if he does, he might not be able to get me in such a position again. He nearly has me. As he bends my head another inch toward the water I pull on his crotch all the harder and he gasps. I know that I have a handful of something that counts. I am trying my goddamndest to rip his dick and balls out and float them downriver.

I have to hand it to the son of a bitch, he doesn't quit. He just keeps bending and I just keep pulling and I know that he is going to be able to duck me before I can twist his balls off. It is about then that I become aware that the other guys are yelling for Ott to duck me under, to bust me, to do something, to do anything. As my face nears the water I look to see who is leading the yelling, or maybe who isn't yelling at all. And the guy making the most noise, the guy yelling hardest for Ott to kick my ass, that guy is Mule, my best friend. Or so I thought.

It didn't occur to me until then that they can't see that I have Ott by the crotch. My part of the action is under the muddy water and they just can't know what is going on. Damn them, I think. Damn them! I can't even show them that I have the bastard by the balls, that I have him as much as he has me, and there never will be any way that I can prove it. My head is only inches away from the water now and I can hear the crying in Ott's breathing. He is really hurting, but so am I and I can't resist much longer. I only hope the bastard doesn't drown me.

My head goes under—for a second. I guess I don't realize it, what with all the grunting, straining, and pulling, but my head goes under and I draw in a nose full of water. I feel it going into my nostrils and I manage to stop it just short of my throat. If I cough, I am done for. Suddenly the back of my head is above water again, and Ott is loosening his grip. My God, I think, he's going to settle for pushing my face under! I must have a better hold than I think! As Ott lets go I duck fully under the water, twist around so that I am facing him and, still holding onto his crotch, pull with all my might—and then shove.

I break the surface and stand up. I have had my beating. He got me underwater. I am a mess, I ache and I pain and I don't think I will be able to get out of the river by myself. But strangely enough I feel pretty good about the whole thing. Because there is Ott, puking his brains out.

Ott has lost face. He has licked me, but it has been a tough job and, if I know what I know, some of the other guys will be looking at him with some new thoughts in their heads. They are all quiet now, taking it all in and not making a commitment one way or the other. I know mentally they are probing Ott, weighing new perspectives. Ott is going to have to build his reputation, if he can, all over again.

But he won't build it on me. I look at Ott, bent over the water, still gagging and holding both hands below the surface around his aching balls. I move in closer, carefully, not wanting to fall into a trap. But his agony is real. He doesn't care where I am, or whether I am there at all. But I am. I line myself up carefully and cock my right hand. I slam the punch into the side of his face as hard as I can, screaming at the top of my lungs as the fist cracks into his jaw and teeth. The punch spins him away from me facedown into the water. For a second or two no one moves, and then a couple of the guys jump off the rock and grab Ott. When they pull him out of the water, blood is running from his mouth and he is still gagging on his puke.

I have been beaten, sort of. At least Ott had pushed my face under the muddy water. But Ott is the one who is sick. Ott is the one whose face is bleeding. Ott is the one who has to be pulled out of the river. So why the hell is everyone acting like I have done something wrong? It pisses me off. It really does. So I want more, I want a piece of those bodies on that rock who have watched the whole thing, who have participated with such certainty. I want a chunk of them and I want it now and I am going to get it.

They know the fight is over and there is no longer any reason to hang around. They slide off the rock and move toward shore. I pull myself together a little and follow them. No one speaks. There is nothing to say. They just start to go home. Nip is already out of the river. He is on the bank, squatting in the sun, his arms wrapped around his knees. I haven't seen him, but he must have been there from before the fight. Then as we move toward shore I see Mule. Mule—sort of one of my best friends—has been yelling just a couple of minutes before as hard as anyone for Ott to kick my ass, to knock my fucking head off. Mule will do just fine, I think. Mule will do just fine.

A couple of the guys are already to the bank and are climbing the sandy slope out of the river. On his feet now, Ott moves slowly up the bank. I am next and Mule is right behind me. I climb for a few steps, maybe seven or eight, then pause until I can feel that Mule is going to pass me. I ease carefully to my right so that he will have to pass on my left. And as he draws even with me I turn and throw a right that catches him on the side of the head, a solid whack that resounds across the river. Mule drops like a rock and rolls to the edge of the water, turns himself over slowly and rises to his knees. He is wobbly and surprised and even afraid. He looks at me as though I am crazy—this isn't part of the game, the game is over. No one else moves or speaks, three of them still in the river, the others above me on the river bank. I back off a couple of steps to make sure that no one can move behind me and then I wait. Sure as hell, I am in for it now but I don't really care. I am full of my new strength and confidence, I have issued a fresh challenge, and now I wait.

Some of them stare stupidly at me, the others stare stupidly at Mule. There is no movement, no sound, no nothing, just the bank and the river and the motionless bodies. Mule regains his feet slowly, the right side of his face swollen, the redness accentuated by the sun. He stumbles slowly past me up the bank, walks into a cane field and is gone. The others turn and follow and I am left alone with the river running a few yards away and the breeze rattling through the cane field. I have lost and I have won and I am confident and I am afraid. But most of all I am alone. Just alone.

The others stand at the top of the bank now, and they look back at me below them.

"Fuck you," one of them says. And they turn and are gone.

1955

Booze Runner

I lean against the railing at the edge of the open-air dance floor, three stories above the huge Dreamland swimming pool, looking out over the acres of empty grounds, most of it lush with grass.

The grounds surrounding the pool are bigger than anybody's yard I've ever seen. Acres of thick, rich grass stretch away toward the bank that rises gently to the top of the floodwall, capped by a chain-link fence. Beyond the fence and across the Big Sandy River, the late evening sun drops down behind the low mountains of Kentucky.

To the south, a two-lane highway bridge rises from the street and flies above the grounds, soaring in a short arc over the brown, sluggish river and then dropping sharply down into Kentucky. During the day, when Dreamland is open, drivers sweating in their old cars always drive slowly across the bridge so they can look down on women in pink bathing suits lying on the cool grass.

There are some buildings scattered around the edge of the grounds—dressing rooms, maintenance buildings, tennis courts, things like that. A chain-link fence surrounds everything, and each day one of us pool humps has to walk the fence to make sure no one has pried it up and made a place to slide, free, into the pool grounds.

The dance floor, on the roof of the main building, must be fifty yards long and ten yards wide, a hard tile floor with metal tables and chairs and a bandstand tucked into one side. There is a curved metal roof, and that is all. Everything else is open to the world.

I lean out over the railing. There is a wide sidewalk directly below, far below, and then the pool. The thick evening air is so still it is almost gone and the surface of the water seems to disappear, a pale blue color that drops instantly to the bottom of the pool.

The pool is big, very big, so big that two concrete islands rise above the surface in the center, with plenty of room left over for a hundred people to swim.

Frank Rizzo tells us that the pool is the biggest public swimming pool east of the Mississippi River. We know that it isn't—there's a bigger pool in Miami—but nobody is going to tell Rizzo that he's lying. We are scared shitless of Frank Rizzo.

Frank Rizzo owns the pool, the grounds, the buildings. He owns Dreamland, and it's the only thing in this part of the state worth paying attention to.

And Frank Rizzo owns our asses.

I work for Frank Rizzo. I'm a pool hump. I do anything Rizzo tells me to do. Seven days a week I'm at the pool at 5:30 in the morning, picking up trash, hosing down the sidewalks, painting anything that needs painting, patching holes in the chain-link fence, making sure there aren't any used rubbers stuck to the walls of the crappers. Sometimes, I put on an ancient metal diving helmet hooked to a leaky hose and clunking air compressor, go underwater and clean the bottom of the pool. While I'm down there, I look for errant turds that might be suspended in the water. When the pool opens for the day I do a magic change—I become a lifeguard, strutting around as though I'm above all that other shit work, never telling the girls that I'm the one who looks for turds in the water, spending hours underwater long before they have gotten up to take their morning pee.

And on Saturday nights I'm one of three bouncers at the weekly dance on the open-air dance floor.

And this is Saturday night.

Seven days a week. And Rizzo doesn't pay overtime.

I'm just a kid, just out of high school, but I'm a big kid and I've always looked older than I really am and Rizzo thinks it's funny, having a high school kid as a bouncer. Anyway, I hardly ever have to bounce anybody, and they're usually so drunk that it isn't hard to do, and Rizzo pays me more for being a bouncer than for being the guy who looks for turds in the water. And I get tips from the drunks. Sometimes, I make more on a Saturday night than I make all the rest of the week.

On Saturday nights the people come to dance and to drink. It is illegal in West Virginia to sell whiskey by the drink. You can buy a bottle in a state-owned store and take it home and drink the whole damned thing, then beat the crap out of your wife and chase your kids screaming from the house . . . but you can't buy a drink in a saloon.

Almost everybody who comes to the Saturday night dances brings a bottle. Sometimes more than one. It's part of the scene for us bouncers to pretend not to notice, pretend not to see that nearly every table has a paper bag sitting on it, the top folded down, the neck of an open whiskey bottle sticking out.

The dances, like everything else at Dreamland, are Rizzo's. He lets the customers bring in their whiskey, but he doesn't let them bring in anything else. At the dances, Rizzo sells "set-ups"—soft drinks and ice in paper cups. He charges almost as much as if the set-ups had whiskey in them. As the night wears on, the dancers run out of liquor, and then

Rizzo sells them whole bottles, which, of course, is against the law. But the law is no problem. Some of the biggest drinkers, and wildest dancers, are cops, and Rizzo makes sure they never pay for their booze.

It's late in the evening. Dreamland is closed for the day, the grounds as silent as a windless forest. From where I am, up here on the dance floor, the water down below seems to have thickened, grown darker, the surface as slick as a pane of dark blue glass. It's an hour or so before the band is supposed to arrive and I'm doing a final check of the dance floor before I change into long pants and the Hawaiian shirt that Rizzo makes us wear. I look under the tables and along the railing. Sometimes kids who have been at the pool all day sneak up on the dance floor to fuck, lying near the edge where they can look under the railing and see hundreds of people down there. Fucking where they can see all those people seems to be some kind of thrill. I think they have a club you can belong to if you've fucked on the dance floor. I don't know. No girl will ever come up to the dance floor with me.

Tonight, I find nothing. No rubbers, no panties. Nothing.

I stare down at the flat surface of the water. And then I climb up on the railing and fling myself as far out over the pool as I can.

You would think it takes a long time to fall three stories, but it doesn't. Your mind only makes it seem that way. I see the main floor go by, and then the maintenance floor, and then the sidewalk flashes by a few feet from my face. Before I have time to be glad that I've missed the sidewalk, I hit the water, the exhilaration of my fall drowned instantly by the power that drives me to the bottom of the pool. I spin lazily and swim underwater to the island in the deep end of the pool, feel its slick concrete side, then swim quickly around to the other side, putting the island between me and the balcony where, I know, Rizzo will be standing, having rumbled out of his office as soon as he heard my body hit the water. If I see anybody jumping off the dance floor, I'll fire his ass, Rizzo told us at the beginning of the summer.

I surface slowly, hidden behind the island.

Rizzo's gravelly voice trashes the smooth evening air. "Hit Man! God-dammit, Hit Man, I know that's you!"

I keep my head tucked beneath the edge of the island. I know Rizzo can't see me, but I also know it's no mystery who is down here in the water. It's a game between Rizzo and me. We both know the rules. If he can't see me, all he can do is yell. If he sees me, he fires me. We've been playing this game all summer.

My only worry is that Rizzo is calling me "Hit Man"; I'm afraid some-body else might hear him. He started calling me that one Saturday night when one of the drunks got mean and took a swing at Rizzo, who just happened to be standing there. I stepped in and cracked a left hook into the drunk's jaw and he went down in a heap at Rizzo's feet. He didn't stay there. He popped up from the floor like a basketball and came after me, throwing wild haymaker punches and driving me back into the bandstand and through the drum set. One of the drums came loose and I grabbed it. I whipped it into the guy's skull. The edge of the drum opened up his scalp and blood flew out into the crowd. But the guy went down and stayed.

Rizzo thought it was hilarious. After that, he called me Hit Man.

But that isn't the problem with him calling me that.

Everybody says that Rizzo is a Mob man, that he knows *real* hit men, and that they sometimes come to the pool to cool off from . . . whatever hit men cool off from. Rizzo knows I have heard the stories. So when he wants to scare the shit out of me he calls me Hit Man.

I hang in the water, trying not to shake so much that I cause ripples. In a few minutes I hear Rizzo's office door slam, his signal that his part of the game is over.

I slip silently from the water and go change into my bouncer clothes. I go upstairs and sit at the corner of the dance floor and wait for the band.

I don't know it, but this is the last day that I will work at the swimming pool. It is the last day that I will spend in West Virginia for a long, long time.

It is almost midnight. The band is tired and the guitar player is drunk, but they still hammer out enough music to make the dancers happy. The dancers don't really care. Most of them are drunk, too, the men cupping the women's asses in their hands, men and women grinding groins against each other, the other two bouncers and me watching and trying to hide our erections. Rizzo will let the dance go on for another couple of hours, maybe more, until the dancers stop buying his set-ups and his whiskey. Then, and only then, will Rizzo signal the band to wind it down. I like working the dances because of the money, but usually I don't even go home afterward. There isn't enough time. I just sleep in the first-aid room for a couple of hours until it's time for me to go look for turds in the water.

It's an easy night. The male drunks are mellow and every now and then the women drunks will flash a thigh or an actual crotch shot in the direction of the bouncers, just to keep us awake. I think everything is going to go smoothly until I see Rizzo, at the other end of the dance floor, holding up a whiskey bottle and looking straight at me. It's Rizzo's signal that I have to make a booze run.

When the dancers run out of booze they buy bottles from Rizzo, and when Rizzo runs out I have to go get more. Across the river. In Kentucky.

The other two bouncers are older, but Rizzo always picks me. I run illegal whiskey across state lines. I could be arrested and go to jail. Rizzo thinks it's funny.

Just across the river, a couple of blocks from the end of the bridge, is a small liquor store. The old guy who owns it sleeps in the back on Saturday nights, hoping that Rizzo will run out of booze. My job is to drive Rizzo's big Lincoln Continental over there, wake up the old guy, fill the Lincoln's trunk with bottles, and make it out of Kentucky and back to the dance, all without getting myself busted, busting any of Rizzo's whiskey, or screwing up the Lincoln. But I never worry too much about getting busted; most of the local cops are at the dance, and they know the routine.

Rizzo gives me a wad of cash and the keys to the Lincoln. And then he gives me the same routine, word for word, that he always does. He grabs my shirt collar, his thick, hairy fingers curling into the cloth.

"You know what will happen, you don't come back with bottles?"

I say nothing.

"You know what will happen, you fuck up my car?"

"You know what will happen, you don't come back at all?"

I say nothing.

When he gets to my not coming back at all, I know the routine is over. I never answer these questions. Rizzo never expects an answer. Rizzo never tells me the answer. He doesn't have to. I am scared shitless of Rizzo.

The Lincoln is parked in Rizzo's private space, orange cones surrounding it. I open the trunk, take out the air pump and top off the Lincoln's left rear tire. There's a slow leak in the tire but Rizzo is too cheap to fix it. He sends a pool hump out to pump it up each evening before he goes home.

I ease the Lincoln out of the parking lot and into the street, then turn onto the bridge. As the bridge rises over the pool grounds I can look to my right and see the damp, green grass of Dreamland glistening in the floodlights mounted on the top of the dance floor. Rizzo likes the floodlights. He says he likes for the dance customers to see the lush grounds of Dreamland, the pool, the tennis courts, all shimmering in the hard light of the floods. But I know that the lights are just to keep the dance customers from fucking, out there on the grass. Rizzo doesn't care if they are out there fucking; he just wants to see them do it.

On the dance floor, people seem to move in slow motion—and I see Rizzo standing at the railing, watching as his Lincoln disappears into the darkness over the river and down into Kentucky, less than 300 yards away.

And suddenly I am part of it. It happens every time. Suddenly I'm not a high school kid who doesn't have a clue; I'm a whiskey runner, driving a big, fat, expensive car, a wad of cash in my pocket, an honest-to-God criminal, a *hood*, a *soldier*, working for the scariest man I've ever known, a man, I think, who can have me killed. And I'm excited as hell.

I finish loading the whiskey in the trunk, twenty bottles of cheap rotgut, plus one bottle of expensive Scotch for Rizzo. Rizzo pays for the rotgut. The Scotch is a "thank you" from the old man.

I hand the old man the money. I never count it. He never counts it. He and Rizzo have everything worked out in advance. I know that if Rizzo ever shorts him on the money, the old man will think I skimmed something off the top. And I'll never be able to go back into Kentucky again. Big fucking deal.

The old man goes back into the store. Through the door I can see a back room stacked with cases and crates, pallets, burlap bags thrown into a corner, a single cot beneath a naked light bulb. The old man closes the door. As many times as I have made the whiskey run, I have never known his name.

I turn the Lincoln back toward the bridge—and something is going on out there, in the center of the bridge arc, high above the river. Twinkling lights.

There are only two kinds of twinkling lights—good ones, like on a Christmas tree, and bad ones, like on cop cars. And I know there are no Christmas trees in the middle of the bridge.

Cops.

I kill the lights on the Lincoln and swing into a side street. I park and walk back to the end of the bridge, creeping up the pedestrian walkway until I can see the lights. It is too dark to see anything in detail, but I can see the roadblock stretching across both lanes of the bridge. The cops are letting cars through that are coming into Kentucky, but are stopping cars that are going the other way, into West Virginia. They are opening car doors, popping trunk lids, raising hoods.

I know what they are looking for. They are looking for me. Rizzo must have pissed off somebody.

They must be state cops, or maybe even feds. They can't raid the dance—too many other cops there, drunk—so they are going the bust the whiskey run. They'll get Rizzo's whiskey. They'll get Rizzo's car. They'll get Rizzo's whiskey runner. Me. Rizzo will wind up in the papers. I'll wind up in jail. And Rizzo won't do a damn thing about it.

Right up until he kills me, I think.

I go back to the Lincoln and think about it. I've never been in shit so deep. If they catch me at the roadblock Rizzo will say that I stole the car, that I bought the whiskey, that I sell the whiskey at the dance, that he doesn't know anything about it. I *know* he will say that. On the other hand, if I don't show up with Rizzo's car and Rizzo's whiskey . . . I think I may never show up again anywhere, ever.

I have to get the whiskey across the river.

I go back to the liquor store and pound on the old man's door. He opens it, holding a pistol out in front of him. I tell him about the cops and what I have to do. He doesn't like it, but he doesn't spend any time trying to think of anything better. He knows Rizzo, and he knows what will happen if I fuck everything up.

I grab some stuff out of the old man's storeroom and we jump into the Lincoln. The old man tells me where to drive and in five minutes we are driving with the lights out on the only road that goes down to the river, a narrow, rutted dirt lane that crawls around some deserted buildings and past a garbage dump. We park on the riverbank, upstream from the bridge.

I unload the whiskey from the trunk and carefully set the bottles at the edge of the water.

And then I unload the other stuff—a couple of gunnysacks, a tire tube from a truck, some heavy cord—all stuff that I grabbed from the old man's back room. I take the tire pump out of Rizzo's car and pump up the truck tube, then use the cord to tie the gunnysacks to the tube. I strip down to my shorts and throw my clothes into the trunk. And then I drag the tube and sacks into the thick, stinking water of the river. Carefully, very carefully, I load the whiskey bottles into the sacks, ten bottles in each, the sacks dangling just below the surface as the tube floats high on the water.

I am ready.

"Don't scratch the goddamn car," I say to the old man, trying to keep my voice steady.

"It don't matter much," he mumbles, "you ain't never goin' ter make it ter the other side, noways."

"Fuck you," I say in my toughest voice. "You just be ready with the booze next Saturday night."

The old man laughs, gets into the car and eases it off into the darkness. And I am left in the night, standing hip deep in the river with bottles of whiskey dangling from an inner tube. I look downriver, beneath the bridge, and I can see the dim lights that mark the river edge of Dreamland, on the other side of the river.

And up on the bridge I can see the twinkling lights of the cop cars. The roadblock. Waiting for me.

I am crazy. I know I am crazy. And I am scared of being crazy. But I am even more scared of Frank Rizzo.

I wade further into the river, towing the tube behind me, feeling the muck sucking at my feet. When I feel the slow current take me I begin to swim in an easy, soft stroke, pulling at the water with one arm, the other towing the tube and the sacks of whiskey.

By the time the current takes me to the bridge, I am only halfway across the river. I quit stroking with my arm and try to hide my head between the sacks, my nose at the surface of a river I can no longer see, only feel. I drift silently beneath the bridge, waiting long minutes before I dare raise my head. There is no one at the rail of the bridge, looking down. They haven't seen me.

I wait a little longer, just to get farther downstream, and then I start to stoke with my arm again, moving slowly toward the West Virginia bank, moving toward Dreamland.

By the time I get to the bank, I am almost at the far downriver edge of Dreamland. Against the glow from the dance floor, I can see the chain link fence at the top of the floodwall.

Thick brush lines the bank and I grab some small limbs, hauling myself into the shallow water. I try to stand and the mud sucks at my legs, the river dragging at the heavy inner tube, the limbs breaking in my hands. I fall back into the river, floating away from the bank.

In a panic I thrash toward the shore, forgetting to be careful about noise, knowing only that if I don't get back to the bank I'll be swept a few hundred yards downstream to where the Big Sandy meets the Ohio River. I'll be in the middle of the Ohio River in the middle of the night in the middle of the worst nightmare of my idiot life.

Gradually, I get back to the bank. There's a small open space and I aim for it. A dead and bloated dog is floating in the oily water and I have to actually touch it to get it out of the way. Finally, I manage to pull the inner tube in until the gunny sacks touch the muddy bottom. Ten minutes later, I have all the whiskey bottles sitting upright in the mud.

I don't know what happened to the dog.

I take two of the bottles and climb the bank, up the floodwall, crouching at the corner of the chain link fence. I look far across the grounds toward the dance floor and see Frank Rizzo standing at the railing, his squat figure almost hidden in the glare of the floodlights. Rizzo stares at the bridge, where twinkling lights still cluster at the center. I know Rizzo is waiting to see them move away, meaning I have been arrested. I hate the son of a bitch.

There's a way to get through the fence, an opening I pretend to wire closed but never really do, a private entry into Dreamland for my buddies, guys who never have the price of admission. Who *never* will have the price of admission.

I find the opening and squeeze through.

Halfway to the tennis courts I am in the glare of the floodlights, but there is no other way I can get to the main building. I slip past the tennis courts and am halfway around the shallow end of the pool before I notice that Rizzo has seen me from the dance floor. He motions me to stay where I am.

Rizzo slides out of a side door. He walks slowly toward me, his hand in his pocket. I wonder if he is fingering a gun. When he gets closer, I can see the anger on his face. And then his mouth opens and he begins to laugh, that Rizzo laugh that makes you think that rocks are being crushed in a metal barrel. Rizzo laughs so hard that he nearly falls down.

Up on the dance floor, people hear Rizzo laughing. They crowd to the railing and look down, seeing Rizzo and me at the edge of the grass, Rizzo still laughing, me standing there, covered in mud, my sodden shorts sticking to my legs and dick, two bottles of whiskey dangling in my hands. All in the glare of the floodlights.

Before he lets me wash the mud off me or even get a dry shirt on, Rizzo makes me go back and get the rest of the whiskey. Then the son of a bitch spends the rest of the night telling the drunk cops at the dance how I outsmarted the other cops on the bridge. It doesn't occur to Rizzo that he is ratting me out. Or that he is ratting himself out. But then I realize that Rizzo doesn't care. Nobody is going to do anything to Rizzo.

The dancers don't go home until almost daylight.

I don't go home at all.

The next day is Sunday. Before I do anything else, Rizzo makes me go get his car. He won't give me a ride across the bridge.

I take Rizzo's spare keys and walk over the bridge and down into Kentucky. I find the Lincoln parked behind the liquor store. The car is covered in mud. I find a hose hanging at the back of the store and I wash the car, drying it with my shirt. The fucking leaky tire is almost flat and I pump it up, then carefully drive the shiny car back across the bridge. I park it in Rizzo's reserved space out in front of Dreamland.

Tomorrow, Monday, is payday, but when I take Rizzo's keys back to him I ask him if he will pay me now. I owe some guys, I say. Have to pay them tonight.

Rizzo pays me in cash.

I walk away from Rizzo and sort of loiter around until he goes back into his office. I climb the stairs to the dance floor and stand at the far end of the railing, overlooking the pool. The dance floor is littered with brown bags, paper cups, empty whiskey bottles and little pools of melted ice. I see at least one pair of panties. One of the bottles has a little hooch still in it and I pick it up and drain it, the foul gunk cutting a path down my throat.

It's well past ten on a Sunday morning and Dreamland is already filling with lush young babes in swimming suits that pull tightly up between their legs. I can see their legs and their tight crotches clearly from where I am, all the way up here, above the pool, on the dance floor of Dreamland. Or at least I think I can.

I've cleaned myself up, have on my good shoes, fresh khakis and a shirt that I keep stored in my locker, in case I get to take a girl home from Dreamland. I have my money in my pocket and I've had a shot of hooch for breakfast.

How much better can it get?

I step up on the railing and pause, waiting for what I know is coming. In only a matter of seconds, I hear a girl scream, her hard plate of sound cutting off the surface of the pool and slicing toward the balcony and Rizzo's office. She's pointing up at me as others turn to look.

I jump.

When I break the surface I can hear Rizzo screaming, his gravel voice pounding down into the water after me. I stroke hard for the side of the pool and launch myself up on the sidewalk. I know Rizzo is storming down the stairs. I run to the end of the building, slip into the water purification room and slide behind the huge filters that are supposed to clean the pool water—but which never do. I hear Rizzo's feet pound by on the sidewalk outside. I slide to the other end of the room, up the stairs and am outside before Rizzo knows he has lost me. People look at me oddly as I go by, my shoes squishing water, my sodden clothes dripping across the tile floor of Dreamland.

"Hit Man! Hit Man! Goddamn you, Hit Man, you show yourself right now . . . !"

It is the last thing I will ever hear Rizzo say.

Within twenty-fours I am gone from West Virginia, hitching, drifting along two-lane highways, wandering into the South.

Into Dreamland.

1956

Dark Swimmer

The beach is a naked dun stripe along the edge of the earth that forces you out into the sunlight or the blackness and keeps you there.

There is no place to hide on a beach, not even in the dark.

I was always good at hiding. Ten feet inside the edge of the woods that surrounded the farms on Black Hawk Ridge and I melted away, flowing down into the floor of the forest as I was born to do. I could stay there for days, living quietly, meeting no one, but hearing and seeing everything. I was a kid, hiding, and they came looking for me, up there on the Ridge, wondering where the hell I had gone and why wasn't I home for supper. When I got bigger, they gave it up. I would come out of the woods, come home, when I was ready.

It was different in Crum. I hid out because I had to and I had my places all picked out and ready. Sometimes I hid in the small old barns scattered around the town, boards hanging from their sides by a single nail, holes in their tin roofs. Or in the little tool sheds that leaned against the houses. But the best places were down on the riverbank and in the woods above the town. Once I got into the brush, into the woods, no one could ever find me.

When I first saw the beach in daylight I wondered where I would hide, if it ever came to that. I wanted to have my place all picked out, be ready. But there was no place. Not even in the dark. In the dark there was nothing on the beach, no glistening bodies, no dogs, no umbrellas, nothing to melt down through. In the dark you stood on the sand and nothing moved except a line of black surf at the edge of a thick ocean and you were out there to be seen by anyone, a dark beacon that could be found by anyone, for any reason.

At first, that's what I think she is doing, trying to hide in the dark on the beach. I lie back in the tiny rental shack waiting for the rain, my feet propped up on a stack of beach floats, my trunks still damp from my last swim of the day. Daylight has faded to that grim light before full dark, a hard, flat gray that makes everything blend together, and I should be able to see her clearly but she moves so slowly that I have to look hard to see her legs push through the edge of the surf as she drifts down the beach, her lithe form seeming to glide above the water. And then I realize she is wearing a dress. She is wading, about up to her knees, and the small waves come up and lap at her legs and soak her skirt and she doesn't seem to care.

Heavy clouds settled in over the beach about mid-afternoon and most of the people drifted away, back to the beach cottages and motels, back to the latest copies of *Life* and *Saturday Evening Post*. Later, some of them come out again, wandering into the open pavilion, dropping coins into the jukebox, some of them dancing on the old wooden floor, some of them just waiting for the darkness. I can hear the music and now and then the slick rolling of the swells beyond the low line of surf catches the pavilion lights and sends quick reflections shooting down the shoreline.

I lie curled up in the rental shack, the door propped open, waiting for the rain to come, waiting for the gray to go black.

She is almost directly below me in the edge of the surf before I really notice her, quick bursts of light from the pavilion finding her, outlining her, then losing her in the darkness between waves.

And then she is gone.

I lie there and listen to the low rush of the surf and the thin sounds of the pavilion jukebox. She is gone and I haven't seen her go. She is a woman in the near-dark and I don't know her name or why she is wading in the surf in a dress and I wish I had gone down to the water and talked to her, all the time knowing that if I went down there she would hurry away, maybe turn and go back. Knowing I would break the mood. Knowing she didn't need me down there, with her, in the water.

I have never seen a woman wearing a dress wade in the surf. I would like to have known her.

A soft wind is building into something stronger and the rental shack shivers a little. I sit up and put my legs through the open door and stare down at the water where she had been, some vague feeling of loneliness washing over me, the female presence of her gone, the beach empty.

The beach empty.

I get up from the doorway and look up and down the strand. The lights from the pavilion help and I can see some distance in each direction, the gray light dropping quickly until the beach falls away under darkness. But I can see far enough and she isn't there, isn't anywhere. She had been walking down the beach, away from the pier, just moping along. I can't figure it out; even if she had taken off running, she still didn't have time to get out of range. No matter which way she would have gone, I should still be able to see her.

And then I know where she is and I don't want to know and all summer long I have been playing lifeguard and drinking beer and chasing girls with plump little asses and now there is a woman in the water and I am going to have to be real and find her out there and I don't know how to do that, don't know how to find a woman in the dark water, a woman wearing a dress, a woman who doesn't want to be found.

I lurch away from the rental shack and stumble about halfway to the water, then slide to a stop. Maybe I should get somebody from the pavilion to help. Maybe I shouldn't. Jesus Christ, my feet are glued to the sand in a growing darkness and there is a woman out there and the only thing she has going for her is a dumb hillbilly who pretends to be a lifeguard.

She doesn't have a chance.

I stand there, my body locked and rigid, the water flicking shots of light from the pavilion.

I am looking too close to the shore. Farther out, just out beyond the end of the pier, I see, caught in the middle of a reflected patch of light, a single arm, lifted, falling back into the water, not even flailing, just moving. And then the other arm. Then the light flicks away and the arms are gone and all the lifeguard bullshit is gone and there is just me and the water and the woman and the blackness and I run, panicked, toward the surf, screaming, screaming . . .

"Heeeaay! *Heeeeaaaaayy*!"

I split the surf as hard as I can knowing that somewhere a very short distance from me something is happening that I don't want to happen, that I can't live with.

I can see nothing. I can find nothing. I keep screaming, knowing she cannot hear me but not knowing what else to do. I scream down and back through all the pathways of all my life and I know that all I am doing is making noise.

I have never swum this far out, beyond the end of the pier. I don't know how deep the water is and when I feel something brush my leg I have one of those moments when everything in my body shuts down, waiting. All the lifeguards have told me shark stories, but I have never actually seen a shark. And now I know, positively, there is one brushing against my leg in the blackness of water at night on the edge of rain.

But whatever brushes my leg stays there and when I shove against it, it moves, and I reach down and grab her.

I haul her to the surface, roll her over on her back, put my arm around her and start swimming to shore, like Hugo has shown me, like we had practiced together. But it is a lot harder than when Hugo and I had been playing at it, and it takes me a long time to get to where my feet can touch the bottom and by the time I get there I can hardly breathe.

I try to pick her up and carry her but she drapes loose and limp in my arms. She isn't large, but her arms and legs hang and slide everywhere, her head lolling backwards, her body folding in the middle and hanging down, her dress dragging the water. I gather myself and try to heave her up higher, carry her higher, but one of her elbows clubs me in the mouth and I can't really get a grip on her. I know if I don't try something else I will never get her up on the beach. I put her back in the water and slide underneath her, rising quickly and draping her over my shoulder, face down, hanging over my back. I crash toward the shore as fast as I can, jogging her up and down, and I feel her twitch and she pukes down my back and down the back of my legs. I can feel it, warm and running, and I hope she is only puking water but I didn't really care. I think probably she has to be alive to puke and I want her to keep right on doing it. But she doesn't.

When I get to the sand, there is a crowd of people, come down from the pavilion, some of them carrying cans of beer, and they all stand silently along the beach, outlined in the lights from the pavilion. No one comes into the water to help.

I put her down like Hugo has shown me, facedown on the sand, her head turned to the side, her arm underneath her head. I straddle her back and push hard against her rib cage and a glob of water comes out of her mouth and nose and I push some more times and some more water comes and I gag and try to breathe at the same time and I keep telling her she shouldn't be wearing a dress in the water and I push some more waiting for her eyes to open, but they don't.

Someone grabs me by the arm and hauls me off the woman. Some guys are there in white coats. They carry flashlights and run around a lot and mess with her, pushing against her, feeling in her mouth, talking tensely to each other, me just there on my knees in the sand, covered with puke. Someone shines a light on her back and there is blood there, patches of it smeared across the sodden material of her dress. They shine a light on me and there is blood painted in streaks down my chest. My lip is split, still pumping blood.

And then she pukes some more water and then some other stuff and her eyes open.

They have her on a stretcher, covered with a blanket. She is breathing.

By the time they start carrying her off toward the ambulance the first drops of rain are blowing in off the ocean. She looks at the faces in the crowd, ignoring the rain, water running into her eyes, her expression blank, recognizing no one, and I realize she does not know who has pulled her from the water.

The crowd splits and moves around me, not wanting to be close to anything that smells like I do, moves away with the stretcher toward the ambulance, some of them sipping beer as they go, hurrying now, pushed by the rain. When they get to the edge of the beach near the pavilion I hear some laughter drifting back from them and then they are all inside the pavilion and the ambulance is gone. None of them looks back.

I sit there on the beach where the woman has been lying, still feeling the presence of her, rocking back and forth on my knees, my arms wrapped around my stomach, shivering, tears forming in my eyes, wanting to hide and knowing there is no place to hide on the beach in the dark, not even in the rain, and telling her she shouldn't have been wearing a dress in the water, *goddamnit,* that was no way to behave on a beach, squeezing the words out into the blackness through clenched teeth, head spinning. And then someone touches me on the shoulder.

I try to stop my whimpering and look at her, at her bare feet, her loose slacks and blouse wet and stuck to her, her hair down and falling around her shoulders in thick strands.

Yvonne.

Her hand is still on my shoulder. She pulls it away and looked at it, her face screwed into disgust.

"You're covered with . . . stuff."

I stay there on my knees, my arms still wrapped around my stomach. Maybe she will just go away.

"Where do you stay? Where's your room?"

I nod toward the rental shack. For a moment, she doesn't understand. Then she does.

"The rental shack? You sleep in the rental shack?"

All I can do is nod.

"My God," she whispers.

She takes me by the arm and pulls me to my feet. I start toward the rental shack but she holds me, pulls me back toward the surf, wading in up to our knees. She dips water in her hands and pours it on my back and chest, splashing it down my legs. She does it carefully, not wanting to touch the stuff that clings to me. It is slow work, there in the dark. She takes off her blouse and dips it in the ocean, rubbing me gently with the silky material, cleansing me. She washes my back and my chest, then down my legs, dipping the blouse and then rubbing me with it, gently, all over, rubbing the stuff off me.

Finally, I am clean.

She dips the blouse in the ocean again, swirling it, cleaning it. She folds it over her arm, and walks away.

I stand in the edge of the surf for long minutes, waiting in the darkness. I can hear voices from the pavilion and now and then a shard of laughter.

And then I realize she isn't coming back.

1957

What Am I Doing Here 1

What the hell am I doing here?

That seems to be the central question of my life, the question that seems to keep coming up, again and again, no matter where I've gone, what I've done.

What the hell am I doing here, on this two lane highway west of Myrtle Beach? I stand here, watching the road fall away to the east as the old Chevy disappears back toward town and the ocean, watching one of the best women I have ever known drive out of my life.

Whatever I'm doing here, I won't be doing it long. I'm leaving again.

Winter is coming on in the Carolinas. The land rises to the west and lifts into the mountains and I can feel the cold flowing down and out of the hills and wrapping itself around me in my beach shirt and old jeans and I wish I were back at the beach with sweat running down into my eyes and a can of cold beer dangling from my hand.

I start walking down and around the mountains and farther into the South, my thumb out every time I hear a car, trying to keep my eyes straight ahead.

I think about going home, but I really am not sure where home is. I know where it is supposed to be, but that doesn't count. I am leaving South Carolina, but this isn't home, even though, maybe, I want it to be. I just ended up here after taking off from some other places I didn't want to be. Places like Bean Camp and Crum.

Actually, I have no intention of going home, ever again. Wherever it is.

1958

Accounting Class

I am a lousy student.

I have no interest in anything. I stumble around the campus not really caring whether I get to wherever I am going on time, or whether I get there at all. I always carry some books. If I do manage to get to class, I want to give the impression that I meant to get there. The books are only a prop. Most of them are novels.

Usually, I veer off from the path to class—any class—and wander into the student union. I play ping pong for hours, gradually becoming good enough to enter tournaments. Once, in a tournament open to the entire student body, I place ninth. It is the crowning achievement of my college career.

Sometimes I go downtown and drink beer. I run into some other guys, and a few girls, doing the same thing. We sit in darkened beer joints and sip at our glasses, trying not to appear to be alcoholics, only to discover that no one cares whether we are or not. The discovery is sobering.

Sitting in a saloon one day I become bored with sitting in a saloon. Even class seems more interesting than what I am doing. I buy a quart of beer, put it in my book bag and straggle off to class. I get the class time wrong; I am actually early. A student asks me if I am a late enrollee in the class; she has never seen me before.

It is an accounting class. Our desks are larger than normal, so that we can spread out the large ledger sheets that we are supposed to use. There is a compartment under our seats where we are supposed to keep our accounting books and the ledger sheets. I have never put anything in the compartment under my seat. I have no idea where my accounting books are. I have no idea why I am in an accounting class.

I keep one ledger sheet on my desk as a prop.

I put the quart of beer in the compartment under my seat.

The professor never looks directly at us. He writes on a chalkboard behind him, then he turns towards us and as he lectures he looks above the heads of the entire class, looking at some spot on the wall above and behind us, his eyes flicking from left to right, never making eye contact.

He writes on the chalkboard and I slip the quart of beer from beneath my seat and take a sip. Some of the students are fascinated, their mouths dropping open. Some are disgusted. Some think it is funny, choking back their giggles behind their books and ledger sheets. I do not intend to be funny. I just want some beer.

Each time the professor writes on the chalkboard, I sneak out the bottle and take a sip. And then I wonder if he would see the bottle if I left it sitting there. So I do.

He never notices.

When class is over the bottle is empty.

The professor is always the first one out the door at the end of class. I think it is because the class bores him as much as me. Or all of us.

One of the girls stops in front of me. I know some shit is coming. I look her up and down. She is wearing a pleated skirt and a white blouse, buttoned all the way to her neck. I think I have seen her before—somewhere else.

"You are the most disgusting example of a college student I have ever seen," she says. "You should be expelled." There are razors in her voice.

She makes no move to leave. She has more to say. Some other students pause to watch.

I keep looking at her, directly, trying to remember. And then I remember.

"That frat house, over on the corner of Morgan Street, didn't I see you there last Saturday night, screwing some guy on that big wooden table in the kitchen?"

Her face begins to glow a frightening shade of red and her mouth opens, then closes, then opens again, but only a sputter of sound comes out, a tiny fleck of foam at the corner of her lips. She looks around at the others. I think she is on the edge of panic. She whips around and plunges for the door.

"Wait," I call after her, "I've always wondered—do you get splinters in your ass when you do that?!"

But I don't think she hears me.

The next day I see on a bulletin board that I have been expelled from the class.

I never find out why they kicked me out.

It's a mystery.

1959

Final Exam

The light comes brilliantly, but softly, as light comes through a scattering of muted crystals.

I think I can see the fractured light, even though my eyes are closed. The light cuts through the edges of my vision and lances its way into my brain.

I know I am lying on a bench at the side of the grassy quadrangle in front of the library. I can feel the bench beneath me. I run my hands along the front of the bench, feeling the smooth, worn wood.

I lay down on the bench an hour or so ago. I needed a nap. I came out of the last exam of the semester, of the year, and the bench was there. Many times, I have seen people napping on these benches. No one ever seems to bother the nappers.

My eyelids seem glued shut. I rub at them with my hands, then sit up, blinking. My book bag is on the bench beside me; I have been using it as a pillow.

I think I should be jittery, but I am not. My head rings with soft pain but my hands do not shake. The reds must have worn off.

The reds, bless their little rounded bodies. They may have saved me again.

I had been to only a handful of the philosophy classes, preferring to just read the books and fake the quizzes. Then I got bored with the books and did not read at all. I am failing the course. I don't give a shit.

We call him Jimmy Bingo and he has the reds. Take a fistful of these, Bingo says, and you can steam through the night, catch up on all that philosophy crap. Pass the final, he says, and you pass the course.

What the hell, I thought, it's worth a try.

The reds cost me all my beer money.

I start popping them at mid-day. I keep at it though the night. I take the last red at three in the morning. Philosophy never seemed so exciting.

I forget my watch and run for the campus, barely making it on time. I do not remember the exam at all. I do remember odd looks from some of the other students, but, what the hell, it's a philosophy class. It's full of goddamn odd students.

The reds start wearing off. I manage to get through the exam and stagger out of the building around noon. The last exam. I am through with this shit for another year. Maybe I'm through with this shit forever.

I start across campus. The reds are fleeing the country. My plane is spinning out of the air, crashing, my head full of sand and my feet not attached to my legs. I see the bench near the library. I am hungry, *really* hungry. But I can hardly walk. I need a nap. I lie down on the bench.

It is getting late, the sun far down behind the buildings and sinking fast. I have slept longer than I meant to, but it does not matter. No one is looking for me; no one knows where I am; I have nothing to do.

I need a piss. Badly. I stand up and stretch, looking carefully around the quadrangle, trying to appear casual. There is no one around. I slip behind the bench, reach over the back and mess with my book bag. Actually, I have unzipped my fly and I am pissing on the ground behind the bench.

When I am finished I sneak another look around again to make sure I have not been seen. Still, there is no one in sight.

Not anywhere.

I wonder about that. There should be someone, some exam-battered student heading for the student union building, some dry slug or two heading downtown for a beer. Somebody. Going somewhere. But there is no one.

It does not register with me until I realize the fading light is not fading. The light is growing stronger. The sun is not setting, it is rising. There is no one on campus because it is just barely first light.

I have slept on the bench all night.

I sit back down and stare at the growing light.

What the hell am I doing here?

I do not even go back to the room in the boarding house. There is nothing in the room that I want. I pick up the book bag, dump the books onto the bench, and walk away in the growing light. Toward the highway.

I find out years later that I passed the exam.

1960

Midnight Pub

I just need to travel.

And so I do.

But I do not mean to end up here, Washington, D.C., late one summer night. Some sort of scene out of a 1940s movie. Three o'clock in the morning and lost in the big city, a light rain falling, dim street lights, my vision blurred, my head aching.

The headlight on the bike keeps blinking on and off as I cruise the street. I know there is an electrical short in there somewhere, but I have never been able to find it. So I ride slowly, peering through the rain and blinking light, trying to make some sense of where I am, trying to recognize some landmark that will lead me out of town.

I ride past a pub just closing, one of those places down a short flight of stairs and through a heavy door into a basement. A couple stands at the bottom of the stairs, in the open doorway. They seem to be waiting for something. I stop at the curb and look down at them. No one wears helmets in these days and the rain pours across my goggles and runs down my face.

"Hey, kid," the man says, "come on down here until the rain stops. None of us going anywhere." He speaks loudly, trying to be heard over the idling of the bike and the sound of the rain.

I am afraid to go down there, but the rain is running inside my shirt and my vision seems to be getting worse. And, besides, I have no place else to go. I shut off the bike and go down the stairs.

We all go inside, leaving the door open, and sit at a low table. In the center of the table is a bottle of some sort of liquor. I am not sure what it is, but somehow I think that it is expensive.

There are four of us—the woman, the man, me, and some guy who comes out of the back room with a pot of coffee. The woman is blonde, her hair hanging in damp, stringy curls. No one says anything.

The guy with the coffee doesn't seem surprised that I am there. He pours coffee for all of us, then adds to the cups from the liquor bottle. We drink, sipping slowly, the heat feeling good inside my chest.

There is a piano in the middle of the floor and the coffee guy goes over there, starts running around some chords with light placements of his hands, long, low, lonely chords that rumble slightly in the dim room.

The blonde gets up, takes me by the arm, walks me to the piano. I shuffle slowly across the floor, walking stiffly from the dampness and the constrictions of my wet clothes.

The piano player grins. "You walk like Walter Brennan," he said.

"Who's Walter Brennan?" I ask, and he laughs.

"Where the hell you been, kid?" he asks, still playing the chords.

"Around . . . traveling . . . in the mountains," I mumble.

"Yeah, I can see that."

"I'm from *West* Virginia," I say, before he can ask me anything.

He doesn't say anything. I don't think he really gives a damn where I am from.

The woman stands behind the piano player and starts to sing, her voice breathing through the room like velvet paint. The softly sculpted sounds flow their images into the room, into my mind, mix and curl with the sounds of the rain outside, crystalline, disciplined sounds carefully thought out, carefully released. I have never heard that kind of singing, not right there in front of me, not right where I can see the rise and fall of her breasts and count the tiny wrinkles at the corners of her eyes. Cool words, combining to make me warm.

One of the best nights of my life is only two hours long.

By five o'clock the rain has stopped, the singing stops, and there is a layer of dull light in the sky above the city. We climb the stairs out of the pub and the piano player locks the door.

The woman takes my arm. "Will that thing carry two?" Her question is soft, as though she is merely curious.

"Yes, ma'am, but the seat's wet and you're wearing a skirt and I don't know how . . ."

"Take me home, mountain boy."

1961

The Dude

In the winter of my twenty-fifth year I raise my hand during a philosophy lecture at a university in Colorado and ask to be excused. I never go back. I go to my room at a boarding house, pack a small gray duffle bag and catch a bus for El Paso, then change my mind and get off in Walsenburg, Colorado. I hitch-hike west to Crested Butte, a town of some 300 people caught in a time warp. The road ends in Crested Butte; once there, there is no place else to go. For fifty dollars I rent an abandoned shack on Maroon Avenue, a single-lane dirt street beside the creek. The fifty dollars pays for the rest of the winter.

I nail up the holes in the walls and heat the place with a small wood stove, burning scraps of lumber I dig from beneath the deep drifts out back. The snow from the high-mountain Colorado winter drifts to the eaves of the house, forming a blanket of insulation that my small stove gradually melts back until I can squeeze along the outside walls of the house in search of wood scraps. I spend the rest of the winter reading.

That summer I get a job with a Gunnison outfitter who takes tourists on pack trips into the high country. We work out of an old ranch up a canyon just south of Crested Butte. I know my way around the mountains, am good with horses, and, since I am getting paid for it, am even good with the tourists. The outfitter has only two other employees, an Indian and a Mexican. The Indian pretends not to speak Spanish, the Mexican pretends not to speak English, and I pretend not to understand either of them. Some days, we don't speak for hours, and it gets so we don't need to.

The outfitter stays in Gunnison and lets the three of us run the pack trips. We make a good team. We make an odd team. I am six feet tall and stocky, with blond hair that hangs down almost to my heavy shoulders. I walk upright, almost too straight—I have a stick up my ass, the Mexican says—and when I move, I go directly about my business. The Mexican says you can watch me move and know what is going to happen next.

But not the Indian. With him, you never know what is going to happen next. He has skin the color of a late sunset in New Mexico, a deep, rusty tint that seems to glow even in the feeble light of early morning. His hair is straight, glistening black, and hangs down even longer than mine. He is slender, tall, with lanky arms and legs that he seems to be able to fold at odd angles. When he gets up to move, there is always a hesitation, a moment when he seems on the verge of changing his mind, a split second when you can't be sure, not of the Indian, not of anything about him.

The Mexican is somewhere in the middle, not as heavy as me, not as tall as the Indian. Quicker than both of us. He wears his dark hair short, held back from his forehead by a red bandana, until the day the Indian trades him a leather thong for it. He keeps the thong on, even under his hat. His forearms are sculpted with muscle and he can chin himself with one arm. As long as I know the Mexican, I never really know whether the man has a temper. I have seen him mad, but it always seems as though the Mexican programs it, makes it happen, doesn't wait for the rise of a temper that isn't there. But that is good, I think. God knows what the Mexican would do if he ever lost control.

In the early fall when the tourists stop coming, the outfitter takes in hunters and turns them over to us, and we lead the dudes by the hand into the mountains to hunt elk.

On the last trip of the season, on a bare ridge that rises far into the West Elk Range, in the early afternoon, with snow beginning to slice almost horizontally through the air, a dude from Chicago shoots my horse. He thinks it is an elk.

I am riding the horse at the time.

The dude panics, gets on his own horse and rides away, leaving me on foot in the wilderness. The dude doesn't know which way to ride, but that is no problem—the horse takes him straight back to camp.

I walk six miles through heavy timber, around steep slopes and through the hard snowfall of an early winter storm before darkness catches me, still and cold on the lee side of a low stand of trees, the temperature dropping, my heartbeat rising. My parka and boots are not heavy enough for what the weather is doing, and I know that I will not survive if I do not find shelter. I spend the night under a deadfall, lying as far back under the fallen tree as I can. Before I crawl in, I pile all the dry forest junk I can find against the back of the tree, trying to block the movement of air underneath the trunk. I spread more on the ground, to lie on. I scrape a wide line in the snow in front of me, down through pine needles and twigs in front of the deadfall, scrape it all the way down to bare earth. The line is the length of my body and I build several small hat-sized fires along it and kept them burning throughout the night. As each little fire dies down I build it up again, working the fire line constantly, grabbing a few minutes sleep between firings. I know the temperature has dropped below zero, but the fires, radiating directly on me and reflecting from the deadfall, sustain me. I stay alive. Barely.

An hour after daybreak the next day I run into the Mexican and the Indian. They are searching in the general direction the dude rode in from, their horses moving easily through the snow that is now almost two feet deep. They give me some hot coffee, wrap me in a sleeping bag, and put me up in the saddle behind the Mexican. I doze on the horse all the way back to camp.

The Indian has the dude tied to a tree. He tied the man there without a second thought, left him, and went off with the Mexican to try and find me. The dude is shaking inside the ropes, an almost terminal kind of shaking, a combination of the cold and abject fear.

They ease me off the horse, my body beginning to stiffen from the night in the cold and the long ride back on the horse. The Indian builds a fire and the Mexican wraps me in another sleeping bag and stuffs me with hot food and more coffee. They leave the dude tied to the tree.

They try to decide what to do about the dude. Finally, the Mexican takes the dude's rifle and inspects it carefully, admiring the grotesquely expensive, hardly-used weapon. He walks slowly and carefully around the fire, holding the rifle in front of him. And then he empties it of its ammunition by firing in rapid succession into the tree next to the dude's head, the dude screaming all the while. When the firing is over, the dude has fainted.

The Mexican tosses the rifle to the Indian, who ties a single feather to the butt, then rams it muzzle-first into the center of the fire. He sits, singing some soft and unknown songs, his own rifle across his lap, and keeps the fire burning for three hours.

1962

Whorehouse

On the ranch, to keep myself from going stir crazy, I order books through the mail, mostly history and biographies, some travel. I read novels when I can find the right ones. I make sure that all the books are paperbacks, so I can carry them in my saddlebags and behind the seat of the pickup truck. The books become worn and fragile from handling and I have to tape them, just to keep the pages from falling out. I wear out three different copies of *FOR WHOM THE BELL TOLLS*. At night, reading, I keep the small light burning near my bunk until the other hands make me turn it out.

The ranch has one big advantage—there is no place to spend money. When I draw my pay I stuff it in the war bag I keep under my bunk and then, once a month or so, Will, Caton and I, and now and then some of the other hands, take the old pickup truck and drive the rutted dirt road out to the highway, then the two-lane blacktop into town. We go to a movie, hang out in the feed store or the town's one saloon. Or maybe visit the whorehouse. But the town is so small that the whorehouse has only two whores, both of them fat, and something about fat whores in tiny whorehouses makes me a little crazy. We drink a little, laugh a little, fuck a little, and then something always comes over me—maybe it is the whiskey, but I always think it is the sight of unrestrained flopping hugely fat breasts. I see a pair of them heading toward me, drooping and bobbing through a doorway, like two small blimps in mating season, and I just fall over, shaking, laughing, out of control. Fat arms rise out of the flesh at the side of the tits and grab me, shoving me out into the tiny waiting room where I rumble toward the door, trying to keep from choking on my own spit and laughter. Always, always, I stumble over some guy's feet and there are some words and maybe a half-assed punch or two thrown and somebody ends up being thrown out into the street. Usually me. Shit. I never learned to get out of there the easy way.

Maybe I should write down some of this shit.

1963

The Journal

My head nods forward and my chin drops down and hits my chest and the notebook slides off my lap again. I pick it up and chuck it at the open door of the wood-burning stove. I am half asleep, the opening is small, my aim is bad, and the notebook bounces off into a darkened corner of the room.

It is one of those hard-backed notebooks with the pages stitched in, the kind kids take to school in the third grade to write their assignments in. The cardboard cover is slate-dark, with flecks of something white floating around in the darkness. The cover is slick and every time I nod off in front of the stove, it slides off my lap.

The notebook is part of my journal. And under the plank-sided lower bunk in the far corner of the bunkhouse there is a small canvas bag with maybe a dozen of them tied in a bundle with a piece of rawhide.

The Indian, Wendell Klah, never really liked the idea of my keeping a journal. He says it is just something you have to lug around, a piece of your life that is already over, something that you probably didn't do well the first time, and now you're carrying it around so you can regret it all over again. Journals are for girls, he says. Don't write anything in there about me, he says. Fucking Indian.

It is different with the Mexican, Caton Baros. He thinks writing in a notebook is somehow special. He has not gone very far in school and, anyway, the schools in Mexico had very few notebooks for the kids to write in. Caton is small, and the bigger kids always got the notebooks. He never got one, so he likes to see me write in mine. Now and then, I will hand the notebook to Cat and he will write a few words in it in Spanish. It is years before I notice that he always wrote the same thing.

El pan de cada dia.

Fucking Mexican.

I don't write in my notebooks every day. What I write tends to be little stories, little memories, more about some instant of my life rather than what happened on a specific day; more about what I feel about what is happening, rather than the happening itself. Maybe that's why, in later years, it turns out there are some big vacant spaces in my journal. I know I should try to find Wendell and Cat so I can fill in the blanks, try to find the only two friends I have ever had, try to make some sense out of the blank spaces. But I know I probably never will.

All in all, it doesn't really matter. Over the years, I lose a notebook, now and then. I lost one last week. I dropped it somewhere on some trail when Wendell and Cat and I were coming down off the high country, racing the snow back to the ranch. I never miss it until days later, when I need some paper to start a fire. Thought I would use the notebook. It is gone.

I pick up the notebook and take aim at the stove again. Out of the corner of my eye I see Cat, lying on his bunk, the firelight glistening from his eyes. He isn't looking at me. He's looking at the notebook.

I close the notebook and tuck it under the mattress of my bunk. When I turn back to Cat, he is feigning sleep, his eyes closed, the hint of a smile on his dark lips.

And I know that I am stuck with the goddamn journal for the rest of my life.

1964

Portland in the Night

I don't know why I head north up the valley, rather than west. I am supposed to meet the Mexican and the Indian in San Francisco.

Sometimes, when you are hitch-hiking, a ride just comes along that you think you should take, no matter where it is going. It always seems like a good idea at the time.

I am standing at the side of the road just outside of Sacramento, it is getting dark, and a trucker pulls over. He is headed north, not west, but, what the hell, San Francisco is not going to go anywhere if I do not show up for a few days. I just want to go, just want to be on the road. The trucker takes me all the way into Oregon.

When he lets me out I think I will go on north for a while, take a look at Eugene. Maybe, in the back of my mind, I think there was a school there that I can tolerate. Maybe not.

I never find out what Eugene is like.

A string of short hitches takes me to just south of the town and then the cars stop coming. The two-lane highway seems deserted, as though somewhere along the way the traffic has been turned off by some unseen hand. I sit on a guard rail at the side of the blacktop and wait. Now and then a car goes by, but the drivers do not even look at me. It gets dark, then windy, and then the wind starts to carry a slight mist that condenses on my face and runs down inside the collar of my shirt. I have on a thin jacket, but it is useless. I start walking up the highway, looking for some sort of shelter.

The big black sedan is past me before I know it is coming. It slides almost silently through the dark, its big engine hardly working. I do not notice the car's headlights as it goes by, only the flare of its tail lights when the driver begins to slow it down. Then I see the headlights beyond the car; I wonder if they had been on when the car went by.

The car does not stop immediately. It drifts up the highway almost a quarter mile, slowing gently, almost as if the driver cannot make up his mind whether or not to stop. Then the tail lights flare again and the car stops. But the driver does not back up. The car just sits there.

I walk up the highway toward the car. I do not shuffle along, but I do not hurry. If the car stays where it is, then I will get in. If it pulls away . . . who cares?

It is still there. I ease up along the passenger side and open the door just enough for the interior light to come on. I peek through the opening.

"Can you drive?" the guy asks. I can hear his words, but they are different, somehow, as though his mouth does not quite fit around the sounds.

I look in the back of the car, look behind the seats, look at the floors. Other than the driver, the car is completely empty. No luggage, not a candy wrapper. Nothing. Just the guy's suit coat dumped carelessly in the passenger seat.

The driver looks harmless enough. He sits hunched over the wheel, both hands wrapped around it as though he is afraid to let go. He has on a white shirt and tie. His head is turned toward me but it nods toward the wheel, as though he might fall asleep at any moment. He looks like a guy in his forties, average size, not handsome, but not ugly either. Just a guy.

"Yeah, I can drive."

"You drive. Portland. Take me home to Portland. I'll give you twenty bucks. Map's in the glove box."

Portland? Hell, I'm only going to Eugene, maybe fifteen miles farther north from where we were.

"Thanks anyway, man, but I don't think . . . "

"Forty bucks."

I hear his door open. He is sliding out of the driver's seat. He doesn't close the driver's door, just pulls open the rear door. He does not bend and tuck to get in—his body just seems to flow inside and fold into the car, his face pressing into the back of the seat. Instantly, he is asleep, not moving, a soft snoring sound barely audible above the idling engine.

I am still standing outside the open passenger door, misty rain dripping down my face, unsure, trying to decide if I should get into the car—and the guy has already crawled into the back seat and fallen asleep.

I close the door, walk around the car and slide into the driver's seat. I think I should not be here, think I should pull the car off the road, lock it up and just walk away. I can search the car, pop the trunk, see what's inside, search the guy, find his wallet, dump him out into the black and the rain. Do anything I want. But what I do is I put the car in gear.

The whole thing is surreal.

I like surreal.

I drive away.

The big sedan is a Lincoln, new, heavy, powerful, quiet. For a few miles I play with the controls, adjust the seat, fiddle with the radio, try to find the dimmer switch for the lights. I turn now and then to get a glimpse of the guy in the back seat. I sniff like a hound, trying to catch a whiff of alcohol. But there is nothing. Whatever the guy is on, it isn't booze. And the guy has not moved.

I mess with the radio some more, find a jazz station, turn up the bass so I can hear the low notes, and drive north as though I own the world. Portland is up there, somewhere. I really do not care where, or how long it will take us to get there. I have been hitch-hiking for four days. This is the most comfortable I have been in all that time.

I do not need a map to get to Portland. It is up the highway. If I don't make any stupid turns, I should hit it head-on. The rain has stopped, the jazz station has faded. I turn off the radio and drive in silence.

I find the city in the tiny, black hours of the night. The big Lincoln is so smooth and quiet I can hardly hear the engine, hardly feel the streets. I love it. I am almost sad to get to Portland.

And then I realize that I do not know *where* in Portland I am supposed to go.

I drive through the outer edge of the city for a few minutes, then pull into an all-night gas station and park under the lights away from the pumps. I take the keys, get out, stretch, try not to look suspicious. After all, there is a guy passed out in the back seat and I don't even know his name.

For all I know, he could be dead.

I walk around the car, away from the station, and open the door. The guy's head is toward me, still facing into the back of the seat. Still snoring softly. I shake his shoulders. Nothing. I pull his arms, turn his head, roll him slightly. Nothing.

I lean farther into the car and put my mouth against his ear.

"Hey, buddy, we're here. We're here in Portland."

He does not move.

I raise my voice.

"Hey, dead man! Wake up! We're here!"

He does not move. There is no indication of any kind that he hears me.

I am afraid to do more. I do not want the guy inside the gas station to wonder if there is something weird going on.

I rise up out of the car and slam the door. I open the passenger door and rummage through his coat. His wallet is in an inside pocket. The wallet is thick, stuffed with bills. I find his driver's license.

John Smith.

John Smith? Give me a fucking break . . .

I take a couple of singles and the license out and put the wallet back in the coat, go into the tiny building and wake up the guy behind the counter.

I am new to Portland, I say, am visiting a friend. I need some help finding his house—the address on the license. Under a naked light bulb covered with fly shit, we look at a map, running our fingers around the paper until we find the street I am looking for. I give the guy a buck for the map and get the hell out of there.

Surreal is beginning to wear thin.

The house sits on a steep bank, a flight of concrete steps leading up from the street to a small, dark, front porch. There are no lights on in the house. From what I can see through the night, there is nothing special about the place. It is plain, unadorned, just a house, like others in the neighborhood, perhaps the right place to live for a man named . . . John Smith. I can see no driveway, no parking off the street. The car will have to sit where it is. I sit in the silent car—the guy's snoring has stopped—and stare up at the house.

What the hell am I supposed to do now?

I take the keys, get out, and slowly climb the stairs. Forty steps upward, the concrete of the steps cracked, bits and pieces crumbling under my feet. There is no furniture of any kind on the small porch, nothing, not even a potted plant. I push the doorbell but hear nothing inside. I wait, then push it again. Nothing. I knock on the door. I can hear the knocking bounce around inside the house, but that is all. I knock again. There are no lights coming on, no movement.

I stand at the edge of the porch and look down at the car. I have the guy's wallet, stuffed with cash. I can just take the money, walk away, leave the guy here. Fuck him.

I don't know why I do not.

I try the door knob. It is locked. I look at the car keys. There are other keys on the ring. I try a couple. One of them fits the door, and I unlock it, turn the knob and eased the door slightly open. There is no sound within the house, no movement.

I go back to the car and open the back door, reach in and grab the guy by the arms. I pull him partly out of the door. He makes no move to help. His eyes are closed, his breathing shallow. I am going to have to carry the son of a bitch.

I manage to get him on the ground and sit him up, lean him back against the car. And that's when I see the butt of the pistol sticking out of the top of his pants.

This is the time to walk away. Leave it be. Disappear into the night in the city.

I don't know why I do not.

I carefully slip the big pistol from his belt and try to look at in the dark. A big, squarish, dark piece of metal. I have seen guns like this in the movies, but I have never held one. I feel the end of the barrel with my finger. The goddamn barrel is almost big enough for my finger to slip inside. The hammer is cocked and there is a little lever on the side that

I think is the safety, but I have no idea if the gun is actually safe. And I don't know how to check. I stuff the gun into my back pocket. It does not fit completely inside, the butt hanging out like the handle of some lethal tool.

It is a struggle, but I finally get the guy up and leaning against the car, then draped across my shoulders, his arms and legs dangling. I struggle up the concrete steps. By the time I get to the top I can hardly breathe.

The door swings open easily when I push it with my foot. I stagger inside and stand in what must be a living room. Just to my right is a small table with a lamp and I manage to reach down and turn it on. The bulb must be small—the lamp throws only a dim light, just enough to create shadows from the few pieces of nondescript furniture that are in the room. In the far wall there is a door. It is the only way out of the room other than the door I had come in.

There is a sagging couch against the left wall and I drop the guy onto it. He is lying on his back, his arm hanging down, his hand touching the floor. I loosen his tie and unbutton his shirt collar. I think he is breathing, but I cannot tell. And I don't care. I have done what he asked me to do—I've brought the guy home to Portland.

I take out his wallet and drop it on a table at the end of the couch.

And I take out the gun.

I can see the gun more clearly, now. It is some sort of automatic, heavy, hanging in my hand like dead metal. I don't know anything about such a gun, don't know how to shoot it, don't even know how to hold it. I grip it in my hand, raise my arm and point the gun at the wall. I stand that way for a while, pointing the gun at the wall, then pull my arm in tight against my waist, the gun slightly tilted on its side, Jimmy Cagney holding a gat on some other bad guys. Suddenly, I feel like an asshole. I put the gun on the table with the wallet.

I go to the front door. The door is still standing open and I put my hand on the knob, step through, and start to pull it closed after me. Then I stop. The guy owes me forty bucks. I step back inside and turn back toward the couch.

The door at the back of the room is open and she is standing there, leaning against the door frame, her arms crossed under her breasts. She is tall, curvy, her hips full and her waist trim. Her long dark hair hangs down the sides of her face, not like she has just wakened, but like she has just brushed it. It shines, even in the dim light. She is wearing some sort of thing that—I guess—rich women wear to bed, long, thin, shiny, and not really covering anything. Her arms push her full breasts up and I can see her nipples above the shiny, thin material, and I realize that the thing she is wearing was never meant to cover her nipples. I do not mean to, but I cannot help myself—my eyes drop to her hips and her crotch and I can see the darkness of her hair under there. She may be the most beautiful woman I have ever seen.

She does not move, does not take her eyes from me.

"Is he dead?" Her voice is barely above a whisper, but it is emotionless, almost as though she is not really interested in an answer.

"Dead? No! I mean . . . dead? Why would you think he's dead? Do you think I . . . ?" I shut my mouth. I can feel some sort of fear growing in dark places inside me.

I wait for her to speak again, but she does not. She stands there, not even looking at the guy on the couch. Staring at me. Seeing my old boots that look as though they need cow shit to hold them together, my old jeans with one knee almost worn through, my cowboy-cut shirt with the top button missing. She does not smile.

"Look, I was hitch-hiking. He picked me up, wanted me to drive, wanted to pay me to take him home to Portland. He never . . . He owes me forty bucks."

She stood silently, her eyes never moving from my face.

I point at the table with the wallet, move a step toward it. She says nothing.

Truth is, I did not want to leave.

I walk gingerly to the table, walking as though at any moment she is going to do something, say something. But she does not. She is close enough that I can reach out and touch her, can smell the scent of her. I think I can feel her heat.

I pick up the wallet and take out two twenties, holding it open, showing her that the rest of the money is still there. I close the wallet and put it down—and realize the pistol is gone.

I whirl around facing her, my breathing gone from my chest. I wonder what it will feel like, being shot.

She is still leaning against the door frame. But now her right arm is hanging straight down and slightly behind her hip. If she has the pistol in her right hand, I cannot see it.

"What do you want?" she says, still with the low almost-whisper voice.

"Want? I don't want . . . I just wanted the money he owed me for driving. That's all . . ."

She raises her left hand and moves the thin strap of the nightgown off her shoulder. It drops away, the gown slips a little, and her full breast glows there in the dim light. I think it produces a light of its own. This is not a whore's sagging breast, like the fat girls back in Colorado. This is the breast of a real woman.

"What do you want?" she says again.

I am not sure I can speak. But I give it my best shot.

"I want . . . you," I say, my voice dragging out of my chest.

I glance back at John Smith, lying on the couch. I want to see if he is moving, if I am going to be caught in some sort of weird game, caught between a man and his woman, Smith roaring up from the couch, maybe another gun in his hand.

But John Smith does not move. I cannot see him breathe. He would have to be dead to lie any more still than he already is.

I look back at her. And she is standing right next to me.

"Don't move," she says, in that voice. "Don't you goddamn move."

She takes another small step forward and her breast touches me, that magnificent breast, that breast that glows with some inner heat. She is so close that I can feel the heat of her breathing. So close that I cannot see her hands, cannot see if she has the pistol.

"Touch it."

"What?" My voice sounds wimpy; I have no strength in my body.

She says nothing, just stands there, waiting.

My hand moves. I do not make it move, it just moves all by itself. It starts at her hip and then gently slides upward, following the curve of her, moving off the thin, slick material and onto her body, finding her breast.

Her hand is on my dick, and she is not gentle about it. She grips it like she is trying to kill it and I wonder what it will be like to have an orgasm with a broken dick.

Without a word, she takes her hand away, moves back from me and steps into a narrow, dark hallway that leads toward the back of the house. As she moves, her gown slips lower until it hangs loosely on her hips and I know that at any moment she will be naked.

She turns back toward me.

"Are you coming?"

"Is that a pun?" I couldn't resist it. This is getting too goddamn serious for my liking.

She does not smile, just moves her hips and the gown slips silently to the floor. And I see the gun hanging heavily from her hand.

I have never seen a body like hers, not real, not in the movies, not in my imagination. But then, I have never seen a naked woman hold a gun, either. I try to sneak back across the room.

"You'll never make it to the door."

She moves the gun out in front of her, not pointing it at me, but ready. Her thumb makes a tiny movement and I heard a snicking sound. It doesn't take a genius to figure out that the safety is off.

And I sure as hell am no genius.

"What about him?" I mumble, nodding my head toward John Smith.

She says nothing. She backs down the hallway and I know I am supposed to follow. And I do.

At the end of the hallway she turns to her left, opens a door and steps through, dim, thick light spilling out into the hallway from the open door. I think I can see her finger on the trigger.

I stand for a moment. She does not close the door.

I can just go into that room, her bedroom. I can be in the bedroom of the most beautiful woman I have ever seen. I can touch her. I can hold her breasts, run my hand between her legs.

And get shot fucking dead.

I wait for the picture show to end . . .

There is no way to piece all this together. I do not even know what all the pieces are. I am into some place I should not be; into something I should not be into. I have no control over anything.

I go into the room and close the door. There is a bolt on the door and I slide it into place.

There are heavy curtains over the windows but I can see the wash of first light creeping around the edges.

She is lying quietly on her side, turned away from me, sleeping, and I just look at her for a few minutes, afraid to touch her. And then I do touch her, gently running my hand along her side, feeling the sweat that is still there.

I am feeling for the goddamn gun.

I slide gently out of bed and put on my jeans. I carry my shirt and boots and walk softly down the hallway to the front of the house. Before I step into the living room I ease my head around the door. John Smith is still on the couch, lying in the exact position where I had dropped him, the lamp still on.

I step into the room.

I don't know what I am supposed to do. So I do the one thing I always know how to do.

I run.

I want her to hear me leaving. I slam the door behind me and charge down the steps. The car hulks in the early light, a huge dark mass, its rear door still open, its dome light still on.

And I still have the keys.

There is no way I can get out of this if I make one wrong move. No fucking way.

I glance back up the steps at the house. There is no movement on the porch, the door still closed. But the light in the living room has been turned out. She is up there, watching.

I grab the map from the front seat, throw the keys onto the floor and close all the doors.

Actually, I slam them.

It takes me two days to get to the city and two days to find them. And then, there they are, sitting on the sidewalk, leaning back against the side of some sort of tourist trap, passing a joint back and forth, people walking off the sidewalk to get around them, not wanting to come close to them. Not wanting to be in the same city.

Wendell and Caton.

They look like hell. But to me, they are beautiful.

1965

Faggot

There is the black silence of midnight in a stinking flophouse. I don't know how long there has been silence. It bothers me. Where are the snoring sounds of the others? I lie there in the bunk, trying not to breathe the stink that slides through the air like oil, but too full of hurt to get up.

I am motionless, almost asleep, trying to let my body purge itself. Confused images float in my mind, twisted fragments of rainstorms and slick city streets, of cars and fire and doorways. I hear the Indian twitch on his bunk next to me and I roll slightly to the side, trying to see him. My shirt is gone and as I roll I can feel my naked skin sticking to the damp, grimy mattress.

Wendell Klah lies flat on his back. Just from the look of him I know his mind is not here, in this room. It is probably back in New Mexico, lost in his being, floating on the winds and soft lights of the mesa. He is not here, not in this room with its stink and its dirty bodies.

Wendell does not hear the soft, fat, shuffling bare feet as they come to the side of his bunk, does not really feel the eyes on him, does not smell the stink that grows more acrid as it flows down from the huge body and across Wendell's face.

But I hear the feet and I smell the stink and I gape at the size of the hulk that looms over Wendell's bunk. It's just that my muddled mind will not accept what I see.

Wendell does not see him, the hulk, but I know he feels the hand. He feels it when it clamps his throat, feels it as it expertly cuts off his breathing, feels the fingers tighten around his neck. And then an arm, an arm the size of a leg, rams under Wendell's back and he is lifted as easily as a doll. And I think Wendell Klah is going to die.

I raise myself on my elbow, trying not to attract anyone's attention. I can see Wendell more clearly now, but I cannot see him breathing. His back rises slightly from the mattress, lifted, bowing upward, leaving his feet and the back of his head on the bunk. It is as if his middle body had decided to rise, to leave, without taking the other parts with it.

In the gloom beside Wendell, a mountain of flesh moves slightly, a log-like arm under Wendell's back, lifting. I can see a hand the size of a prime ham sticking out from beneath Wendell. The mountain of flesh, the hulk, is a giant, a towering mass of blubber. The giant leans over the Indian, gripping him, turning him like a sack of laundry, one huge leg lifted to the edge of Wendell's bunk. Except for a filthy, sagging sweatshirt, the arms cut off at the shoulders, the giant is naked and his trunk-like leg toys with the edge of the bunk, tilting it.

Behind the giant, outlined against the light, a tall, thin man stands, shifting back and forth on pole-like legs, dancing from foot to foot, elbows flapping, his hands held up in front of him like a fighter, fingers curled, except, oddly, his palms turned forward. A stickman.

I wonder why Wendell isn't doing anything. Why is he just lying there? What the hell is this? Wendell's an Indian—maybe this is one of his angry gods? Okay, god, whichever one you are, we won't ever drink that much again. I promise. But, god or no god, I'm not making any promises about fucking.

Wendell brings his hands up to his throat, trying to pull the huge hand away. Both Wendell's hands did not really fit around the hand that is there, choking him, a hand that seems to fit around Wendell's neck like my hand would fit around a broomstick. Wendell tries to pry the fingers away, but can't. I know that if he panics, jerks, thrashes around on the bunk, his neck will break like the stem of a wine glass. I can hear him making tiny strangling sounds.

My mind is clearing. Wait, Wendell, I think. Wait for me.

"Stop making noise, Little Beaver, and you won't git hurt," a voice said from somewhere above the hand. I have never heard a god talk. It's not a god. Must be some sort of man, I think. But, Christ, what sort of man is that big?

I am wide awake now, and I can see more clearly in spite of the ache in my head. The voice comes from a puffy face that bulges as much as the hand. The face sits atop a neck that seems to be rolls of fat stacked on top of each other, pushing up and out of the filthy cut-off sweatshirt, a shirt almost as wide as the bunk the Indian was sleeping on. I know I should do something, but in spite of myself I spend a long second trying to remember if I have ever seen a man this big, a mountain of fat, a hulk. I can't remember.

And then, turning the Indian fully on his side, the big man pulls his arm from beneath him and began to fumble with Wendell's pants, pulling at the waistband, feeling for the zipper. Wendell whips his legs up, curling his body.

The fat man leans forward, his face almost against the Indian's. "Goddamn it, I said don't make trouble! Just lay still, you red asshole, and I said you won't git hurt!" The voice is jagged and grating, but with an odd cast to it that rings in my mind, an alarm, a terror. The hulk grunts the words into Wendell's ear but they force their way into my mind. The hulk grips Wendell harder, turning him, pressing down against him. There are months of sweat, spit, body grease and dribbled, rotted food ground into the giant's sweatshirt, and I think I can smell his rank, green, almost-liquid breath. Wendell tries again to move, but he is held in a grip and under a weight that presses the strength and breath out of him. He is helpless.

And then the giant's hand is inside Wendell's pants, searching, prying. Wendell rolls his legs up tighter, trying to bring his knees up as far as he can. From somewhere behind the giant I can hear a thin voice, high, nervous, and giggling.

I start to push myself up from the bunk. The giant catches my movement.

"You jist lay still, cowboy. First I git me some red, and then I git me some white. I ain't seen no blue yet, but I lay odds there's one'a them in here somewhere's, too."

"Don't hurt both of them, Ollie. Don't ream 'em out too big. Save some for me," the thin man giggles in the background, weaving, back and forth, back and forth, his voice like fingernails across a tin roof.

I look back at the giant holding Wendell. Holy shit, I think, that's got to be the biggest faggot I've ever seen. I have always thought of faggots as dainty, limp-wristed pussies, thin little guys who pour drug store toilet water over their asses and waggle them in the wind. Jesus, this is no pussy. This is the biggest faggot ever created, maybe the biggest anything. I am almost frozen just from the sight of the guy. Flesh hangs in folds from his stomach, from his hips, from the one leg that I can see, thick creases and humps of fat that swing and bump in the night. His lips flap when he talks, spittle spraying from them each time they slap together. The arm that holds the Indian is trunk-like, a side of beef that seems the same size from shoulder to wrist.

Somehow, the other bunks have emptied, whatever bodies sleeping in them ghosting out through the dirty light and fading silently down the far stairway. Wendell Klah and I are alone with a stickman and a giant faggot.

Oh, God, I think, I think we're about to be fucked. And panic hits me.

I do my best to explode from the bunk, grabbing the edge of it as I came out and lifting my body off the floor. I rise above the Indian's bunk and drive my body straight, legs shooting out in a hammering blow in front of me. I catch the giant in the chest with my right leg, the sound of my bare foot against the compressing flesh a whacking vibration that claps across the room. The giant moves. About an inch. He casually shifts his hold on the Indian, moves his hand to the base of Wendell's neck, and turns slightly to face me.

I drop to the floor and bring my arms up to cover my head, expecting the stickman to be there. He isn't. I roll under my bunk, come up on the other side. The stickman hasn't moved; still giggling. Let Ollie have all the fun, I think. I jump on the bunk and aim another leg at the giant. The giant sees it coming and simply raises his arm, swatting me aside. I land on the foot of the bunk and it collapses in a screech of bending metal. I come off the mangled bed as fast as I can, but I can feel myself slowing; the last few days have left me weak. The giant's hand is back inside Wendell's jeans, still rummaging and pulling, Wendell gasping from the thick fingers at his throat.

Wendell can hardly move. The air is precious now. I know it won't be long until he passes out, but I also know the giant doesn't intend to kill him. At least not yet. The giant wants him alive—groggy, maybe, and not in any condition to fight back, but alive.

". . . ther . . ." I hear Wendell rasp.

I quickly look around for a weapon, briefly consider the wrecked bunk, reject it. I see one of my boots. I grab the soft top and wad it in my hand, leaping directly in front of the giant and picking my target as I move. I swing, cracking the boot like a whip, snapping the thick Western heel straight into the center of the giant's face, watching as the giant's nose and upper lip disappear into the mass of flesh.

The giant screams and roars upright, his arm flailing and catching me across the chest. The impact shoots me across the room past the stickman. I hit the floor and ricochet into another bunk. The giant's huge leg comes off Wendell's bunk and slams into the floor, driving a cannon-like sound from the wood and bringing clouds of dust up from the filthy boards. In his left hand he still holds the Indian by the neck, shaking him like a rabbit.

"You goddamn redneck muthafucker! That hurts! That hurts good! Good! You hear me, muthafucker!? Let's hurt each other some more!"

Holy shit! I think. He likes it!

". . . other . . ." the Indian gurgles.

The giant starts to waddle toward me, his thick gut swinging back and forth as his legs move, each leg having to come out around the other in order to move forward, his hard little dick sticking straight out and swinging from side to side, flapping with each leg movement, always in danger of being crushed between the grinding thighs.

I can hardly stand. I think maybe I have enough energy for one more shot at the giant, maybe not even a good one. And I don't know what kind of a shot to take. Fragments of memory begin to glow again through the polluted haze in my mind, and I don't like the glimpses of what I see. I begin to feel that cold weight in the pit of my stomach that always forms at times like this, a solid, freezing mass that plugs my body. Solid fear.

From across the room I hear the strangling voice of the Indian again, the words forced out from beneath the giant's fingers, squeezed, gagging, ". . . other . . . faggot . . ."

Jesus, I think, the other faggot. The *other* faggot! The stickman! I search for the giggling man through the dirty light.

And find him.

I rush the stickman. The giggles stop as the man pushes a thin arm toward me. I slip past the arm to the outside and hook an elbow into the stickman's ribcage as I go by. I feel bone move, maybe break. There is not a sound from the stickman. I spin, intending to go for the stickman's neck, maybe a chokehold.

I never make it. The stickman is facing me and his arm shoots out, a bony fist landing on my mouth, my lips splitting, teeth loosening. My head snaps back and my feet pop out in front of me. I land on my ass on the floor. Shit, my mind screams, I thought at least this one would be a pussy! Through the pain I hear Wendell strangling.

The stickman comes in, leaning over, cocking another punch. Instead of ducking, I lean forward, still on my ass, and grab the man's other arm, pulling him forward and down. I roll backward, pulling my legs up, planting my feet in the stickman's stomach. I pull the bony body over me and fire both legs straight up and out. And then I let go of the stickman's arm.

The jangling body rises and flies, making an odd, broken curve over a bunk and into the wall. It hits feet-first and then collapses almost silently into the old brick, the head finally stopping against the wall with a soft, crumpling thud. With the last of my strength, I am on the crumpled body. I grab it, raise it, hold it in front of me, wrap an arm around the scrawny neck, all the time screaming.

"Drop him, you fat motherfucker! Drop him now, or I'll break this faggot's neck!" I jerk my arm and the stickman's head bobs sharply, weirdly. I think maybe his neck is already broken.

"No, don't do it, don't hurt Stanley! No, don't!" the giant yells, his grunting voice rising in pitch. He drops the Indian. Wendell falls in a tangle of arms and legs, his head hitting the floor.

I back up, dragging the stickman in front of me. The giant begins to follow. I can see Wendell start to untangle himself on the floor, gagging.

"Put Stanley down, you muthafucker! You put him down right now!" The giant's voice is still rasping, but there is a pleading note in it now, almost desperate.

I turn between two bunks and back farther toward the wall. The giant follows. I can see that Wendell is crawling now, fumbling along the floor, trying to get to his feet. The giant is between me and the light at the end of the room, blocking the way out—and I have no idea what I will do when my back finally hits the wall behind me. The giant is closer, blocking even the light now, and I can't see Wendell at all.

I have never heard anything to match the high-pitched sound that comes from the giant. It is a scream, a pig-like squeal of pure pain and it makes me blink just from the volume, the pure ripping cut of the sound. The giant's rolled lips curl and retract, tiny rat-like teeth showing for the first time in the dank cavern of his mouth. His arms shoot out to his sides and then whip behind him, clamping tightly to his enormous ass. He spins, and then spins again, and as he turns blood squirts from between his fingers and sprays thickly out into the room. He falls facedown across a bunk and it collapses instantly beneath him. He doesn't seem to notice. The mountainous cheeks of his ass are covered with blood and as he thrashes on the flattened bunk the blood sprays out and over the floor.

I can see Wendell on the floor, on his knees. He must have crawled up directly behind the fat man. Wendell's head is back and his arms are held rigidly, straight out to his sides. In his right hand I can see something shiny. And blood runs from the Indian's fingers and down across his wrist.

I fling the stickman in the general direction of the giant and start for the light at the end of the room, grabbing Wendell and pulling him to his feet as I go by. Then we are down the stairs and out into the street, stumbling in another darkness in another time and in another frenzy of running away.

Running away. We are running away again. Somehow, it feels comfortable.

Later, in a darkened doorway, I try to wipe the blood from Wendell's arm and hand. Wendell's throat is loosening up and he can get a few words out.

"I thought you lost your knife in the whorehouse," I said.

"Did," Wendell muttered.

"Then how . . ."

"Belt buckle," the Indian rasped, holding up the huge, oval rodeo buckle. "One time I filed a little sharp place on the bottom edge, just in case. Worked just fine. Must'a laid his ass open a couple inches deep."

1966

Dying in San Francisco

I get drunk in San Francisco and fuck away all my money and then the Mexican burns the police car and we lose him. None of it is very hard to do.

We don't belong in the city. We don't belong in a lot of places. Truth is, maybe we don't belong anywhere.

But, what the hell, it could be worse. Hell, I could be back in Bean Camp, or Black Hawk Ridge. Jesus H. Christ on a bicycle, I could be back in Crum.

Later, in the army, I would come to understand that, yes, it could be worse. It could be much worse.

In the alien darkness of nights in the city, the Indian and I walk the steep wet streets and try to find comfort in our own company. We lean together in black doorways and blacker basement stairwells of hard-faced buildings that offer nothing more than the cold touch of brick and stone. The days bring fog and then rain and even the doorways and stairwells fill with a coldness that goes straight to the bone, and to the heart. We steal ragged clothes from Salvation Army boxes and nothing fits and our steps drag and our jeans sag so that the cuffs wear against the grinding sidewalks, tattering, like kites left too long in the wind. In less than a week I know that we both have assumed the anonymous and sightless attitudes of street people. Bums.

We don't know how to make a living in a big city. We steal some more stuff to wear and then steal something to eat. We think about begging, but there is no way either of us can do that. We'd rather steal than beg. We know it is only a matter of time before the systems of the city catch up with us. And then people might ask about a whorehouse and a police car and a tough Mexican with a flaming whiskey bottle and an enormous faggot with deep slashes across his ass. And we didn't want to talk about any of that.

The Indian and I walk the streets, mostly looking for the Mexican, but there is no way of finding him. We take newspapers from busted racks and read them through, but there is no mention of the police car or the Mexican. I borrow the phone in a pizza shop and call the police, asking about the Mexican. The cop on the other end of the phone seems more interested in finding out exactly where I am. I hang up and we walk away, quickly. But not before I steal a pizza.

Once, we come across a soup kitchen run by the Salvation Army. We go in and stand by the door for a while, just trying to get the hang of the place. The lighting in the big room is uneven, different light bulbs hanging from the electric cords. The light drains down over rows of long tables and narrow benches that sag and tilt. Silent men move in grim shuffles past large kettles where steam drifts up and washes among them, men moving through a soup of fog to the benches, hunching over their bowls.

We get in line and get our soup and sit on a bench on the far end of the room. The little man sitting next to me takes his spoon and pours some hot soup down inside the front of his pants, holding his pants out from his belly and dribbling the soup in, a little at a time, letting the hot liquid splatter down inside his pants, soaking them, steaming his penis. When the spoon is empty he does it again, this time blowing on the spoonful of scalding soup before he dribbles it in.

The Indian eats his soup and does not look around.

As the little man dribbles the soup into his pants he hunches back and forth on the wooden bench, his mind not in the room. Then he makes a little grunting noise, stiffening on the bench. In a few seconds he relaxes, almost folding forward onto the table. He never eats a single spoonful of the soup. He puts the spoon down and leaves, soup dripping from his pants legs.

The Indian gets up and walks away. And so do I. We never go back to the soup kitchen.

We are bottom feeders. We steal bread from a truck delivering early in the morning to the back door of a deli. Raid a milk truck parked behind a small hotel. Grab a pot of some stuff a Chinese cook sets out on a rack, run into an alley and eat it. But both of us vomit before we get out of the alley.

And then we realize that no matter what we steal, what we eat, we were still hungry. Not just hungry like when you don't have any food, when you miss a meal, but hungry like when you miss a life. Bone-deep hungry. A kind of hungry that needs more than food. A hungry that needs some vision of a future. We begin to carry a gnawing that goes deeper into us than we understand, that empties out our resistance and hollows out our eyes.

It is only a matter of time until we die.

1967

Helen 1

I hate it here.

The wind screams down from Hudson Bay, carrying snow across the flats of Canada, then roars across the lake, whipping the water into slush ice. Once across the lake, it seems to seek out the town, pounding down out of a sky so thick that late afternoon light is filtered to a thin frigid gray.

The storm captures the small town like an alien invasion, driving at a hard lean through the streets, along walkways and over roofs. Drifts begin to form and within minutes traffic disappears.

I have no place to go.

I arrive in the small dark hours of the night before at the small Army base nine miles south of the town, a place so barren and chilling that I don't even go to bed, just sit in the room staring at the one duffle bag I have dragged along. Finally, a wicked early light comes over the stand of trees to the east and I pull on my only coat and get the hell out of there. I catch a ride into town.

And then the storm hits.

They had warned me about the storms, but I didn't believe them. I sure as hell am a believer now.

I stand on the sidewalk, shivering inside my coat, the weight of the heavy pistol hanging under my arm a reminder that I am not a tourist here. I am a watcher, a hunter. But not now. Not in this storm. I watch through windows as storekeepers huddle against their back walls, their brightest lights on, waiting for customers. But the people are gone.

Across the street I see a store with fishing tackle in the window. And bats and balls. Gloves. A tent and a volleyball net. Something for everybody, something to take us to summer, to take us out of the snow, here, on the last day of February.

I trudge across the street and push through the door, closing it quickly against the swirl of snow in the entryway. The store is long and narrow and warm, lit with the yellow light of incandescent bulbs drooping beneath a painted tin ceiling. Tables, shelves, counters and racks sag under the weight of gloves, balls, hunting jackets, tents, fishing rods of every known length, hundreds—maybe thousands—of lures, duck calls, wool hats . . . A sporting goods store. A store of fantasy, of every woods-born boy's dream. I have never seen anything like it.

But the place is empty. Not a customer, not a clerk. No one.

Just inside the door I shake the snow from my coat and walk slowly down a side aisle, my fingers trailing over wool shirts and insulated underwear, things that I want to put on, right now, right here, against the storm that presses against the front windows.

I'm halfway to the back of the store, standing next to a rack of guns, before I realize that I am not alone. At the very back, where a counter bars the way to a last stand of shelves that hold the largest collection of ammunition I have ever seen, a ladder leans against the top shelf. At the top of the ladder a woman is trying to pull a box from a far corner, stretching out from the ladder, her skirt tight against the curves of her hips and legs. Her legs are so long, so perfect . . . I realize I have never seen such legs before. Even though her head is turned, I can tell she is beautiful. I watch, unable to turn away, my eyes fixed on the small of her back. She doesn't know that I am there.

Her long, slender fingers finally tip the box into her arms and she climbs gracefully down the ladder. And she sees me.

I see her eyes flick over my shoulder, checking the store, learning that we are alone, just the two of us, at the back of the store, warm with the essence of wool shirts and heavy hunting jackets, the storm battering the glass of the front windows.

She knows we are alone. Her eyes come back to me and I can see clearly that she is not afraid. She puts the box on the counter, smiles, and says, "Did you bring the storm, or did the storm bring you?"

In a single sentence, in a single moment, she knows who I am. She knows that I am always brought by the storm.

I stand there and look at her. I am seeing something I have never seen before. I am seeing the future.

I talk with the woman for a few minutes and then, stunned by what I think is happening to me, I leave, pushing out into the storm and stumbling toward the bus station. I catch the last bus south toward the Army base. It takes the bus almost an hour to cover the nine miles.

I am a criminal investigator. Shit happens. Shit happens that night when I get back to the base and I am in the middle of it.

I don't get back into town until the first day of April. I go straight back to the store.

"What kept you?" she says, her voice full and deep.

1968

Ruker and the Bikers

I am a criminal investigator for the Army, and idiotically I think it is a job that matters.

I am new. I'll get over it.

It is that time of day when the light dies willingly behind cracked buildings and trash-strewn vacant lots, as though it cannot wait to cover the city with darkness to keep decent people from seeing what crawls there. The sun slides down behind the highest buildings, leaving a thick, tired heat that boils through the streets and seeps into the gaps of the boarded-up windows that stare vacantly into a neighborhood where no sane person ever walks alone.

Ruker and I sit quietly in the car, sweat running down our faces and soaking our shirts. We move only when we must, staring vacantly at the abandoned cars and dented garbage cans that line the sidewalk. The cans seem to be a permanent part of the street, overflowing with trash so old that it has become solid, petrified, and I know the cans have not been emptied, or moved, in weeks. Months.

We are parked between two cars that have their windows broken, one of them with all the wheels gone. Once, about an hour ago, Ruker got out of our car and pretended to be looking at something on the back of the car in front of us. Actually, he was pissing on the car. When he got back in his seat he said, "I should'a taken a shit. They'd never notice it, this part of town."

But they would notice us. We are wearing civilian clothes, but no one would ever take us for civilians.

I have to take a leak. Even though lights flicker only dimly in the near-dark and I know I will not be noticed, I am determined not to take a leak in the street. I am, I tell myself, more civilized than Ruker.

Ruker is my boss. I am on temporary duty, just a fill-in, muscle, new meat, another pair of hands, somebody to keep Ruker company. I don't know what Ruker's rank is, or even if he's in the same Army as I am. I have never seen him salute anyone, refer to anyone as "sir," take his hat off when he enters a building. On the Army base, he comes and goes whenever he wants, never reports to anyone, always carrying a briefcase that he never seems to open. The briefcase is with us now, behind Ruker's seat. All I know is, Ruker is supposed to be an investigator and no one gives him shit, not the officers, not the enlisted men, not the civilians.

We are watching the bar across the narrow street, one of those pathetic saloons that seem to be painted into the landscape by a set designer for a low-budget horror movie. The door of the bar is set back from the sidewalk and there is black grillwork on the windows. A single, flickering neon beer sign glows dimly, almost unreadable through the smoky smudge that covers the glass. I wonder why anyone would ever go in there.

I'm keeping Ruker company while he stakes out the bar. This is the third day of the stakeout and I am bored to a level of actual pain. But

Ruker doesn't seem to be affected by anything. He is six-feet-four, with heavy shoulders, thick arms, massive hands that close like vices, his body so thick that he barely fits behind the wheel of our government car. His face is craggy, split by a large nose that was broken in some long-ago bar fight. When he smiles, his mouth doesn't turn up; the smile forms a jagged slot across his ugly face and, for a moment, makes you forget that he isn't really smiling at all.

Before this is over, I will see him smile. Once.

We are chasing a rapist, an Army sergeant who kidnapped a civilian employee from the post exchange and held her in an abandoned farmhouse for three days. He raped her so many times she lost count. In between the rapes, he beat her. And then he disappeared. She was pregnant, but not any more.

It happened within five miles of the base, happened right under our noses. Right under Ruker's nose. I was there when they told him. I don't ever want to be there again.

We have tracked the sergeant to this city on the West Coast, to this bar, and to a snitch who has promised to tell Ruker's real partner, Garcia, where the sergeant is. Inside the bar, Garcia is sitting at a filthy table, trying to drink enough to be a customer, and not drink enough to be drunk. Garcia and Ruker have been partners for ten years. He is as handsome as Ruker is ugly, as graceful as Ruker is crude, slender where Ruker is thick, the kind of guy who tailors his uniforms to fit perfectly on a perfect body. Except he never wears uniforms. For this stakeout, Garcia went to a Salvation Army store and bought some crappy clothes to wear so he wouldn't stand out. He looks like shit.

Not stand out? Bullshit, I think. We don't live here. We could be dead, and we'd still stand out.

The snitch is supposed to meet Garcia in the bar. We parked our car here four hours ago and we just sit here, waiting, smelling the stink of the street and waiting for the lights to go on behind the blinds that are drawn down over every window we can see.

For the last hour we have seen no one on the street so we stay where we are. I'm edgy, but Ruker isn't. That's fine with me. I don't like being around Ruker when he's edgy.

And then we hear the rumbling.

The noise starts in the far distance, a growl that grows in your stomach before you actually hear it, slowly and steadily edging up until you can feel it in the metal of the car. The sound climbs your spine and crumbles into your brain and you know that whatever is causing it is not going to be good.

"Bikes," Ruker says, trying to squeeze his bulk farther down into the seat.

I slide down, tucking my knees under the dash.

There are six of them. They roll slowly up the street toward us and then turn in toward the bar, wheeling out again, finally backing the bikes into the curb. They kill the growling engines. The riders swing off the bikes and strut around the machines. Three of the bikes are shiny, glistening even in the pale light, mirrors twinkling, chrome burnished. But the other three bikes are different. They have pieces of leather, feathers, chains, beads, hanks of rope, studded belts and other crap of unknown use or origin tied, bolted and strapped to every square inch of surface. They look like garbage magnets. They look like shit.

"Rat bikes," Ruker mutters. "I didn't know this was a rat bar. What the fuck."

I own a motorcycle. I ride every chance I get. But I have never seen a rat bike. I don't know what they are, or what Ruker means. In fact, I seldom know what Ruker means.

The bikers are mostly big guys, fat, greasy hair hanging down to their shoulders, wearing heavy boots and studded leather vests with no shirts.

Only one guy wears a helmet, a World War II German type with a spike sticking out of the top.

The bikers strut into the bar.

Ruker is suddenly tense, nervous, balled up like a pending explosion. I know he wants to go into the bar. But he doesn't.

The bikers come out of the bar in a bunch, jostling each other, joking, laughing. They seem . . . high. They amble to their bikes, fire them up, ride away.

"How long were they in the bar?" Ruker wants to know, his heavy voice sounding like it's from some inarticulate throat.

"Seven minutes."

"Seven minutes is not long enough to be in a bar because it's a bar," Ruker growls.

Before I realize it, Ruker is out of the car and halfway across the street, his heavy legs and huge feet pounding the rutted pavement. I jump out of the car and run after him. Ruker pushes through the door of the bar. I know he will not charge into the middle of the room—he will immediately slide to the left, just inside the door, quickly sizing up what, if anything, is going on. I go through the door and move a step to the right.

The bar is as dim as a crypt. A haze of smoke hangs from the ceiling and the smell of stale beer, stale bodies and piss seems to ooze out of the woodwork. There is no one at the tables or on the stools. The bartender is behind the bar, smoking a cigarette and leaning on a broom. The three of us stand absolutely still. And then I see Garcia on the floor.

The hospital is one of those that sit on the edge of hell and, nightly, scoop up broken humans.

Garcia is on the third floor. He is in a coma and the doctors don't know if he will ever come out of it. The bones around both eyes are scattered fragments, ribs cracked, spleen ruptured, one lung collapsed. Somewhere inside Garcia a bleeder is oozing into his guts and the doctors don't know where it is.

I think Ruker will stay at the hospital and wait for the end, but he doesn't. He looks at Garcia, talks with the doctors, paces the hallways and, once, punches his fist into a tilted serving cart, scattering dishes crusted with day-old food. He goes to a pay phone and talks for a long time. And then he leaves before I know it. He doesn't wait for me and I have to run to catch him in the parking lot.

We stop the car at a grassy park and we sleep in the car. We eat greasy sandwiches and drink weak coffee and sleep in the car some more. And then it is almost night again.

We sit quietly in the same car in the same place across the street from the bar, the car now beginning to stink from the sweat of our bodies, and from the hate that bleeds out of our eyes. The street is the same, except for a trashed-out deuce-and-a-half that I notice about half a block away. The huge, blocky truck has one fender missing, its windshield cracked, its paint faded, and I dismiss it as another piece of shit that belongs in this neighborhood.

Last night when the ambulance left with Garcia there were wraith-like people in windows and doorways, watching. I could see their eyes and sometimes their teeth but I knew they were not smiling. They saw us get into this car, parked in this same spot, and follow the ambulance. And here we are again, obvious and exposed. Ruker doesn't seem to care. For 24 hours, he has not spoken to me, or to anyone, and I know enough not to ask questions.

So I am surprised when he speaks.

"We're going inside. Follow my lead and don't get in the way. If there comes a time when you don't want any part of this, just walk away."

As usual, I don't know what he means. I don't *want* to know what he means, but I follow him into the bar.

Two guys sit on stools, talking with the bartender. The rest of the place is empty.

The bartender is surprised to see us. He starts toward the other end of the bar.

"No," is all Ruker says. The bartender stops.

The two guys get up and start around us toward the door. Ruker holds out his arm, like he's directing traffic.

"Take your beer and go to the back. Stay there and keep your mouths shut." Ruker's gravelly voice is so low I can hardly hear what he says. He walks slowly down the bar toward the bartender.

"Make the call," Ruker says, nodding toward the phone at the end of the bar.

"What call? I don't make calls for . . . "

He never gets to finish. Ruker grabs a barstool and whips it into the bottles behind the bar. Shards of glass and sprays of cheap whiskey flash toward the bartender. The guy flings his arms up to shield his face and doesn't see Ruker come across the bar. Ruker is on him like a giant on a gnome, picks him up and throws him toward the phone. The bartender slams into the wood and sinks to the floor, bleeding from a hundred cuts. Ruker drags him up, grabs the phone and smashes it into the guy's face.

"I told you, make the call," Ruker says quietly.

Ruker is still inside the bar.

I am back across the street in the car, where Ruker told me to be. Cover the street side, he said. I take out my .45 and jack a round in the chamber. I don't put the gun back in my shoulder holster. I snap on the safety. I sit holding the heavy gun in my lap.

I don't have long to wait. I hear the rumbling again.

The same bikes. The same riders.

When the bikers shut off their machines and swing down, Ruker is standing in the doorway of the bar. And suddenly there are two things that I know clearly—that Ruker may be the angriest man who ever lived, and that we are no longer investigators on official duty. We are straight out of the history books. We are vigilantes.

There are six of them, and two of us. I don't want to go across the street. I argue with myself: this is Ruker's fight; Garcia is Ruker's partner; Ruker is not thinking clearly, or not thinking at all. Why should I pay the price for that? I'm more civilized than Ruker. Why should I go over there to be beaten so badly that not even my dental records will identify me?

And then I realize I am halfway across the street. At some point, I have jammed the .45 back into its holster, and I have a military baton stuck down inside the back of my pants.

The first biker, the guy with the spiked helmet, rushes the door and I see Ruker's right hand shoot out at his neck. Ruker grabs the man and spins him, slamming him against the doorway, fingers digging into the guy's throat. The biker is sagging, knees bending, the air, and the fight, gone from him. The other bikers seem stunned.

I see a flicker of motion to my right and suddenly there are two guys standing on the sidewalk, not bikers, guys who wear loose black pants, black t-shirts, boots, their hair cut so short they are almost bald. They move at the same time, using their feet, and two bikers are on the pavement. It happens so fast I don't know what those guys do, or how they do it. The bikers just go to the ground and stay there, each of them clutching body parts and screaming.

The other bikers are moving, one toward Ruker, the others toward the two guys in black. Ruker has been holding his man with one hand. Now, he drops him, unconscious, to the ground and moves out of the doorway, shooting a straight right at the face of the man in front of him. The guy throws up his arms to block the shot and doesn't see Ruker's right leg coming up at the same time. The leg, as big as a tree trunk, thuds up between the guy's legs and he doubles over instantly, puking on the sidewalk. Ruker kicks him in the ribs and the puke shoots all the way to the front of the building.

One of other bikers reaches the guys with the black pants. He never gets to raise his arms. One of those guys whips out a short piece of heavy cable and, spinning, slashes it across the biker's face. Blood splatters all the way to where I am standing.

The last biker breaks away and runs for it, toward me. I drag out the baton and whip it across his face. I feel it sink into his skull and he screams, grabs his nose and rolls off to the right. I catch him, whip him with the baton again and again, his ribs, the sides of his knees, his collar bone. When he goes down, his feet fly up and I whip the baton through one of his ankles, hearing the bone shatter.

One by one, Ruker drags the jangling, bleeding bikers onto the sidewalk, two of them still unconscious. The guys in the black pants do nothing, just stand there, expressionless, as though viewing a boring movie.

The bikers all carry heavy wallets hooked by shiny chains to their belts. Ruker rips the wallets off their pants and tears out the insides. He finds driver's licenses and collects them all, looking at each in turn. He turns to me.

"Four licenses have the same address," he rumbles. "That'll be the clubhouse."

Ruker keeps the licenses, but kicks the wallets down a sewer at the curb.

The first biker groans and sits up, his spiked helmet pulled back on his head. Ruker carefully, almost gently, unbuckles the helmet and lifts it from the guys head, puts his fist inside and drives the spike down into the bikers thigh. The guy screams and goes limp. He's unconscious before he slumps sideways and hits the sidewalk. He doesn't move and I think he is dead.

The two guys in black check the street, the front of the bar and a couple of the abandoned cars. They seem to find nothing that concerns them. They do not speak to Ruker, or to me. In fact, they do not speak at all. They turn and walk away and I think we are rid of them.

I am wrong.

They climb into the junked-out dual-wheeled truck and start it up. I can tell from the sound that the engine of the truck is not junk. The truck pulls away from the curb and eases toward us and I watch as the driver takes the truck easily over the row of bikes, the huge wheels crushing frames, tanks and spokes like an angry child might crush cheap toys. The truck rolls over the last bike, stops, and then backs over them. And then again. And then the truck is gone.

Ruker disappears inside the bar. In less than a minute he is back, dragging the bartender. Behind him, inside the bar, he has turned the lights up and started music playing on the filthy jukebox. He leaves the door open.

He handcuffs the bartender to the heavy grating that covers the windows.

"If any of their friends show up, you'll be the first thing they see. They're going to wonder why you're standing up, when everybody else is on the ground. In the meantime, this place is open for business to any neighborhood patrons who might want to drop by."

The bartender starts to cry.

We climb back into our car and pull slowly away. As we leave, I turn in my seat and watch as two winos materialize out of the darkness, edge around the bartender and wander in through the door of the bar. A few people have opened their bolted doors and are peering into the night. In the distance I think I can hear sirens, but I am not sure.

It's a neighborhood that I wouldn't be caught dead in. But it occurs to me that I might be.

Ruker looks across the near-dark street at the piece-of-shit house, a two-story frame that leans slightly toward the sidewalk. One of the front windows is broken. A flight of mismatched steps leads up to a front porch that is held together with nailed-on two-by-fours. Rusted pieces of what appear to be engines and other motorcycle parts are piled against the cracked railings. Inside, a naked light bulb shines dimly in a narrow hallway. Four bikes—two of them showroom-shiny and two rat bikes—are parked on the bare earth below the porch.

The lots on either side of the house are vacant, weeds growing knee high, piles of old tires and random pieces of metal sticking up like insane tombstones.

Ruker takes out a tiny flashlight and looks at the drivers licenses clutched in his huge hand. He looks at a few of the nearby houses, most of them dark, their doors probably bolted against the other evil and moving things of the neighborhood.

"That has to be the place. Even without a street number, you can't miss a fucking shit hole like this."

He pulls out his .45, presses the slide slightly to the rear, making sure there is a round in the chamber, clicks on the safety and stuffs the gun back into the holster on his belt. He looks at me.

"You don't have to be any part of this. If I step in shit in there, I'll tell 'em I sent you back to the hospital, check on Garcia. That is, if I'm in any condition to tell anybody anything."

I look at Ruker and say nothing. Darkness tics heavily against the windshield. And then I know that I *am* in this, that I'm *already* in this, that I was in it back at the bar when I first got out of the car with a gun and the baton, and that no matter what happens I will *never* be able to separate myself from what happens here. This is a time, and a place, and a weight that will be in front of me, on me, forever. I know what is going on inside Ruker, because it is going on inside of me.

This is judgment day, and I am one of the judges.

I am tensioned, a spring bent to the breaking point.

I am calm.

I drag out my .45 to jack a round into the chamber, only to remember there is one already in there. I check the safety and jam the gun back under my arm.

We take our batons and climb quietly out of the car.

There is no one on the street. I feel eyes on me, but, then, I always feel eyes on me when I'm with Ruker.

We cross the street and stand in front of the house.

I can hear Ruker breathing.

"Want 'em all?"

"Yeah," Ruker growls, "I want 'em all."

"Then I'll take the back."

"Two minutes," Ruker says.

I check my watch and then ease away and slide along the side of the house and around the back porch, feeling weeds grab at my pants and stumbling now and then over metal junk. The back door is closed. I slip up a short flight of creaking steps to the porch and try to see through a back window, but there's something covering it on the inside.

I look at my watch. Fifteen seconds to go.

The first thing I hear is a crashing sound and I know Ruker is through the front door. There are a couple of screams, some cursing, one curse cut off in mid-curse, as though the man's throat has closed. None of the screaming and cursing is Ruker's. He's working silently.

So far, no gunshots.

I move back toward the railing and try to relax, try to be ready.

The back door explodes.

A huge man thunders through and I know instantly that if I give him a half-second to act that he can take me. I dive to the side, whipping the baton across his shins as I go down. I lose the baton. I hear him scream. He pitches forward and slams face-first into the porch, bouncing forward and down the steps and before he can get up I'm on him, wrapping up one of his arms and twisting and I feel the arm come loose from its socket. He screams again and I drive the heel of my hand into his nose, feeling the bones flatten. He twists hard toward me and swings his good arm at my head. I catch his forearm on the side of my head and the hit rolls me over backward. As I'm rolling, I'm dragging out the .45 and trying to swing it toward him. His face is directly in front of me and the swing of the .45 catches him on the ear. He goes down and goes quiet, his head back and an odd angle. I rip the .45 across his throat, hearing something tear in there.

I didn't want to hit him with the .45, I wanted to blow a hole in his fucking head. I point the gun at his chest and I think about it. But I do not fire.

I leave him on the ground, charge up the steps and blow through the back door, the .45 in front of me.

Ruker is standing in the middle of the room. Two bikers are crawling down the narrow hallway toward the front of the house, and Ruker is watching them go. Almost casually, we follow behind them. My eyes flick from door to door, the .45 on the door as my eyes get there. But there is nothing.

Just inside the front door, Ruker reaches down and grabs an unconscious biker by his leather vest. The two crawling bikers are on the front porch, trying to get to their bikes. Ruker kicks them down the steps. We follow, Ruker dragging the last biker down the steps.

The bikers never get to the bikes. Ruker sees to that. He grabs one and jerks him up into a sitting position, leaning close into his face.

"You tell your 'brothers', I'm dissolving the chapter." He shakes the biker. "You understand?" He shakes the biker again. The biker says nothing. Ruker slaps him so hard snot and blood fly from his nose. "You understand?" The biker nods his head, Yes.

Ruker brings his fist down hard on the bridge of the guy's nose, and I know the guy will never breathe properly again.

Ruker looks at me. "Where's your guy?"

"Out back, maybe strangling."

"I'm going to light it up."

"I'll do the bikes."

Ruker disappears inside the house.

I find a heavy piece of scrap metal with a pointed end. I kick the bikes over and drive the point through the tanks, gas dribbling out onto the bare ground.

Ruker comes out on the porch. Behind him, a light begins to flicker in the hallway.

I have matches in my hand. Ruker takes them and, almost casually, drops a lighted match on the gasoline-soaked earth. The flames that shoot up are so heavy that the bikes disappear inside them.

We climb into the car and Ruker starts the engine.

"You clear?" he asks.

Something jumps in my mind. "Wait a minute." I roll out of the car, scramble around the flames that are eating the bikes, along the side of the house to the back. I pull the .45 and step around the corner. The biker is where I left him. I cannot tell if he is breathing, and I do not check. I ease up on the porch. Inside, I can see light flickering and hear popping sounds. I scout the porch and find nothing. I jump down to the ground, take out a small flashlight and do a quick search. I find the baton in some weeds.

As I run back around the house toward the car, there is a small explosion and a window blows out behind me. And then I am in the car. Ruker drives slowly back to the hospital. There is plenty of time.

And I realize that he is smiling.

Two days later, Garcia dies.

I work with Ruker for two more years.

He never mentions Garcia.

I never mention the biker at the back of the house, never mention that I don't know if he had been breathing.

Ruker covers our trail, saying that we pulled out of the surveillance before the fight at the bar. He says Garcia was working alone.

We are never connected to the fire at the biker pad, where two bikers died.

For two years, unofficially, I try to find out which two bikers died—whether one was in the backyard. But no one knows. When the fire department arrived, they just scooped up the bodies and got them out of there. They knew one guy had been in the backyard, but did not know if he was one of the dead ones.

I never find out who the other two guys were, the guys in the truck at the bar. I ask Ruker, but he does not answer.

I am done with the Army.

When I leave, Ruker gives me the briefcase. I am afraid to open it.

Two days later, just at nightfall, on a narrow two-lane blacktop that crosses a high ridge in the Appalachians, I pull off at a wide spot in a turn, kill the engine and get out, looking at the mists beginning to form in the hundreds of valleys I can see stacking away in the distance. I take out the briefcase, lay it on the hood of the car and open it. Inside, the case is lined with something like velvet, and nestled into the bottom is a .45 caliber sub-machine, a "grease gun" we called them in the Army, a cheaply made, almost disposable piece of shit, one of the most dangerous weapons the Army ever handed out. Fitted into the lid of the case are six magazines, long black sticks of terror, each holding thirty rounds of ammo.

I take out the gun. I have fired grease guns before, but this one seems . . . different. It is polished, almost shiny, as though it has been worked on. Worked on? What the hell would that mean to a grease gun? I raise the bolt cover, stick my finger into the hole and pull the bolt back. The gun works smoothly, no slop in anything that moves. I jam one of the magazines up into it, pull out the wire stock and clamp it, point the thing out over the ridges and lean on the trigger. I run off all thirty rounds. The noise is a string of connected explosions that pound through the mountains over the scream that I realize is mine. When the gun stops firing, I am still screaming.

Thirty rounds in memory of Ruker. And Garcia.

Not nearly enough.

I cradle the empty gun in my arms, pressing it against my chest, a tiny curl of smoke drifting out of the muzzle.

And I know that I am not more civilized than Ruker.

I am not more civilized than anyone.

1969

Toy Beggar

It is my birthday and I am alone and from somewhere along the coast a wind blows down on me, picking up spray from the tops of small breakers and driving it, needle-like, across the narrow strand of deserted sand and into my face, a cold storm of the mind. The chilling water runs down my forehead and past my eyes, and I know there are some tears there, mixing with the sea spray. A man shouldn't be alone on his birthday, I don't care how old he is.

I am sorry that it is my birthday. I didn't want it to come, to crawl up on me with the weight of another year, another load of long hardscrabble months that keep loading my shoulders, pressing me flat. Another year of waiting.

I am just . . . feeling sorry. It is total bullshit, to feel sorry, but it is my right, on my birthday. I think I will do it just this one time, here, alone on a beach at the edge of a jungle that I have been sleeping in for weeks, and will continue to sleep in until they let me get the hell out of this fucking country where hot storms rage in from the ocean and into the countryside, twisting La Ceiba trees from the soil and flinging them whole into the tarpaper shacks of the people. People who had nothing before the storm, and have less afterwards.

The beach runs for miles, finally blending into the jungle. I walk toward the far end, knowing I will never get there, the sun falling into the jungle behind me. Finally, I turn and walk back toward the miserable little town, walking on the far edge of the sand, close to the water, feeling the force of the wind increase, blowing hard against my thoughts. If this scene were in a movie, I think, it would be edited out, a cliché rightfully left on the cutting room floor.

An hour later I am nearing the town and can see the long stone breakwater that juts into the gulf, a tiny part of it lit by a single bulb mounted on a leaning post.

And then I see him, sitting under the light on a broken wooden crate, waiting.

On bright warm days people from the town walk out on the breakwater. They fish, talk, hold hands, drink beer and look at the few tourists who manage to find their way into the town. Probably lost.

And some of them beg—always the young ones. As he is doing. Only he is sitting there in the near-dark, with no one to beg from, all the people blown back into town by the hot wind.

I move closer.

He is maybe eight, maybe ten, no older, although it is difficult to tell. He wears shorts and a t-shirt that are too large, making him look smaller still. His skinny arms and legs stick out of his clothes like the articulated limbs of a puppet. He is barefoot. He is dirty beyond belief, a grit and grime that have become part of his skin, part of who he is. His skin and hair are of such a color that I have difficulty seeing where the hair begins. He does not move. There is no need. There is no one else on the breakwater, no one for him to move toward.

I watch him from a short distance, see that his eyes do move, following me, waiting for me to come closer. As I then do. I catch his look and hold it, not wavering. Closer. When I am but two paces away, he holds out his hand, palm up. I look around, looking for the other children, other adults, looking for someone, anyone, anyone who is with this tiny beggar, waiting.

There is no one.

The boy is a toy beggar in the warm tropical night. Alone.

I reach into my pocket. I have a handful of "Limps," the local currency, virtually worthless. I put the money in his hand. He closes his fingers around it and slowly withdraws his arm, the hand holding the money coming to rest in his lap. After that, he does not move.

I wait, but he does nothing, says nothing. It finally occurs to me that he is waiting for me to leave. And I do.

I walk slowly down the sandy street, then turn into an alley and into total darkness. I stop, ease back, and stand in the blackness of a wooden building that leans out over the edge of the street, its tin roof rattling in the wind like a cheap kettle drum. I hear a noise from the darkness behind me and I slip the huge pistol out of its shoulder holster and ease the safety off. I wait, but there is only the one noise and no one comes. I holster the pistol.

I lean out of the alley and look back at the breakwater.

The toy beggar is gone.

I step out into the street and see him walking slowly and carefully away toward the river, his back straight, his hand stuffed into his pocket. I know that he is still gripping the money, deep in his pocket.

I let him get almost out of sight and then follow, far back, ghosting along in the black of old buildings in the night. I follow him until he turns down over the riverbank. There is only one reason for him to go to the river. He lives there.

At first light I am sitting on a low bluff overlooking the river. People live there, maybe a half-dozen families or so, scattered along the bank for more than a mile. They sleep on the bank, piss in the water, drag old boards to place on top of stones to make shelter, bathe in the pools knowing that, upstream, others have pissed there, too. They burn damp driftwood to heat the pots they have salvaged from the flood plain above the low canyon and the smoke begins to rise above the river like fog, hanging above the crumbled banks like a thin roof, trapping the people below.

I wait, and I watch, but I do not see him.

As the light grows stronger I move up the canyon, toward a small stream that I know is there on the other side, running out of the jungle and into the main river.

A few yards up the small stream, I see him.

I squat on the bank, lean back against a small tree and watch. I don't care if he sees me.

He is on the bank on the other side, at the edge of the jungle, trying to roll a small boulder into the river canyon. The stone must weigh forty pounds and he can barely move it. But he does, rolling it slowly toward the edge of the bank, grunting, his face screwed up against the effort.

He stops when he sees me, the *Norte Americano*, the *gringo*, who was on the breakwater last night. He stands silently, staring at me, and I know he thinks that I want something. But I make no move and he returns to his task, slowly rolling the huge stone toward the edge.

The stone drops over the lip and rolls in slow motion down the bank, thumping to rest against other stones and I realize that he has rolled them all there, a pile of rocks on a flat place halfway down to the water. There are some old planks there, a piece of tin, some tree branches.

He is building his home.

He slides down the bank to the pile of rocks and just stands there looking at them, knowing the effort it will take to move rocks into place, rocks that weigh more than he does.

And then I move, and he goes motionless, calm.

I drop over the edge, onto the soft earth of the stream bank, slide down to the bottom and wade slowly toward the river, and the boy. He stands quietly, watching as I move across. The water never reaches above my knees.

The boy makes no noise. He does not put up his hands. He makes no effort to run. I am a *gringo* coming at him, and he knows I can do with him what I will. Anything that I will. Maybe *gringos* or other men have come at him before.

I stop within a few feet of him, the rocks between us. He does not take his eyes from me, but he shows no emotion. He will simply wait.

I look at the placement of the rocks and see the outline of the room that he is building. Bending over, and using all the strength I have, I manage to pick up a rock and drop it into line. And then another. And another. I squat beside the next rock and suddenly he is there, on the other side of the rock, his small dirty hands digging underneath, getting a grip on the stone. Together, we lift the rock and drop it into place.

I take off my shirt and he sees the pistol, but if he is afraid, if he cares at all, if there is any emotion in him caused by the weapon, it is hidden inside the boy. I take off the holster with its long straps and hang it in a small tree, within easy reach.

We go back to work. We work all morning, rolling rocks into the stream canyon. At noon there is nothing to eat and so we pretend that we are not hungry, staying with the rocks.

We pile the rocks, one on the other, until there is the semblance of a room. A room with no windows, no doors, with only the sand of the canyon for a floor, but a room, nevertheless. We add the old planks, the piece of tin and the dead tree limbs that we will use for a roof. We leave a small dip in the wall that faces the stream; it will be his door. He will have to climb in and out, but that is a small price to pay for a room of his own.

At the end of the day the roof is on, the door is made. There is nothing more that we can do with what we have. The room is finished.

I stand up and walk out into the shallow stream. The water is cool and I splash it into my hair, on my face and down my back. Although I have been thirsty all day, I have not drunk the water. Afraid.

The boy walks into the water and stands beside me. He cups his hands and drinks, looking at me over the edge of his hands.

I reach down, cup the water, and drain it into my mouth. Then again and again.

We simply drink, the boy and I.

I put the holster on and, out of habit, check the pistol. He watches, but says nothing.

I wade back across the stream and climb the other bank, my feet slipping in the soft sand-like earth. The sun is dipping below the high jungle ahead of me. The sun dies quickly when it hits the jungle and I know that in only a few minutes it will be too dark for me to be wandering through the brush. I will have to go to the river and follow it back to the town.

I turn and look back at the boy. He is out of the stream and sitting in front of his room, leaning back against the wall, watching me.

His room. His home.

In the dying light I lift my hand to him.

Goodbye.

He does not move.

I turn and head for the river.

1970

Reunion

It is the best café I have ever been in. I want to stay here, to live here, to drop out of the minds and sights of any who are in search of me, who know that I am alive.

Heavy wooden tables and benches nestle into the sand floor. The wood has been scrubbed so many times with sea water that the surfaces are velvet to the touch. The roof is made of banana leaves and palm fronds, stitched together with some sort of tiny vines that twist and bind like miniature snakes. The roof is held aloft by heavy timbers of wood so hard that there are no nails driven into it. There are no walls. The café is open to the air, to the beach, and the sea. The counter is bamboo, and meant only to keep customers out of the kitchen. There are no stools at the counter. The kitchen is an area directly behind the counter where a length-wise half of a 55-gallon barrel rests atop a stack of concrete blocks. Lying across the top of the barrel are pieces of heavy metal grill that look as though they might once have been the shelves of refrigerators. At the other end of the counter is the café's cooler, a heavy wooden box lined with thick pieces of foam that have been picked up along the beach. The box is half-filled with ice left over from the fish truck that leaves the village before dawn each day. As the ice melts, it simply runs out of the box and down into the sand. There is no electricity in the café. There is no gas, not even propane. When night falls, the only light is from the glow of two kerosene lamps attached to the center pole that supports the roof. The lamps do little to hold back the night. In this café, at night, you eat mostly by touch.

I sit at a small corner table near the front—the side nearest the ocean. I am less than twenty yards from the water. There are only three other customers, all men, all sitting at separate tables off to my right, and as the shadows of the jungle darken the café and the beach, I am not able to see any of them clearly. Even so, I sit turned slightly so that they are in my field of vision.

I dig my rubber sandals into the cool sand, sip a beer from the cooler, watch the small waves, and wait on my food. The menu is simple, never varies, everything cooked on the barrel-grill: fish—whatever has been caught that day—rice, flat bread, coffee and beer. The cook is also the waiter, and also the owner, and when he brings my food he brings a small pottery bowl filled with something that can only be described as liquid fire, the hottest salsa I have ever tasted in a public place. He smiles when he puts it on the table. He knows the salsa will demand that I have another beer.

I have been coming here every day for almost a month. It has become a habit, and I know I am not supposed to develop such public habits. But the café is, after all, the best café I have ever been in, and that has to count for something. I have begun to feel less tense, less hunted, less the hunter. I have begun to fantasize about living here, sleeping under a *palapa*, wearing nothing more than I have on now—sandals, shorts, large floppy shirt—fishing for my food . . . Coming here is a habit. It is a habit I will risk.

The cook brings my second beer, and I pay him, and I know he will simply go home, leaving everything as it is until he comes back tomorrow. If he decides to come back tomorrow.

I sip my beer, listening to the soft sounds of night at the edge of the jungle, hearing the overlay of light surf. Two of the other men are gone. There is only me and the one other guy. I keep him in my peripheral vision. He does not seem to be eating and there is no beer bottle on his table. He sits and stares at the ocean, now a black, moving sheet beyond the beach.

I tip the bottle up and empty it and realize that the other man is moving toward me. I have not seen him get up from his seat. He is in no hurry, walking casually, but there is no doubt that he is coming to me. The man is large, bear-like, with long arms and huge hands. I can see the size of his hands even in the kerosene light.

I try to stay relaxed, turning slightly away from him and reaching up and under my shirt, my fingers wrapping around the grip of the pistol that hangs under my arm. I slip the pistol out of the holster, move it down to the bottom of my shirt, ease off the safety and transfer the gun to my left hand, away from the man who is still ambling toward my table. I turn slightly toward the man, my left hand pointing the gun at him under the table. I put my finger on the trigger.

He stands at my table, looking down at me.

He seems thinner, now, but not really smaller; his bulk blocks out the light from the lanterns.

He sits down at my table, turning slightly so that I can see his face in the gold light of the lanterns. The lines in his face are deeper, the crooked nose somehow more crooked, bent more to his left, as though it is over there by accident and he never really cared to put it back.

He leans forward slightly, puts his elbows on the table and folds his big hands. I can see his gnarled knuckles and the scar tissue that runs down from them.

It is a full minute before he speaks . . . try that sometime, just look at someone across a table for a full minute without speaking. You'll think an hour passes.

"You don't need the piece," he says, his voice a rumble in the night.

"I'll decide that."

"What are we, enemies now?"

"I don't know. I know what I'm doing here. What are you doing here? Are we doing the same thing?"

He turns his head slightly and stares off toward the ocean. I think he has lost some of his intensity, some of the hard covering that has always been part of him.

"Looks like we've both graduated to other things . . . chasing different kinds of bad guys, now," he says, still looking at the water.

"Depends on your definition of 'bad guy,' I guess."

"You're not as careful as you used to be. Pretty obvious of you, eating here every night."

"Maybe I don't give a shit anymore." I wait for him to say something, but he does not. "Maybe there comes a time when . . ." I don't finish.

Ruker turns his face back toward me.

"The two dead ones . . . you ever get that figured out?"

For a moment I do not know what he is talking about. And then I do.

"I got their names, but not their locations. I don't know if one of them was in the backyard."

"Did it matter then? Does it matter now?" He is not being sarcastic. He really wants to know.

I think about it.

"It mattered for a while. But not now," I mumble, angry that he has made me think about it. "Nothing much matters now."

We sit silently for a while, and then he looks back at the empty counter.

"You think there's a beer back there?"

I nod.

He gets up slowly, as though his legs are tired of moving his big body. He shuffles across the sand floor to the cooler. All the time, I keep the gun on him.

He brings back two bottles and puts one down in front of me, unopened. He puts the cap of his beer bottle against the table and pushes. The cap flips off. He drinks long and slowly.

He looks at me.

"It takes two hands to open a beer bottle," he says.

I do not answer, and do not touch the bottle.

He reaches across, takes the bottle and opens it, putting it back in front of me.

"So, it has come to this?" he asks.

"I don't know. You did not find me here by accident. You've been tracking me. What do you want?"

He drinks again, long, slow swallows.

"Maybe nothing," he says. "Maybe nothing."

He pushes back from the table and stands, sensing that the muzzle of my gun is still following him under the table.

"You once thought you were a civilized man," he says softly. "You read Whitehead. Whitehead said that civilization was a very fine veneer—the more you rub it, the thinner it gets." He looks away down the beach. "Who you been rubbing up against, partner?"

"I don't remember that you read much."

"I don't. Never read the man. Whitehead. You told me what he wrote, about the veneer."

He picks up the beer bottle and walks out from under the café roof and stands at the edge of the light from the lanterns. He turns slowly back toward me.

"You still have the briefcase," he says, a small note of lightness in his voice.

My left foot automatically nudges the case sitting on the sand under the table.

"Yeah. Same case. Same contents."

He stands quietly for a moment, then raises the beer bottle and holds it there, above him.

I don't want to, but my arm and hand seem to move without my will. I take the beer bottle in front of me and hold it up.

"Garcia," he says.

"Garcia," I say.

He drains the bottle, turns, and throws the empty out into the ocean.

He shuffles away down the beach, his huge body growing smaller as he moves away, until his size seems almost normal. And then the night takes him in.

I never find out what he wanted, why he was tracking me.

And I never see Ruker again.

1971

Horizon

We search all of our lives, some of us, for that one great thing that makes us.

But maybe that isn't how it really works. I remember Willi saying . . .

"Be careful where you set your sights. If you reach your ultimate goal too early in life, what is there after that?"

Maybe life isn't *finding* that one great thing.

Maybe it's already here.

(Damn, I think, here we go again. More psycho-babble bullshit.)

It's the *search*. It's the *journey*.

Maybe it's here, in this jungle, on this beach. Sitting here in this café that will not be here another year. Maybe this is what defines me, *has* defined me.

It is *not* one great thing. It's . . . a slowly gathering wave of experience until, one day, riding its crest, you can see the horizon.

I can see the wave coming.
Within the day, I am gone from here.

1972

The Patience of Dead Men

There is an end to the desert somewhere but I am afraid I will not find it before I am dead.

Yesterday morning, I drank the last of my water.

I know I am in Mexico, but I do not know where, only that somewhere to the north the Rio Grande cuts through earth and rock in a slow grinding dance to the edge of the world. There is water in the canyons of the Rio Grande. The water is thick, muddy, and stinks of rotted human life, but I will drink it if I can get there. But I think that I will not.

The moon has been nothing more than a sliver, spilling hardly enough light to keep me out of trouble, so I wait until early morning, moving only when it is light enough to see the spines of cactus and the hard spikes of Spanish Bayonet. I pick my way carefully among the sharp things of the desert, heading north, always north, thinking maybe, over the next rise, on the far sloping ridge, from the top of a heat-soaked rock that I climb in clumsy fashion—thinking maybe that I will see the dark gash of the canyon of the Rio Grande. But days have gone by and I have not seen it.

When the sun is a hand-width above the eastern horizon I start looking for shelter, a place to curl up in some sort of shade, a place that I know I will have to clear of desert life, all those small and spiny things that are doing what I am doing—getting out of the open furnace of the sun. Usually, I find a rock outcropping that leans out over a sandy piece of earth, a place where I can move with the shade, easing myself along the rock, keeping the sun at bay. Sometimes it takes me hours to find it.

I see a likely place about a half-mile ahead, a spire of rock rising from the desert floor. It is not due north, more to the northeast, but I will make the detour if it will provide me with shelter. I know I cannot be in the sun during the long hours of middle day.

I reach the spire and walk carefully around it, looking for tracks. I know there will be no human tracks, but I am not looking for humans. I am looking for something to eat.

I see the curling, rhythmic signs in the sand, a graceful trail etched from a small *arroyo* directly to the shade of the rock. I take off my small pack and pick up a heavy, twisted mesquite stick. Edging toward the rock spire, I lean carefully around a corner and see the rattlesnake there, coiled loosely on a flat rock in the shade. I smash the snake's head.

For an hour I write in my journal. One of the things I write is a will. Last Will and Testament, it is called, although I always thought the terms redundant. I get past the first paragraph, the one about being of sound mind, when I realize that I am not, I cannot be, I probably never have been, of sound mind. After all, I am sitting by a tiny fire in the desert, eating a snake. But I write the will anyway.

The sun has slipped off the shoulder of the sky and is hanging in the west, the main force of its mid-day fire reduced to something bearable. The air is breathable again. I bury the ashes of my small fire and pick up my pack. I know I should not have eaten the snake. I know that eating will only increase my thirst. But I think that I cannot get any more thirsty, and I need the food. So I ate the snake.

Before I put out the fire, I burn the pages that contain the will I have just written.

I start north again.

My legs move without my knowing. I find it odd, being able to look down at my feet, to see them move slowly forward, rising barely high enough with each step to keep from catching, stumbling, sending me into the face of the desert. I watch them, my feet. But I do not feel them.

It is later now, but not much cooler. The sun falls down off my left side and the light begins to thicken and I think that I could feel the light if only I had some water. The light begins to shimmer among the hard desert growth, moving in slow rivulets along the depressions and piling up against small obstacles . . . and I realize that my mind sees the light as water and that I am going slowly down that mystical path where nothing is real and reality is nothing.

I walk until it is full dark and then I simply sink down onto the dirt and fall asleep.

In my dream, I am in the Grand Canyon, far up a side canyon. It is early evening and I am lying down, my head propped on my pack. Less than a foot from my left shoulder a tiny, clear, cool stream runs softly down the canyon, so steadily, so easily. I do not hear the water. In my dream I only know it is there. I turn toward the stream and lower my face into the water . . .

When I awaken, I have rolled over, my face in the grit and sand.

The night is fading. I can see the dim outlines of cacti and yucca. I get up, sling my pack over one shoulder and move off across desert.

The soil seems to firm up. I sink into it only a little and now and then my feet brush against scraggly blades of some sort of grass. The land rises slowly and I top a low ridge covered with spiny brush. I do not bother looking at the brush or trying to identify the grass. Nothing matters except that I keep moving forward, moving north.

At the top of the ridge I stop, trying to stand erect, trying to stand still, but my body weaves in the mid-morning light, pushed by the movement of hot air that snakes across the sand. I cannot call it a wind. It is only air that touches the skin like sandpaper. I weave like a slow-moving metronome, keeping time for unheard music in another universe not of my making. I stare to the north, seeing the cut of a canyon in the distance, knowing that a river made the cut.

Water.

I move forward, desperate now, stumbling. But there is no cut, no canyon.

No water.

Maybe on the next low rise I will see a canyon. Maybe. I start forward again.

A movement curls into the corner of my eye. My eyes are sticky from lack of moisture and the tiny unseen things carried by the breeze and I want to rub them, but know that I should not. I stare intently a little off to the east, in the direction of the movement. Of the movement I *thought* I saw. For a moment there is nothing out there, just more low rising sandy ridges, hard brush, everything baked to porcelain by the sun. I stand quietly, trying to be motionless, watching. And I see it again.

I see it now, farther east, an agonizingly slow passing of . . . something . . . between two house-size rocks that rise from the land. The movement is constant, tiny flickers of rhythmic light breaking through.

I want to keep moving north, but I know that I will not. I will investigate the movement. It is the way of things. It is my way.

I drop off the rise and down into a shallow basin and lose sight of the movement. I walk slowly, but not steadily, and not exactly in a straight line, toward the rocks in the near distance. The acid breeze pushes against my face.

The desert rises slowly and I rise with it, finally leaning against one of the rocks. I wait, listening. At first I hear nothing. But then I hear a faint, thin sound, a tiny squeaking, something turning on a dry axle. But it cannot be.

I ease away from the rock, ease to my left, and stare down the gentle slope into the salvation of men dying in the desert. I am looking at a slowly turning windmill.

I collapse onto the slope, my ass sliding into the soft loam, my eyes bound to the windmill, watching the corroded blades turn slowly, making the faint squeaking sound. But there is another sound, the soft bubbling made by a wire-thin run of water pulsing slowly from an ancient pipe and dripping into the stock tank below the windmill, a tank that must be twelve feet across and four feet high, a tank so old that sand has drifted almost to the top of the rim.

A tank full of water.

Suddenly the thirst that has been in my body and my mind for days, thirst that I have struggled to keep in back of me, thirst that I know will kill me—suddenly that thirst will not remain behind me. I want to leap up and run to the tank, vault over the side and into the water.

But I do not.

Patience, Willi said, back there, when we were in the mountains. Patience. In times of stress, we are men, not animals. We do not stampede. We will proceed to stay alive, but we will proceed with style and grace. We are men. We are men.

I push myself up from the dirt and walk slowly, and with all the dignity I can muster, to the side of the water tank. A narrow sheen of water runs slowly down the side and into the desert, thick grass growing where the water makes life possible. I look carefully around at the ground, at the grass, at the nearby desert. There are no large tracks—no cattle, no horses. There are only the tracks of every desert creature known to man. But none in sight.

I look into the tank, sniff the water. There is some green stuff growing in there but the water is clear. I dip my fingers into it. It is cool.

It requires resolution that I do not know I have, but I do not jump into the tank.

Patience, Willi said. Patience. We are men.

But . . . perhaps . . . we are dead men.

I drop my pack and take off my clothes. I walk to a drift of sand and rise to the rim of the tank, slowly put one leg over, and then the other. I ease down into the water. I put my head under, but I do not drink.

Patience.

Underwater, I rub my face with my hands, feeling the coolness of the water.

I lift my head above the surface and move toward the dripping pipe. I put my face under it and let the water run into my mouth.

Tomorrow, I will figure out what I will do next.

But not today.

Patience, Willi said.

1973

Low-Rider

The air drafting through the open windows of the cab of the pickup truck is soft enough to sleep on. The air is loaded with the fragrance of near-desert countryside and lies in the bottom of the small canyons and covers the twisty little road like the worn blanket you had when you were a kid. The sun is almost down behind the western ridges and the slanting light seems to make the air dance on the narrow, two-lane blacktop in front of me. I am driving with my elbow sticking out the window, the radio tuned to some country music station that keeps fading in and out. I do not really care about the music; it just seems that I should have the radio on. I have not seen a car, a house or a barn for miles.

It is the best I have felt in months.

I am less than fifty miles from the state line, driving below the speed limit, poking along. When I get there, I think I will stop the truck, get out, stand right on the line, take a sip of bourbon, and just breathe the air. Then I will climb back into the truck and sleep until dawn. And then I will find the mountains. The real mountains.

The big sedan eases up behind me. I have been watching it come for a couple of miles. The driver, like me, seems in no hurry, drifting along, the big car low on the curvy road. Really low. A low-rider, maybe. I try to figure out the make of the car, but so much body work has been done to it, it does not seem to be anything specific.

The driver hangs back about fifty yards. I keep an eye on him in the mirror for a while, and then I forget about him. More or less.

We come out of a long, looping curve and into a straight stretch and I realize that the car is in the lane next to me, his front bumper coming even with mine, his speed matching mine. Four doors. I try to see inside the car but the windows are darkly tinted. I can see only the outlines of heads against the pale western light. Maybe four.

We drive that way for half a mile. Then I ease the pickup forward a few feet, just to see what he will do. He matches me. I am reluctant to punch the accelerator; the truck has an engine that will tear up most cars, and I don't want the low-rider to know that I have some real punch under the hood. Not just yet.

But I punch it, just a little.

I have caught the low-rider off guard and before he can recover the truck jumps a full length ahead of the car.

I watch him in the big side mirror.

He comes on hard, roaring past me, cutting in front of me a little too close, close enough that I have to back off to keep from tagging his bumper. He keeps going, pulling away and storming into the next curve, out of sight.

I stay backed off, but I am wary now, feeling the old reflexes pull my nerves into tune. I roll into the curve, watching the sides of the road, looking for anything that does not belong there. But I see nothing.

Through the curve and then a few more and then a straight stretch and there he is, idling along, all the time in the world. I close on him slowly, waiting to see what he will do. When I am a few yards behind him, and he has kept his slow speed, I drift the truck out into the left lane—and he immediately drifts out in front of me.

Twenty miles an hour, tandem, in the left lane, not more than four or five feet separating our bumpers. We ride that way for a while, and then I drift slowly back into the right lane. And so does he.

He's beginning to piss me off.

I sit up straight, cinch up my shoulder harness, turn off the fucking radio, put both hands on the wheel, and twitch the wheel slightly to the left. As he sees my truck start to the left again, a little faster this time, he jumps hard into the left lane, the big sedan mushy in the quick move.

It is what I want him to do. As the car moves to the left, I correct, move to the right, and punch it. The big engine seems to have been waiting for this—it roars into full life, the rear wheels burn on the pavement, and the truck shoots past the sedan on the right, leaving the big car behind in a jolt of speed that I had almost forgotten about.

I watch him in the side mirror. I can see that he is trying to accelerate, but the car's value seems to be in its looks, not in its engine. In seconds, I am into another curve. I keep up my speed, driving now, really driving. The road stays curvy for a few miles and I keep driving, putting more and more space between us.

The road tops a mesa and rolls away straight into the distance, a black line running toward the far mountains in a series of dips and rises that resemble an almost-flattened roller coaster ride. Halfway across the mesa I slow down, again below the speed limit, poking along, the sun barely above the horizon. I'm curious now. I want to see how stupid this guy really is.

He is very, very stupid. I am looking in the mirror when I see him appear on mesa behind me. It is difficult to tell, but I think he is coming hard, having managed to get the clumsy sedan up to some barely manageable speed. I know that I can outrun him, easily. But I do not. I keep the truck loafing along, waiting. There is a game going on here, and I am a willing player. I think of the times when I should have walked away from the game, whatever the game was at the time, and I did not. I have thought about it, but never figured out why I do these things. I know that I will die without an answer.

I wait.

I watch him coming, coming on strong, dust, or maybe smoke, streaming behind the car. He is in my lane and I think he is going to ram me. But at the last moment he swerves to the left and blows by me, his speed and the closeness of his pass rocking my pickup. As he passes, I see his arm rising out of the driver's window. He flips me the finger as he rams off into the distance.

I feel the chase coming on, feel my leg tense up and my foot begin to tighten on the accelerator . . . and then I back off. The laughter rises in my chest and I let it come, laughing as I slow down even more, content to let the mountains up ahead in the near distance wait on me. I'll be there soon enough.

Okay, pal, I think—you win. Still laughing, I know I have walked away from the game. Maybe it isn't too late to change.

The road rises into the low hills in front of the mountains and makes gentle, swooping curves upward into the higher elevations and I am again truly enjoying the ride, knowing that I am closer now, anticipating the bourbon. There is a fairly sharp turn to the right, and then a long, easy turn back to the left and in the middle of that turn, on the right side of the road, there is a pull-off at the mouth of a small side canyon. And in the middle of the pull-off sits the low-rider.

They are standing in front of the car, four of them—two guys, two girls. One of the guys stands out in front. The driver, I think. Even in the bad light I can see that he is tall, skinny, a dark bandana around his head holding back his longish blond hair. One of the girls clings to the other guy and actually bends her leg at the knee and raises her foot behind her, something she has seen in a movie. As I approach them I am smiling. As I pass them, I wave. As I wave, the driver raises a small, shiny pistol and fires.

I hear the popping sounds of the pistol. I am stunned. I duck my head and stomp the pedal. The pickup lunges forward but I am in a curve and the rear wheels break out and the truck starts to spin to the left, turning my side back toward the shooter. I get off the gas and cut the wheel hard to the right, then on the gas again. When I think I am out of range of the pistol, I pull over and stop. There is a bullet hole in the right side of my rear window.

Son of a bitch.

I open the door and slide out, the engine still running, keeping part of the truck between me and the shooter. I can see him back there, waving the pistol, laughing, the other three dancing around like warriors, celebrating. I cannot believe what I am seeing.

And then the skinny bastard raises the pistol and pops off another round. And another.

I can only stare.

I have gotten out of all the places I have been in, out of all the messes I have been in, out of all the pain I have been in, and now, a couple of dozen miles from a place where I might want to spend the rest of my life, some skinny son of a bitch is popping at me with a goddamn toy pistol, holding his elbow tight against his hip and pumping the gun dry, a scene out of some old Cagney movie.

JESUS H. CHRIST I AM PISSED OFF!

He is reloading, taking his fucking time. He looks as though he is stuffing rounds into a magazine—the goddamn hick doesn't even have a spare magazine!

I choke down the anger and the heat and go cold. I grab the latch and release the back of the seat, pulling it forward. I grab the hook-and-loop straps that are bolted to the back of the cab, pull them loose, and the briefcase falls into my hands. I shove the seat back and put the case down. I stare at it. But not for long. I pop it open.

In a matter of seconds I have the grease gun out, pull out the wire stock, ram a magazine into the hole, raise the cover and pull back the heavy bolt.

What the hell am I doing?

I don't give a shit what I'm doing. I stick another magazine in the back of my pants.

I hear another pop and I know the driver has his little midget gun loaded and is back in action. I step out beside the truck and raise the grease gun.

Trigger manipulation. That's what Ruker called it—touching the trigger of the grease gun quickly and then getting your finger off it. Properly done, you can fire a single round.

I must be out of practice. Two rounds boom out over the head of the shooter—I'm not trying to hit them.

Everybody back there freezes. The heavy report of the grease gun is unlike anything they have heard, and the whip of the bullets above their heads is unmistakable.

Before they can move I start walking toward them. As I walk I fire two more rounds over them, but a little closer this time.

They break and run, all of them. There is a narrow trail up the side canyon and they jump onto it, feet flailing at the dirt. They disappear among the trees. For a moment or so I can hear them thrashing through the heavy undergrowth.

I raise the grease gun, sight carefully on the trees along the trail, try to calculate where they might be and where they are running, and fire a sustained burst into the woods above their heads. I can hear the heavy bullets tearing through the limbs and I know that wooden shit is falling in there, above them, each bullet driving them forward, farther up the trail. I move forward toward the car, and I keep firing until the magazine is empty.

Out of habit, I pop the fresh magazine into the gun.

I stand silently, listening. I think I can still hear them running through the woods, but I probably cannot. It is just that I *want* to hear them running through the woods.

The light is almost gone now. I look at the shiny car, sitting only a few yards away, a hulk with a silent heart in the coming dark.

There is absolute silence. I can hear nothing—no running feet, no approaching cars, no birds. Nothing. Only the slight ringing in my ears from having run off thirty rounds of .45 ammunition.

I do not plan to do it. It just happens.

Yeah, right.

I tilt the gun toward the car's left headlight and try that trigger manipulation thing again. I touch off a single round.

Dead center. The headlight seems to explode.

I ease the wire stock up under my arm, grip the magazine up high, and lean on the trigger. There are twenty-nine more rounds in the magazine. I use them all.

I turn the car into a pile of shit.

The incredible, horrible noise rolls through the mountains like some unwanted storm. And then it is silent again. Nothing moves. Nothing makes a sound.

I walk back to the truck. The engine is still running. I put the gun away and slide in.

I drive ten miles without thinking a decent thought.

The road drops sharply to a short bridge that crosses a steep, narrow little canyon. I am across it before I really pay any attention.

At the end of the bridge I pull off to the side and for some reason turn off the engine. I sit in the dark, listening for something. I don't know what I am listening for. All I can hear is the faint sound of the river, far down in the canyon.

I get out of the truck and walk out on the bridge, leaning on the rail, trying to see the river far below. I see nothing in the darkness.

I walk back to the truck and get the briefcase and go back out on the bridge, trying to judge when I am in the exact center. I set the case on the rail and hold it, tilted slightly over the water, knowing that all I have to do is relax my hand. The case will be gone, will just disappear into the dark, as though swallowed by its own history. I will never hear it hit the water.

But although I stand there until I feel the tension building in my legs and arms, I do not drop the case.

I carry the case back to the truck and secure it behind the seat. I drive slowly away, farther from the bridge and higher into the black mountains.

I have not changed at all. I know that, now.

1974

The Buick

The Buick goes away in the middle of the night in the heat of late autumn in Los Angeles.

I drive down Sunset Boulevard, the Buick cruising with the windows rolled up and the air conditioner on full blast. Up ahead, a gang of people stands in the street, blocking my lanes. A couple of cars ahead of me turn quietly out to the left and drive around the crowd, speeding through the intersection once they get past.

But not me. I pull up to the crowd and sit there, trying to see what is going on. Sometimes I do really stupid things.

Harley riders, maybe thirty of them, most just standing around, but some still sitting on their hogs. They look at my car, my *Buick*, look through the windshield at me, and then a few of them, grinning like fools, move farther out into the street, really blocking the Buick, now. Maybe they think Harleys belong on the Boulevard but Buicks don't.

Bastards. Harley riders are the same everywhere.

Everybody unsaddles and stands there, looking at me. They have no reason to block me off like this. They have no right. I'm not a biker any more. I am an executive, goddamnit, wear a camel's hair coat, smoke a pipe, drive a Buick! A *Buick*, goddamnit! In short, I am totally fucked up.

And then one guy sits on the hood of the Buick. *The fucker sits on the hood of the Buick!*

I spin out of the car, slam the door, rip off my suit coat and grab the guy by his vest. We grapple and wrestle, trying to fight, flopping around in the street while the others laugh and break cans of beer out of saddle-bags.

Nobody wins. In the final twists and jerks of the grappling I feel the swoosh of several cans of beer being poured over my head and I realize that it is over. Everybody calls it a draw, and everybody is still laughing. We let go of each other and shake hands. The biker's hand wraps around mine, and then around half-again, and I finally take a good look at him and know I am lucky to get out of this one with all my organs in their original locations; I realize the guy hasn't really been trying.

We sit on the curb with our arms around each other, swapping stories, the smell of my beer-soaked clothes blending with the smell of the beer we are drinking. The hog rider's stories are a hell of a lot more interesting than mine. The value of a camel's hair coat and a Buick begin to fade into the back of my mind.

There is no wind and the stillness of the thick air makes it seem as though we are all in a room, friends, sharing company. Imaginary walls shut out the freaks, gawkers and hookers on Sunset. In the background, a thin cloud of blue smoke begins to rise above the bikers and then someone hands a thin, gray cigarette to the biker, who passes it to me. The smoke picks up on the beer and drives into the back of my brain, killing a few too many cells back there.

And then it begins to rain. A soft, cleansing, easy rainfall that can hardly be felt forms tiny drops on my face and gradually soaks my clothes. My two-hundred-dollar pants are soaked and dripping and I notice that they seemed to be getting longer. Or I am getting shorter. It doesn't matter; the fight has already ruined them.

We don't really notice the rain. We sit in it, drinking beer, talking and laughing, telling lies. It keeps raining but no one rides away. The bikes sit like the shining armor of knights, guardians of the Buick, silent metal horses motionless in the dark and the wet.

Sometime shortly before dawn I auction off the Buick. I don't get much for it, but it seems like the thing to do at the time. A hog rider pays me cash, peeling the bills from a roll that must have been three inches thick. His girl gets into the Buick and drives away and I know I will never see that car again.

The next morning I call Tris, a buddy, a rider I haven't seen in a long time. He brokers bikes now. Almost respectable. Some of the bikes almost legal. I tell him I am dropping out again, maybe for the last time.

What took you so long? he wants to know. Tris can be a smartass.

But he gives me a job delivering a vintage bike to some guy up north. When I get to Tris's place and see the bike, my mind goes into a soft spin that peels away years and floats long-buried images to the top of my head. I sit in dim light in the small garage beside Tris's house and stare at the motorcycle. It is a Vincent, a show-room-condition black mother of a machine that looks as real and as promising and as vital as any motorcycle has ever looked since men have stopped straddling horses and started throwing their vital parts across the top of narrow internal combustion engines. It is a Black Shadow, a near-twin brother of a Vincent I had once picked up in a small town in New Mexico. It is the freedom machine of my youth. Oh, God, I think, I'm going to do it again.

My deal with Tris is simple. The bike is to be delivered to some guy in San Francisco, I can take any route I want, take as many days as I want, and I will be paid a hundred bucks. All I have to do is deliver the bike, collect the money from the buyer, send it to Tris, and I am free. Again.

I pick up the bike, pick up some gear, borrow a pair of soft saddlebags from Tris, and ride out of town in the rain. I am on the road again. And I am on a Vincent.

Within the first ten miles, I completely forget about the Buick.

1975

The Typewriter

Now and then . . .

. . . when I don't know where I was last night; when I don't know the name of the last town—or the next town; when every café looks like the last café and I am sure I recognize the tired, washed-out woman behind the counter but I know that I do not and never will; when the whine of the engine buzzes in my ears even when the tank is empty and the bike is still . . .

Now and then, I get down off the motorcycle and try to go straight.

I tried it in Denver once. For two years. It didn't work. It never has. Maybe it never will.

Going to work is the worst time, even worse than the nights. I feel as though I am on the down side, that a weight is being dropped on my shoulders and is falling forward to crush my chest, that my mind is slowly shrinking. I feel my number of tomorrows begin to count down. I am wasting them.

I can't afford a car—I don't *want* a car—so I ride an old Honda CB 350F, a rusting, rattling, wired-together beater that somehow keeps running even beyond the day when the odometer, terminally fried from turning, finally sticks at some unknown mileage and never moves again. When I feel that way, riding to work, I gun the Honda and look over my shoulder at my life and realize that I am, in fact, riding away from it.

I work in a gas station that specializes in oil changes. For hours, I drain the oil from the big cars of mouth-breathing fat boys and from the sports cars of skinny women in flint-hard hairdos and from the low-slung sedans of guys with knives in the waistbands of their ass-tight pants.

The boss won't let me park the Honda where anybody will see it.

Every evening I go back to the creaking boarding house that has been my home for as long as I have been in Denver, stash the Honda under the porch, and sit in my tiny room on the second floor.

And stare at the typewriter.

The typewriter never moves, and neither do I. Once, when I was younger, there was enough light behind my eyes to write by. Now the light is gone and the eyes are bloodshot.

And so, in the last hour of the last day of the worst two years of my life, I sell the typewriter. And I sell everything else in the room that belongs to me. It takes all weekend to get rid of it all; it takes a long time to sell shit no one wants. But I don't sell the Honda. It is a piece of junk, but it is freedom.

Selling the old manual typewriter doesn't matter, I think. It is a vintage Royal, a square, heavy, black box manufactured in 1936, a monolith that squats stolidly on the corner of the small rickety table by the bed, darkly, silently, reminding me each day of how useless I am when I sit in front of its keys. When I do manage to punch the keys they lunge slowly at the paper. Sometimes they bounce back, sometimes they don't. And once, when I hit the carriage-return lever a little too hard, the carriage launches itself from the typewriter like a torpedo. It crashes down onto the desk, hits a full bottle of beer and drives it neatly off the edge of the desk and into the wastebasket. I think maybe it is the only mess I have ever made in my life that I don't have to clean up.

But selling the typewriter *does* matter. It is *my typewriter*, my only link to creativity, and I have had it for a long time. The last thing I wrote on it was a list of all the things I wanted to write, had to write. It isn't a very big list—one small scrap of paper. I folded the list neatly and tucked it inside a worn, leather money belt that now lies on top of an old blue laundry bag that is my only piece of luggage. Inside the bag are my last few pieces of clothing. On the floor are my faded leather jacket and my motorcycle helmet. It is a good helmet. There is only one small crack in it.

I sell the typewriter for five dollars. I am glad the damned thing is gone. It is embarrassing to own a typewriter the same age as I am. The lady who buys it says she is going to paint it yellow and use it as a door-stop. With any luck, maybe she will drop it on her fucking foot.

The five dollars is the most money I ever earned with that typewriter.

I put the five-dollar bill in the money belt with the writing list and the rest of my money. The old money belt, with its shiny brass snaps, now contains everything that is valuable to me.

There is nothing else in the room except the sagging bed and the bureau with one drawer missing. I sit on the bare floor and lean back against the laundry bag, watching the light fade through the dirty window, feeling the aches and the tension running through my body.

It is time to move on.

1976

Tommy Hatfield 2

The beautiful old lodge sits on the edge of a canyon, looking out over miles of forest. Inside, we are gathered in a large, bright room, probably a hundred of us, waiting to hear the governor make a speech, a speech about hunting and fishing, about the environment. A speech I have written.

The governor walks in—cameras click and reporters flip open their notebooks—sheets of paper clutched loosely in his hand. As we get to our feet and politely applaud, he catches my eye, raises the paper and nods. He likes the speech.

I glance around slyly to see if anyone else has caught the governor's motion, to see if anyone else knows that the governor will be reading my words. But no one is paying any attention to me.

Except Tommy Hatfield.

He is standing in the back of the room. He is taller now, even more handsome, his face mature, more rugged. If he didn't smile, he could be on magazine covers. But when he smiles his mouth forms a dark slash that breaks across his face like a scar. His eyes are not part of the smile.

A dark light seems to show in them, some sort of hellish luminescence that has no good purpose in life. And Tommy Hatfield is smiling at me.

I am an adult. I have a college degree. I have been in, and out of, the Army. I have started, and ended, a lot of shit. I have a wife now, and a responsible job. I am, goddamnit, an *adult*.

And all I can think of is that I want to hit Tommy Hatfield. No, that isn't it. I want to *kill* Tommy Hatfield.

As we sit down, I turn back and fasten my eyes on the governor. I turn on the clunky state-issued tape recorder. As the governor delivers the speech in his usual monotone, not really knowing what he is reading, I can feel the eyes of Tommy Hatfield raking the back of my neck.

The speech ends and people crowd toward the podium to shake the governor's hand and I can feel Tommy Hatfield standing right next to me. I step to the side, away from him, and turn. He has some buddies with him, buddies I remember from high school, buddies who know about Tommy Hatfield and me.

We stare at each other, Tommy still smiling. Some others in the room begin to notice the tension, but they don't know me, and they don't know Tommy Hatfield.

The governor is still trapped by a crowd of people, but I see him motion to me to come to the front of the room. It's my job to "rescue" him, to take over the conversation with the crowd while the governor eases away. I start toward the front, and I feel a hand grip hard on my arm, spinning me.

"Jist wanted to tell you there ain't no hard feelin's," Tommy says, in a voice slightly too loud. I wonder if he's been drinking, or if he just wants his buddies to hear. He fumbles for my hand and grips it.

At the front of the room, some people hear Tommy and turn toward us.

I say nothing. There is nothing I want to say to Tommy Hatfield.

Tommy steps closer, still holding my arm. "You git back down home way, you be sure to stop in fer supper. We'll catch up on old times." Still talking loudly, still smiling.

And then I feel his grip turn to iron as he tries to crush my arm, and I realize he is quietly saying something else through the smile, squeezing the words through teeth that, up close, I can see are tobacco-stained. " . . . and after supper," he half-whispers, "I'll stomp on yer balls 'till you squeal like a girl."

I hear him, and his buddies hear him, and they grin like idiots.

I drive the tape recorder into the side of Tommy's skull.

The machine shatters, pieces of plastic digging into the side of Tommy's face. He is too startled to yell, just staggers backward, grabbed and held upright by one of his buddies. As the buddy holds him, I step in and hook an elbow into the other side of Tommy's head. Tommy Hatfield goes to sleep.

Cameras click.

I sit alone on a hand-hewn wooden picnic table not far from the empty lodge, breathing soft, late-evening air, watching darkness fill the canyon. I grip a copy of the governor's speech.

At the end of the table is an empty charcoal grill, crusted with the black residue of a thousand fires. I put the speech in the grill and touch a match to it.

From my wallet, I take my official state ID card, personally issued by the governor. I look at the card, at the simpering smile on my pictured face. I never really liked that picture. I spin the card into the flames.

1977

The Funeral of Cousin Elijah

I am going back to Black Hawk Ridge to watch them bury my older cousin, Elijah.

I say I am going to watch them—I'm not going to help, I'm not going to attend the wailing funeral service that I know will be held in the old slab-sided Baptist church. I'm going to watch them dig the grave, watch them lower the box into the black earth, listen as the dirt hits the top of the box. And then I'm going to get out of there, just like I did before, before the pull of the raw earth can rip at my heart.

The black earth.

On Black Hawk Ridge when we turned the earth to grow the scraggly corn and the thin runner beans the dirt was gray, sometimes black, and always loaded with stones polished by the wearing down of mountains and the wearing down of men. At the edge of the small fields and into the woods there didn't seem to be any dirt, just layer upon layer of the stuff of which forest floors are made, the refuse of hundreds of years of the grinding turn of life in the near-darkness of dense stands of Appalachian hardwoods. The woods made their own floor, their own dirt.

The dirt of Black Hawk Ridge seems sometimes downright personal. Like the dirt they take, now, out of the grave when they bury old Cousin Elijah.

Cousin Elijah died with his face between the legs of one of the widow women from down on the lower end of Turkey Creek. His heart gave out at the very time the widow woman was giving out and Elijah began to thrash and twist, driving his face harder into the crotch of the widow woman, making sounds like the grunting of a pig, his head almost buried inside her, jerking. She had never known anything like what Elijah was doing and in her eagerness to help she raised her legs and wrapped them around Elijah's head. All summer long the widow woman had plowed her own ground and worked her own bottom land, walking the long furrows behind the mule, and her legs were like bands of iron around Cousin Elijah's head.

Elijah died just like he wanted to, and just *where* he wanted to. Some said it was his heart. My uncle said he suffocated.

When they dig Elijah's grave, the men swing their mattocks against the black earth in the hole, then shovel it out into the pale light just beside the grave. In the hole the dirt had been alive, black with loam and time and all manner of living things. But as it dries in the sun it turns gray, the right color for being stuffed back into a grave.

The next day, when they bury Elijah, the rain mists through the trees and into the grave, turning the gray earth black again and then making it thin. A small rivulet of the runny dirt spills down and spurts into the grave, splashing into the dark water already gathered there. And then more earth slides in and then more and the preacher is afraid the grave might cave in, so he cuts the preaching short and the men just grab the long wooden box and try to slide Cousin Elijah into the hole but the rain sluices through their eyes and the black-slick mud climbs their legs and runs into their stiff Sunday-meetin' shoes and they stumble against themselves like corn stalks twisting together in a high wind.

The soft edge of the hole gives way under Cousin Inis' feet and he flops, arms flailing, into the grave in front of the coffin. The other men, already sliding the thick pine box into the grave, drop it in on top of him.

It takes them a while to get Cousin Inis out and he nearly drowns in the liquid mud before they do. They have to put a rope around the box and raise one end of it, and one of the men stands on the coffin in the process, adding his weight to the coffin and dead Cousin Elijah, all pressing down on Cousin Inis, who is screaming from underneath the coffin that he can see the devil down there. His voice makes bubbling, gargling sounds and we all think maybe the devil has actually grabbed hold of him. Turns out to be the mud in his mouth.

They finally squeeze Cousin Inis around the side of the box and drag him up out of the grave by his coat. One of the coat sleeves rips off as he comes sucking up out of the mud. Cousin Inis stands there in the rain by the side of the grave, blowing mud from his nose and digging chunks of black stuff out of his ears and eyes. He appears to be angry.

The man who has been standing on the coffin takes a shovel and levers the box flat again, then climbs out of the hole. By then, all the commotion has caused the mud to partially refill the grave, most of the mud under the coffin, and dead Cousin Elijah is in the hole only about half as deep as he is supposed to be.

And that's when they realize the coffin is lying flat, all right, but it is upside-down.

Cousin Inis, who didn't really like Cousin Elijah all that much anyway, rips off his one-sleeved coat, throws it into the grave, grabs a shovel and begins to fling mud down on top of it. He has completely covered the coat and the box before the others join in.

And so Cousin Elijah ends up in a shallow grave exactly as he has spent his last hour on earth. Face down.

Before the hole is full I slide to the back edge of the people standing there in the rain, all of them dressed in their Sunday-black, all of them staring at the hole.

I am on Black Hawk Ridge once again and I feel it grabbing at me. I ease off through the woods, away from the old graveyard and down past the Baptist church.

And then I am gone from Black Hawk.

1978

Ice

The wind, heavy with moisture, comes in off the Pacific and drives hard across the land, dropping snow where no one expects snow to drop. The snow falls in a hard, driven slant until it hits the thick evergreens and then it breaks into swirling, crazy patterns that make you dizzy if you stare at it too long.

We keep our heads down and slog along the trail, gaining altitude, wondering if we are going to break out of tree line before we find the old lean-to. Wondering if we are lost. We will use the lean-to as a base camp for the summit attempt we will make tomorrow. But only if we find it.

The snow builds quickly until we are knee-deep in it. At first it is thick and heavy on the ground and our bodies heat up from the effort of moving through it, from the effort of the climb. As we gain altitude, the temperature drops and everything around us become hard and fragile; the snow gets lighter. I notice that flakes that had melted on my pants have begun to freeze. Later, we will learn that the temperature dropped more than twenty degrees in little more than an hour.

We are traveling light. We are prepared for the mountains and the cold, but not for this much snow, not this late in the spring. Knowing we will be on rock once we have left tree line, we brought no skis, no snowshoes. We take turns breaking trail, one of us plowing through, the other two following close behind. Whoever breaks trail can only last about fifteen minutes, and then we have to trade off. We can see no more than a few feet in front of us. I am leading when the trail seems to flatten out, to become eerily smooth, as though we are walking on a snow-covered sidewalk. This can't be right, I think. There are no such trails as this.

And I am right. I am walking on a frozen stream and I realize it only when the ice breaks and I shoot down into the water. I hold my breath, thinking I will be in over my head, but the stream is less than two feet deep, enough to cover my boots, to soak my legs to my knees. I stand in the water, stunned that I am wet in the mountains in a spring-winter that is not supposed to be here, thankful that I can breathe, grateful that I can walk out of the stream. I backtrack as quickly as I can, breaking ice as I go. In less than two minutes I cannot feel my feet.

The snow on the bank is deep and dry and I throw my pack into the drift, pull off my gloves and begin to work at my boots. The others offer help, kneeling in the snow beside me, but there is little they can do. The laces are already stiffening and I have to fumble for a knife in my pocket, my fingers no more limber than the laces. I get the knife out and cut the laces all the way down the center of the boots. There are ice crystals on the boots before I get them off and my socks make tiny crackling noises when I pull at them. I am barefoot in the snow. I hang the socks in a tree: I know they will not dry; I just do not want to lose them in the snow.

The others are still trying to help, but they are only in the way.

I rummage in my pack and pull out some extra clothing and wrap my feet and legs. I have two extra pairs of socks.

The snow gets thicker. If we are going to find the lean-to we will have to forget the trail and navigate in by map and compass. We can hang our ponchos on the open sides and create a type of cabin, protection from the storm. And we know we can make a fire there.

We take shelter beneath a large evergreen that has lower branches held to the ground by snow weight, with more snow piling up. There is snow under the tree but not as thick as outside the branches and we think we might be able to hold out for a while, at least until we study the map and get our bearings.

There is just one problem. There is no way I can move from the tree until I get the boots thawed and dry. We think about building a fire; desperately wanting a fire. In the end, we know we can't. There is no real protection for us or the fire, too much fuel everywhere, and there is the constantly increasing weight of the snow. We have to get to the lean-to, and to do that I will have to figure out how to move. How to walk with no boots.

As we scoot around under the tree I realize we are sitting on a thick layer of forest duff—dry needles and tiny bits and pieces of twigs that have fallen from the tree over the years.

And, somehow, it all seems very simple.

I pull out my poncho and cut two large pieces out of it, each maybe two feet square, then two more pieces, a little smaller. I spread the two larger pieces on the snowy ground. I carefully scrape away the snow until I get to the dry duff, then spread a layer of it on each of the large pieces of poncho. Carefully reaching up into the tree, I slice away tiny, green fingers of fresh greenery, layering them in with the duff. When the duff on the pieces of poncho is about four or five inches thick, I cover it with the smaller pieces of poncho. I tug on my two extra pairs of socks. Placing a foot diagonally in the center of the duff "sandwich," I carefully fold it up around my feet and ankles. I have cut the pieces large enough so that the poncho ends up wrapping around my legs almost mid-way to my knees. Using parachute cord, which I always carry in my pack, I wrap and tie the pieces of poncho until my new footgear resembles some sort of Viking boots held in place by sinew. By the time I get things tied in place, my feet are numb.

But I can walk. In fact, I walk better then the other guys, my overly large foot-wrappings not sinking as deeply into the snow.

We waste no time. I don't know how long my "boots" will last and I want to get on with it. We start for the shelter. As we move, my feet slowly warm up, the tingling sensations gradually lessening. I discover that the insulation in my new boots is more than enough to keep my feet warm, and it stays in place. My footprints are so large that they resemble the tracks left by Inuit mukluks, which, I know, is more or less what I have manufactured.

We are losing the light. I never carry a flashlight—figuring that I shouldn't be rambling around in the dark anyway, and a flashlight is just something else to carry—but now I wish I had one. We have taken a map reading and a bearing and are trying to follow it, but the darkness is growing against us. The terrain begins to flatten out and I think that we may have reached the last ridgeline before the mountain. If it were daylight, I thought I should be able to see the mountain through the trees.

We stumble upon the lean-to, tucked inside a stand of trees. In minutes we are stringing ponchos against the storm, scraping away the forest floor down to bare earth and rock, a tiny fire dancing against the darkness, water boiling in a small pot.

Maybe we will live.

We are in the lean-to for three days.

It snows off-and-on for the entire time and we give up the idea of climbing the mountain, disappointed, but knowing that the mountain would probably have killed us in this storm.

The shelter is barely large enough to stand up in. The first morning, I hang my boots and socks from a small timber supporting the roof and I watch them carefully. It takes them two days to thaw and dry.

On the fourth day the storm dies and the sun shines so brightly that it is painful to pull a poncho aside and look out into the glistening world.

We know we have to go. We are low on food and there is always the chance of another storm. If we are trapped here again, we will never leave.

I can use parachute cord to make bootlaces, but I do not. My mukluks have not been off my feet since I made them, and I will wear them out of the mountains. I put the boots in my pack.

I have a much easier time walking than the other two and I break most of the trail until we are low enough that the snow is thinner and the air warmer. Only when we reach bare earth and rock do I put the boots back on.

I can't throw the damned things away, the mukluks. I am alive because of them. For years I keep the scraps of poncho and the frayed parachute cord tied in a bundle, hanging from a nail in the rafter of a storage shed. I seldom look at it. And then, one day, when I do, the bundle is gone.

1979

When Will They Find Me Out?

I don't belong here, in this town, in this job.

I wonder when they will find me out.

I wonder when they will know that I know nothing, can do nothing. I wonder when they will know that all I am is a reflection on the surface of a fragile glass jar, a distorted image looking back at things that have passed me by.

I wonder when they will know that I am hollow.

I always run hard, trying to keep one step ahead of that inevitable time when they will find me out, discover I am nothing but a hillbilly kid from Black Hawk Ridge, West Virginia. Just a kid who never really made it out of the hills, the hollers. A part of me is there still, sitting on the ridge, looking down at the cars that mutter along the narrow, pitted highway.

Maybe there is a Black Hawk Ridge for most of us, some place back there that has us by the throat.

I wonder if Black Hawk Ridge will ever let me go, and then I look in the mirror and know that it makes no difference anymore.

It is far, far too late.

I wonder when they will find me out.

1980

Hornets 3

There is a softness in the air so warm and sweet that when it pushes gently against my face I think I can taste it.

I sit under the portal of the ancient adobe house and watch the white puff seeds of cottonwoods floating thickly through an afternoon so quiet that I think I can hear them when they find the earth, a landing so gentle that, I know, cannot be heard by anyone or anything.

There is no one else in the old adobe. I am alone. I have come out to sit under the portal, read another chapter of *The Delight Makers* and sip good bourbon from a short glass so shiny that the bourbon seems to float in mid-air.

I am tired, so tired that I can hardly lift the book, or the glass. I sit and watch the cottonwood puffs drift, hear a bird somewhere down in the *bosgue*, the book lying unopened on my lap.

From somewhere out in the sunlight I hear the buzzing of an insect, a heavy sound, made by large insect wings beating thousands of times against the warm air.

And a huge, stinging insect—some sort of hornet, I think—lands on my bare arm.

I feel a catch in my chest.

I stare at the insect. It seems to be preening itself, although I am not sure that insects preen. Its heavy thorax carries a stinger so large that I can see it, waving gently as the hornet rests on my arm, perhaps trying to decide what to do next about all the warm flesh underneath its legs.

I can feel my aunt's old washtub under my bare feet. I can feel my tears. I can hear the buzzing of the hornet in the back window of the old Chevrolet. I can feel my tears. I can hear my father's words, and I know that the words, not the hornets, brand me, drive me, hollow me out.

And then other images push through my mind—swimming rivers, clinging to rock faces, sleeping under a deadfall in a snowstorm, sliding over jungle waterfalls . . . a grease gun.

Maybe it is the bourbon that is working on me. But when I look at the glass I realize that I have not taken a single sip.

And, finally, I am able to articulate it, even though there is no one there to hear me . . .

I am not defined by a fucking hornet. I am not defined by my father. I am not defined by anyone, other than myself. Whatever I do, or do not do, it is all on me. All on me. I am the only one who can do it, change it, be responsible for it. Me.

Fuck you, hornet, I think. And I gently flick the insect off my arm and watch it spiral away into the light.

It is all on me.

And I know that it isn't over yet.

1981

The Prayer Horse

I am in a hurry, and it is a mistake. A place I want badly to get to, a mistake trying to get there.

The plan is simple. In the early hours when the tops of the highest trees are still lost in darkness I will leave my truck at road's end, step across the log barrier and walk away.

I will walk across the Gila Wilderness in Southwest New Mexico.

The Gila. To be in it is to be free. Its countless ridges and canyons are what the world is supposed to look like and even after half a lifetime spent outdoors I can't seem to look at it enough, as though human eyes and a human brain are not enough to take it all in, to cope with it. I want to inhale it, to drag it inside me and hold my breath until it becomes part of my bloodstream.

But it is the Gila in midsummer, the heat of a relentless and unforgiving sun pouring into rocks and ridges and trails, baking my skull, cooking my feet.

At mid-day I pass a side trail that I know goes to a remote hot springs, steaming pools where I had once soaked for days in the heat and wildness and the company of hawks.

I stop, drink some water, and for the first time begin to notice the heat in my boots.

The boots are not new. I have had them for some weeks, have worn them around the cabin, around town. I have walked in them, run in them, done some easy climbing in them. I thought they were ready for the Gila. I was wrong.

For the rest of the afternoon I try everything I know; stop and air my feet; put on extra socks; quicken my pace; slow my pace; tighten the laces; apply bandages. Nothing works. But I am committed to the trail, wanting to do what I had set out to do. I walk on, the boots like live sandpaper.

The sun drops into dusk and finally I can stop. I am a full day into the wilderness. I take off my boots and socks and pad around on the soft forest floor, the first time since noon that I can walk normally. Before the sun dies completely I sit on a rock and inspect my feet. I count eleven blisters, near-blisters and hot spots. I doctor my feet as best I can.

An hour after dark the heat is still boiling through the high country. I lie nude on my sleeping bag and feel the electric buring of raw flesh in my feet. But I am in the Gila again. And I am glad.

At first light, I check the map. I have come twenty miles across an impartial and unforgiving wilderness larger than many eastern states. I quickly pack my gear and put on the devil boots. The pain is instant.

It is a simple decision. An "expedition decision" we call it. I will never make it across the Gila. If I continue, I may die. I turn back down the trail. I eat while I am walking.

I am not limping. What I am doing is far beyond limping. I am walking as though barefoot on hot, thin glass, a gingerly placing of each foot a short distance ahead, flat-footed, trying not to let the flesh of my feet move any more than necessary.

The trail loses altitude and leaves the tall pines and as it flattens out into the main drainage of the Gila River it becomes more open and rockier, by mid-afternoon the sun baking it to a fine searing edge. I know I cannot walk without the boots. And I cannot walk in them. Somewhere up ahead there will be the river to cross and then, still, more than five more miles to go, back to the truck. I am barely moving. I know I am not going to make it.

The river is somewhere ahead. As I shuffle and stumble I keep listening for the water. I count birds. Look for snakes. Try to remember lines from Tennyson ("to strive to seek to find and not to yield"). Anything to keep my mind at least above my ankles. But nothing works.

A new sound sucks its way into my consciousness, a sort of pulling sensation more than a sound, and I realize it is coming from my boots. I stop, sit on a deadfall, hold my feet out in front of me and look at the crimson oozing from the eyelets. If I take the boots off, I will never get them on again.

The trail comes out of the brush and straight into the water. The river is only about twenty yards wide and less than knee deep, flowing down from the Mogollon high country through narrow shaded canyons. By the time it gets to me it is still icy and I can't wait to feel it against the baking flesh of my feet. I never think twice about stepping into it.

When the water pours into my boots the cooling sensation is replaced immediately with a thousand lance-like stabs, steel points that seem to puncture every blister, probing between raw layers of skin. My feet feel as though they are dipped in acid. I am so surprised that, for a few seconds, my mind blocks the pain and I stand there, betrayed and angry. This isn't the way it is supposed to be. The water is not supposed to hurt.

Only twice in my life have I screamed uncontrollably from pain. This is one of them. The sound of my screaming cuts through the canyon and when the echo dies away so does all the natural sound. I cannot hear a bird, not an insect. I sink to my knees and then fall forward on my face into the shallow water. Anything to get the weight off my feet.

And then, because there is nothing else to do, I get up and stagger across the river.

Since there is no rational solution to my problem, my mind begins to create irrational ones. The answer, obviously, is . . . a horse. If I just had a horse, I could simply ride out, my feet would no longer be a problem . . .

I begin to implore, like Richard III, "Give me another horse! Bind up my wounds! Have mercy . . .!"

What was the next word . . . oh, yes, "Jesu." It was a prayer. I repeated King Richard's lines, again and again.

When people hallucinate, do they know it at the time? Am I like Richard? Would I ask God for help only when everything else is lost and only when I can scream it out into the hills? Unheard. I go forward on the trail and begin to laugh, tears streaming. I know I only have another hundred paces in me, and then I will be done. I will stop, sit, pull off the devil boots and wait. I probably will see no one for days. I have food for one more day.

The laughter dies. The sun is low against my back and my shadow reaches out far down the trail, flowing unsteadily over the stony ground. I will never get to the end of my shadow. I will fall before the sun. I stop.

The right shoulder of my shadow moves, a bulging darkness down there on the trail. I am not moving, but the shadow moves anyway. I hook my thumbs under the shoulder straps of my pack and force my legs to turn. I look back up the trail. A huge mass, motionless now, blocks most of the low sun, a dark silhouette against the flowing gold, an elongated head bobbing up in attention to my presence.

It is a horse.

I do not move and neither does the horse. I know it is not real, an apparition, a thing assembled of bits and pieces of agonized yearning, a ghost born of pain.

"Give me another horse," I mutter under my breath. "Jesu."

God, I think, the mind is an amazing thing—it will be a beautiful ghost while it lasts, but, to clear my mind, I will have to make it go away. So I wipe the sweat from my eyes and confront it directly, drag myself right up to it, to the horse; grab its halter.

It is a real horse.

The horse stands quietly. It wears a halter and a lead rope but no saddle. There is something going on here that I do not understand, but I am not going to question it. I gather up the lead rope, put my foot on a nearby rock and struggle up across its back, my head hanging off one side, my feet off the other, my pack riding up over my shoulders. If the horse takes a step I will slide forward and off, head-first down into the rocks. The horse never moves.

Gradually, I get myself upright and sit the horse.

"A horse, a horse . . . " I mumble, and the horse calmly carries me away down the trail and into the falling darkness.

The horse walks through the night and does not stop until we get to the trailhead, and my truck. I take off the hated boots, bandage my feet, hobble the horse in a patch of grass and lie down near him and sleep.

At first light two wranglers on horseback, outfitters, show up looking for the horse. They say it has never wandered off before, don't know why it did this time. They lead the horse away, back up the river and back into the wilderness. I stare after them until they are gone, and then I keep staring until my eyes begin to water. I am not crying, I tell myself.

I drive away, the boots on the seat beside me. At the first bridge I come to, I fling the boots far over the railing and into the water.

The wranglers said the horse had a name. They called him "King."

1982

The Gift

We call them "Baja days," those of us who drive down the peninsula looking for deserted beaches, our sea kayaks strapped to the top of every sort of sand-going vehicle known to man . . . these mornings when the Sea of Cortez is a bright plate of blue glass stretching away toward paradise, and the air is hot and still and sweet. Now and then, on a Baja day, in the far distance we can see the gentle ripples made by whales breaking the surface, quietly going about their ancient business. Nothing else moves except our kayaks and the tiny waves growing out from the bows, the sea so flat and still we can see the dimples left by our paddles for twenty yards behind the boats. The kayaks move effortlessly across the glass with a speed and agility that make us feel a part of the sea, as though we have joined with another world, become creatures of the water.

It is a Baja day, December 21, and I have come to Baja alone. I leave the old Jeep parked at the edge of a tiny beach, my sand-scrubbed tent pegged down next to it. I paddle out onto the silky surface of the water, drift slightly south into the early morning, crawl up out of the cockpit and lie back across the rear deck of the big kayak, contemplating the depth of the Sea of Cortez, the height of the sky and the width of the universe, glancing now and then back at the desert shore where there is not a single man-made thing to blink in the sunlight.

I have the right to this adventure. Any adventure. It is what I believe.

I paddle farther out. Time slides by.

It is my storm and it knows I am there and it must have been waiting; I am no more than a quarter-mile off shore when it hits. It comes in low from the Pacific, hidden by the peninsula, then vaults the desert ridgeline and lands crazily and violently on the water and on the kayak and on all the days of my life, shattering the glass of the Sea of Cortez and pounding the breath from everything it touches. The wind comes first, screaming down across the low bluffs in the distance, pulling black masses of sky down to the very deck of the boat. And then the air is thick with water.

A handful of yards off shore . . . and I never make it back.

The waves are taller than I have ever seen in Baja and the wind stacks them up, one against the other, until they break against themselves in total confusion and there is no room for the kayak in the troughs, the boat squeezed, bridging, bow and stern almost always underwater.

The feeling is gone from my fingers, the paddle nothing more than a weight hanging at the end of my arms. I keep pumping at the paddle, trying to drive the kayak into the waves, punching toward shore. But the wind and rain and waves are growing stronger, pounding me back.

The turmoil and the distance to the beach keep growing and even though I am working as hard as I can, I lose distance with each stroke of the paddle, moving steadily backward toward *Isla Carmen*, twelve miles across the channel. I know, sooner or later, I will be at the point of no return.

I don't know when I lose sight of the shore. It just isn't there. I twist in the cockpit and look behind me but the island is not there, either. The shorelines are lost in a low dome of black-gray violence so filled with sound that, for brief moments, it seems almost silent. I am alone in a sea that does not want me there. I only hope I am still lined up with the island. If I miss it, there is nothing else until mainland Mexico, a hundred miles to the east across open sea.

I wear a watch with a built-in compass. I try to grab a periodic look at it, try to keep track of the time since I have lost sight of the shoreline, try to keep the boat pointed in what I think is the right direction. But I am losing the fight for the beach and at some point I give it up. I spin the kayak awkwardly and drive with the waves, using the storm to hurl the boat toward the island. The change in speed is exciting and the kayak seems to skip over the sharp crests, hardly leaving one before the next is exploding on the stern. I don't know how long the ride goes on but my arms go numb and my body begins to shut down everything but the vital parts, becoming nothing more than a machine, lifting the paddle, lifting the paddle.

Hours pass. It is late afternoon but it is late-evening dark and I can see nothing but the storm. If I am still in the water when night falls, I will not notice that it gets any darker.

Sometime later, for a brief moment, the ocean seems to go soft and I should recognize it as that deceptive small quiet space before a truly large wave. But I do not. The boat nestles into the near-calm, then rises sharply on a rushing mountain of water. The bow dips and the kayak drops steeply forward and down, as though slipping over a dam. Suddenly the ocean is directly down there in front of me, a solid floor waiting to catch the boat as it drops like a stone off the front of the wave. But the boat never punches fully into the water. The bow hits something.

It is a glancing blow, enough to slam the kayak sharply to the side, shooting it out in front of the wave. The world and the storm come to an instant halt, freeze-frame, silent, and I hang in the air, free and alone, looking down at the water and wondering at the stillness and the beauty of it all, hanging motionless in air thick with foam. The storm and the sea can't touch me. I am flying.

I hit the water. I feel something slam into my thighs and realize that it is the edge of the kayak's cockpit. I am being torn from the boat, paddle gone, spray deck up around my waist, water sucking at the air inside the boat. My hearing seems to flick on and off and it is a few seconds before I realize I am upside down, the waves thrashing at the smooth bottom of the boat.

I don't know when I come out of the kayak. The boat is simply gone, and I am alone in the storm, sagging in my life vest, my hands cupped in front of my face in a type of mask, an attempt to keep the water from slamming directly into my mouth and nose.

I clear my mind of everything else and concentrate on hanging on, breathing, trying not to flail my arms and legs, trying to keep my body still and quiet in water that now seems too cold to let me live.

Hanging on to life. If I am going to die, something will have to kill me. I will not willingly die.

Somewhere out there in the darkness is an island. If I don't miss it.

My knees scrape the sandy bottom, catch, and pitch me head-down into the foam. My face hits the sand. The island. I have hit the island.

It isn't like in the movies. I don't pass out, only to awaken in the warmth of the morning sun, the surf lapping gently at my ankles, coconuts and bananas within reach, just up the shore. Not like that at all.

I come out of the storm as though driven by demons.

I don't know that I am near the shore and I have my legs pulled up tight against me, trying to keep my body warm. My arms move slowly, as in a dream. But when my face hits the island I have sudden visions of not making it, of being pulled back into the surf and dragged down, of somehow losing the land. I explode out of the water, thrashing up on the sand, arms flailing as though swimming in the wind. It is black-hell-dark, the water driving over me even as I plunge up the slope. I stay upright for several steps and then lose control, pitching forward onto the sand. Gradually, tumbling like a sodden, heavy ball, I roll onto the blackness of the beach.

I crawl farther up the slope of the sand, the scream of the wind cutting across the top of the deep pounding of the surf, all the sound hammering into a high bluff beyond the beach and seeming to shake the island.

I don't know whether it is high or low tide, how far the water will rise on the beach, how long the storm will last. But I know I am alive.

I claw up the sand away from the water, then crawl until the sand begins to turn to small gravel and I see a low bush directly in front of me and I am beyond the usual reach of the salt water. I keep going until I find a car-size slab of rock that leans at an angle away from the beach. I crawl around behind it and snuggle into the base of the rock, into whatever stored heat it has left. Some small critter is already under there. I feel it move against my back. I roll over, smack clumsily at whatever it is and it moves away into the storm. I fall asleep.

Dawn, December 22. The storm is still with me. There is a hard chop on the water and the wind howls in across the top of the breakers, flinging foam far up on the beach. A rusty haze hangs above the island and thickens off to the west, hiding anything that might be out in the channel. Somewhere across there is the tiny town of Loreto, hunkered down beneath the wind, the *panaderias* open and fresh bread, some of it thickly crusted with raw sugar, is loaded onto open, slanting shelves, the people coming in, smiling, stocking up for Christmas. But I am not over there. I am here, on this island.

And no one knows I am here.

I unfold stiffly from the base of the rock, walk down to the beach and look back at the island, a rocky pile of desert puncturing the storm. I try to gauge where I might be along its coast. I have visited the island before, know it runs generally north and south, with a tiny, almost-circular, jewel-like cove on its northwest side, a favorite stopping spot for fishermen. If anyone were to visit the island, it would most likely be there.

I still wear my life vest and spray skirt. I have on a long-sleeved, light-colored shirt, nylon shorts and old high-top basketball shoes with the tops cut off—my usual paddling outfit. My hat and sunglasses are gone. A sheath knife is laced to the front of the vest, and stitched on the back, just below the neck, is a flat nylon pouch that holds the basic tools of survival: another knife, rudimentary fishing gear, 150 feet of parachute cord, a fire kit and a few other things. And that's all. Everything I own in the world, I am wearing.

I check my compass. I think I am south of the cove but I have no idea how far. I build a cairn at the edge of the beach and start off—south. I figure, if I know the cove is north, I should find out what I don't know, by going south. I can't stand the thought of not knowing what is down there.

For more than four hours I scramble the beach. At some places, crumbled rocky points jut out into the water and I have to climb them. Small canyons appear to my left, rocks sloughing from their edges, their mouths open to the wind that keeps coming out of a foul sky. I find nothing that will get me off the island.

What I do find is water. The rocks of Carmen Island, their pocked faces turned to the sky, hold tiny glistening pockets of water left by the storm, each pocket a tiny *tinajon*, a jar for catching water. I put my face into them and suck them dry, every one of them, bugs and all.

Carmen Island is maybe 10 miles long. I think. I will never be able to cover it all. I head north.

When I came to the cairn I don't even stop, just keep going north, my feet dragging in the sand, head down against the wind, the flat light beginning to fade. I haven't gone 200 yards past the cairn before I find the kayak.

It is high on the beach and upside down and I almost miss it. The fiberglass hull makes tiny crackling noises when I try to roll it over and I discover it is full of sand. I start digging it out, hoping to find something, anything, of my gear. I never go kayaking, not even for a leisurely paddle, without basic equipment, but when the sand is gone from the boat there is nothing.

Now that the kayak is empty it is in danger of being blown away. I drag it behind a pile of rocks and anchor it, noticing that the bow seems to have an odd wobble. I sit in the lee of the rocks, my arms wrapped around the boat. Finally, I lie down beside it, pull the vest up around my head, and go to sleep.

Daybreak, December 23. I remember a small sign hanging behind Layne Longfellow's desk at Prescott College: "Either it is calm here, or the storm is the right size."

When I open my eyes I am covered with a sense of calmness. On any other day I would have thought the weather too dirty for any useful purpose, but, in comparison to the day before, the storm is now the right size. It is calm here.

The storm has pounded the island through the night and then simply has gone on to other places, leaving in its wake a flat, heavy sky and thick, dim morning light that makes me want to stay curled against the side of the boat. But the light is better than yesterday and the wind is gone.

I recheck the boat. A few inches back from the bow, a crack runs down the left side of the deck for about two feet, then makes a jagged turn directly across the boat. I have no idea if there is anything I can do to fix it.

I leave my life vest and spray skirt tied to the boat, take my knife, and head north again, tiny gravel working its way into my shoes.

Dark rocks stand guard at the southern edge of a narrow gap in the shoreline, silent watchers of the water. I scramble through them and ease around a small rise and there is the cove, pond-like, almost perfectly round, its surface hardly rippled, its shallow sea-green water lapping gently on a thin beach, the inland edge carving itself into the rising spine of the island. It is beautiful.

And deserted. There are no signs of recent visitors to the cove—not a footprint, no fresh ashes. Nothing. The storm has scoured the island of all things human and I am Robinson Crusoe except that there will be no man Friday, not now, not for days. Maybe never.

I walk completely around the cove. Tiny canyons, rock outcroppings, dry washes and clumps of *palo verde* are everywhere. I look in them, behind them, under them. I hike up the canyons, crawl the washes, scramble up the side of each ridge, go around the cove and back again. I look everywhere and find nothing and then the day is gone.

There is plenty of firewood among the scrubby desert growth and I have my fire tool—a piece of soft magnesium with a spark-striker embedded in the edge—but it isn't firewood I am looking for. In my island universe there is no piece of wood, no piece of anything, large enough to use as a paddle.

I go back to the kayak.

Daybreak, December 24. A brilliant sun in a glistening sky.

When I awaken there is a sense of alone-ness so thick and real it covers my body like the gentle warmth of fleece. I have been alone many times in my life, but I seldom have been lonely. I am not lonely now.

I think of my friend, Felix, and his annual winter trips, alone, into the high Sierras. He might even be there now, wrapped in layers of insulation, dark glasses on against the hard glitter of fractured sunlight skittering across the ice crystals, water boiling for tea on a tiny stove in front of his snow cave. Felix knows about aloneness. If I can be Felix, I will be okay.

I have to get myself a job on this island, plan something to do. The kayak is no good back here—maybe it is no good anywhere—so I carry it to the cove, its nose wobbling with each step I take. There is a rock outcropping on the south side of the beach and I set up camp there, the kayak tied to a bush just above the high water line.

I will sleep under the outcropping, which angles far enough out over the rubble to form a sort of lean-to. I build a small fire under the overhang. When the fire has burned for a while, I dip some small clumps of brush in the water and put the wet wood on the fire. The smoke fills the overhang, drifts back and forth, creeps into every crack and crevice. I see various small desert critters scuttle out of there, heading for places where they can breathe. I keep the smoky fire burning all day.

I try fishing with my simple equipment, but catch nothing. I have never thought much about fishing, and I think little about it now. Catching fish doesn't seem to matter.

I inspect the boat again, turning the deck toward the sun and sticking my head into the cockpit. Tiny blades of sunlight come through the crack and light up the inside of the boat. The crack is substantial. Finding some sort of tree sap, heating it and stuffing it into the crack is the only thing I can think of. And then I notice the small plastic bundle taped inside the very nose of the boat.

It has been in there for a couple of years and I have forgotten about it—a roll of duct tape wrapped in heavy plastic, rammed into the nose and taped in place. I can't even reach it—a neighborhood kid had crawled up into the boat and put it there. I get a long stick and poke it loose. When I cut off the plastic wrapping the tape is dry, like new. I spend the next two hours very carefully taping up the crack in the bow of the boat.

Christmas Eve. The sun seems to hang in the sky, suspended in clear light. But I know it is moving. I turn inland and gather some firewood, and when I drop it in front of my shelter, the sun is gone behind the peninsula, leaving a pale sheen painted on the gulf and flowing up on the sand and across the rubble at the base of my camp and off into the hills beyond.

I sit on a high rock and stare out across the channel. I have come to Baja to be alone, to sort through the sharp and heavy jumble that has cluttered my mind for years. And so here I am . . . alone. Maybe I have been alone on another Christmas Eve, but I don't remember. No. That could not be so, I think. A man would remember being alone on Christmas Eve, would remember the special pain that such aloneness would bring.

Across the channel the fishermen will be home with their families, maybe at dinner, but most likely in church. The church doors will be open and the light of dozens of candles will spill into the street. The small houses of Loreto will be at peace, the storm gone, Christmas arrived, the New Year coming. I think I can see tiny lights twinkling across the channel but then they are gone and maybe it is just lights flickering in my mind, after all. For the first time since I have turned off the engine of the Jeep, I am lonely.

Christmas Day. First light. The dawn is always softer on this day, easing the light onto the earth with a gentleness that can't be explained, except that it's Christmas morning.

There is an absence of sound, something more than mere silence, as though the parts of the world I can see and touch are quietly awaiting the most famous day in the Christian world. I can hear my heartbeat.

I crawl out from under the overhang and stand by the boat, looking across the channel. It is a Baja day, the sea flat and cellophane-wrapped, shimmering in the early light. So flat . . . that I wonder if I could paddle the wounded kayak across the channel, using only my hands. It is an idea I quickly reject.

I am wearing only my shorts. The sand at the edge of the cove is already warm to my feet as I walk back toward the inner shore. A few yards from the beach there is still water in some of the *tinajons* and I drink every one I can find.

I already have decided that I will do nothing on this day, Christmas. I have shelter, firewood, water, and good weather. What more can I want? What more can I do?

I shuffle slowly back to the boat. Even under the layers of tape its nose still seems to wobble slightly and I wonder if there is damage I haven't found, can't see. Still, I think the kayak will float and be relatively watertight. But it doesn't seem to matter. It is highly unlikely that I will ever be putting the boat back into the water.

I go to the dark rocks at the entrance to the cove, climb the highest one, and sit facing west across the Sea of Cortez. There is not a ripple on the water, the air thick and still, the sun climbing up behind me, warming my back, brightening the peninsula across the channel with thin golden light. I think I will simply sit here, waiting, becoming whatever it is I am to become, being respectful of the day. It is, I think, not a bad way to spend Christmas.

I don't see it for an hour.

It is at the edge of the water about 20 yards from me, floating, hardly moving, gently touching the sand, waiting.

The paddle. My paddle.

The storm took it away. The storm gave it back.

It is Christmas.

I suppose there should be something more, some ceremony, some parting ritual involving me and the island, something to send me gallantly and proudly off the beach and onto the water. But there is nothing—only adrenaline and a sense of going in a broken boat now, now, now, before I lose my nerve. Within ten minutes of finding the paddle I am on the water, stroking hard.

I have no equipment in the boat to weigh me down and it feels as though I am flying. Halfway across the channel a breeze comes up and small chop begins to lick at the bow, making it wobble harder against the tape. I can feel water in the bottom of the kayak and know the hull is leaking. None of that matters. I am committed to the crossing.

Christmas. I hit the Baja beach not more than a half-mile south of my camp. A man, his wife and young son are there, watching my crossing; have been watching for hours. The woman and the boy hang back but the man walks over to the boat, smiling.

I stick out my hand. "*Buenas tardes, señor.*" We walk toward the fire. They have had a picnic on the beach and there are warm tortillas, an iron pot of beans and chile, a cooler of beer.

I look at the iron pot and make a very simple decision. "*¿La canoa para usted . . . para el niño?*" I smile. "*¿La comida y cerveza para mi?*"

He laughs softly. "You don't have to give your boat, *señor.* Please, eat with us."

When I turn around, the boy is sitting in the kayak.

The woman fills a bowl with beans and chile, hands me a stack of tortillas. It is, I think, one of the best meals of my life.

When I can eat no more, I pick up the paddle and look at the boat. The boy is still there, turned now to face the water, his eyes on some far shore.

I walk around the boat. The boy does not raise his eyes to me. Carefully, I lay the paddle across the cockpit, just in front of his hands.

And I walk away, leaving them there, the man talking with his son, the woman watching.

I do not look back.

"*Feliz Navidad,*" I hear the man say quietly behind me.

The clutter in my mind seems to be gone.

1983

Lowenstein 1

Time can be suspended. I know it can. I have always been fascinated by those moments when it happens. The neurologists tell us that time is not suspended at all, that during those moments we merely think it is, because our brains are processing information at many times normal speed. Science is very unromantic. I prefer to think that *we* suspend time, bend it to our will, hold it back against the flow, prevent it from rushing forward and completing whatever it is that we don't want to happen. I know we can do this.

I know I can do this.

Now and then I can stuff time into my fist and squeeze it. I try to hold tight, but small pieces of it escape between my fingers and flash out into the passage of reality. The pieces hang there in the air, floating, shining, as I watch things unfold that I do not want to be a part of.

Like now.

I stand outside the door. I have never been so afraid.

His office is in an ugly house on the east side of town. The house looks benign, a squat collection of adobe and plaster stacked together to make rooms and offices. I have no idea what waits for me inside.

In his office, Lowenstein keeps the curtains drawn, the shades partially pulled down. The effect is to make any outside light force its way in, terribly diminished in the process, the room overly muted, funereal, as though Lowenstein is afraid I will see him clearly. Or that he will see me. There is a chair beside me but I do not sit.

He drops a large envelope of x-ray film on the desk.

"Do you want to look?" He doesn't look at me.

"If I look, will anything change?"

"No," he says. He sits behind the desk and folds his hands. I can hardly see his face. I know he cannot see my eyes.

"I'll give it a year, maybe a little more, maybe a little less. But a year's about it." His voice is uninflected, uninterested, as though he is discussing a problem with auto parts.

He is discussing the rest of my life.

"It?"

"You know," he says, "your . . . time."

"What will happen? How will it end?"

"Oh, well," he says, "nothing very special. Gradually, those particular organs will lose their ability to function. You will have certain choices at that point, of course. Transplant, perhaps. Maybe some other procedures. After all, who knows what treatments will be available in a year."

He sounds almost cheerful, as though he is giving me good news. On the corner of his desk is a small picture frame and next to it a clock with a glowing dial and I see him glance at it. I have been given my allotted time in his office. I have been given my allotted time in life.

I feel my hands ball into fists. "No one has ever said anything as important as this to me, so casually, and in so little time, and with as little caring."

For a long moment he says nothing. He glances at the clock again. His hand goes to his hair, smoothing it. "I have a lot of patients. I do the best I can." He clears his throat. "Thanks for dropping by," he says.

I glance down at his clock and realize that the picture frame next to it is actually a small mirror. Lowenstein has been glancing at himself. I go to the door.

"Oh," he says behind me, "you might want to schedule your next appointment with the nurse before you leave."

I open the door and light floods into his office. I stop and turn. "Doctor Lowenstein," I say, "when will you die?"

He is startled. His chair jerks backward.

"When will . . . I don't . . . I'm not the one . . . why would you ask that?" There is animation in his voice and I hear a catch in his throat.

"I do the best I can," I say. "Be sure to schedule an appointment with your nurse. You never know."

1984

What Am I Doing Here? 2

What am I doing here?

I have to get the hell out of here.

I'm at 13,600 feet and the wind is blowing a steady 30 knots.

I remember Willi opening his parka and showing me what he had scrawled inside in heavy black marker: "Life begins at 10,000 feet." I believe him. Life begins when you can look up and all the trees are below you. Life begins when the storm is over and there is still time to summit.

But there are other times, other places. Life begins when you can hear the white water before you see it, know that it is there, living in your mind, waiting. And then you turn the corner and you are in it and you know that life begins at the head drop.

Life begins when the raft is standing on its tail in the back wave and for a brief moment life is suspended—time is suspended—and there is time to consider many things, among them the grave question as to whether the boat will drop downriver or fall backwards and upside-down into the hole. While life is suspended, you can consider these things at your leisure.

Life begins when the sails go up and the wind snaps them full and the boat takes on a life of its own.

Does life only begin in those times and places that make me ask, "What am I doing here?"

I am coming down, tired from climbing, running from the storm, the summit far above me. It begins to rain. I make it just inside the tree line and hunker down at the base of a rock overhang, watching the rain drive slanting from a sky I cannot see. The air is alive with the water and now and then it dances into my shelter, misting my face and dripping from my beard.

The temperature is dropping so quickly I can feel the skin crinkle on my forehead. It is only a matter of time until the rain hardens, turns to snow, and I am trapped at 1,000 vertical feet above the thin shelter of my tent. It is late in the season. I huddle hard against the stone and bury my head deep within my parka. I know I am alive only because I am breathing.

What am I doing here?

Usually, the question rushes through my mind at times and places where I can least afford to answer it.

What was I doing there, back then, falling off the mountain, on a day full of light and magic and the rushing air of emptiness. It is not true that you scream when you fall. Your throat clenches and not even the crying sound of "God . . . " will escape before you get to the bottom.

What was I doing there, on the river, when the hard swift hand of the rapid took me out of the boat and I was hurtling free and captured through a world in which I could not see and could not breathe, in which survival was nothing more than chance and the world was much too loud and wet for the question that slipped out of a huddled place in the back of my mind . . . "What am I doing here?"

Long spans of sun-streaked days and broken nights in the wilderness. The whipping stings of scorpions. The snapping of bones. Dehydration so severe my eyes stung when I tried to cry. Adrift in a broken boat in a cold sea watching the last lights of a distant shore fade into the night.

What was I doing there?

For once, here, on the mountain, I have time to think about it.

Perhaps I *shouldn't* be here? But that is a question I never seem to ask.

I put myself into these places. I always seem to make it through and when it is over all I can do is wonder at the thrill and that I am still alive and immediately start to plan for that next place.

It is a life I chose to live.

Perhaps, I think, it is a life I have to prove.

Other than that, I have no answer.

The rain grows thick with sleet. I break out a poncho, cover myself, and dig into the driest part of the overhang. I will sleep out the rain and sleet here on the mountain.

Mountains do not ask questions. They do not provide answers.

They are mountains.

What am I doing here?

If I don't get out of here, my life may end.

Perhaps that is why I am here, after all.

1985

Scorpion

I buy the battered KLR 650 motorcycle from the priest at Loreto and we push it under the *ramada* where we can work on it in the shade, safe from the Baja sun.

The motorcycle will not run and we work on it, using the priest's collection of odd tools, bits and pieces of metal and wire.

And then, one day, there is a coughing sound and a ball of smoke from the tailpipe. The bike is running.

At the end of the street a smooth sand track stretches away into the hilly desert, eventually, the priest says, connecting with the Baja highway somewhere to the north.

I ride out of Loreto.

It feels good to be riding north again. Somewhere up there I will find the highway, and then miles later I will find the border and then San Diego. I have a patched-together bike and a couple of pesos and I am healthy. Maybe I will just keep going.

I make the turn into the *arroyo* automatically.

I am deep into the desert, the highway nowhere in sight, the motorcycle sluggish, the heat boiling up from the sand and rock and baking my legs. When I see the small canyon leading off to the west I think maybe it might take me to the blacktop. My auto-pilot takes over and before I know what is happening I wheel the motorcycle hard to the left and rise on the pegs, feeling the wind rushing between my legs. I shift down, wanting a little more gear until I get the feel of the softer surface. Everything feels good so I turn the throttle and in a few seconds my goggles are pressed against my face and the KLR is moaning in its low, flat voice, the speed up and the wheels floating on the surface of the sand, drifting.

The *arroyo* narrows. The walls creep closer until they are a horizontal blur, layers of motion streaking past the edges of my vision, so close that I can smell the heat of the rocks.

The heaviness of mid-day in the desert wrings the sweat from my scalp and it runs down from inside my helmet, down the back of my neck, small tracks of moisture soaking my heavy shirt.

And then I hear the music again. It rises in the back of my mind, fed by the sound of the engine and the tearing whip of the wind. I don't know where it comes from—I never know where it comes from—but it is mine and I stay on the pegs and dance with the big bike, blind from the speed and the heat and the rush of the air, joyous from the music, dizzy from the passing rush of the rock.

I always hear music at times like this. Later, when I try to remember it, I never really know what kind of music it is, only that it is there, in my mind, high pitched and screaming, driving me on. I used to tell people about the music but I couldn't seem to make them understand, couldn't make the words come out right. And they would nod their heads and smile knowingly at their friends.

I quit telling people about the music.

After a while, as the *arroyo* gets tighter, I know it will not lead to the highway but I don't really care. I have an oversized fuel tank full of gas, saddle bags stuffed with food and water, and my camping gear strapped on behind me. It is simple. I will ride until I feel like stopping.

I keep pressing, twisting the throttle, fighting back my fear of the speed, the turns and the drift, glancing down and watching the jump of the needle, feeling the bike leave the ground in short bursts of flight.

The music rolls on and so do I, free in the desert, free in the wind, crazy with the heat and the speed.

Until I hit the ditch.

It is cleverly placed, about fifty feet beyond a small turn, just far enough out to let the bike regain its speed. It is dug straight across the *arroyo*, its sides smooth and sharp, the dirt thrown further back up the narrow canyon, the area smoothed. It is as though the ditch has simply appeared, a divine rift across my path, reaching neatly from side to side, unnoticeable and unavoidable. There is no warning.

I see it at the last second. I turn the throttle hard, lean back and try to pull the front wheel off the ground, but there is no time. The wheel drops sharply into the ditch, the forks snap, and the rest of the bike and I cartwheel over the ditch and into the rocky dirt beyond. Through the blur of the speed and the instant burst of fear, I watch as the scorched earth comes up to meet me.

I don't remember how I hit the ground. Maybe I bounced. Maybe I hit in several places at the same time. The dirt and rocks catch me, slow me. The dirt and rocks should have been hot, but when I land there is a blackness that is cool and gentle, a velvet touch of night that covers me and makes me safe. I wonder how it got so dark in the middle of the day. I remember wondering why I did not hear the music anymore.

I don't know how long I lie there. The first time I open my eyes the blackness is still with me and I think I am dreaming, that I have not regained consciousness but only think I have. In my dream I am on my back, my head twisted hard to the left. But then, out of the corner of my eye, I can see the stars hanging in a clear desert night and I know I am awake. I think about trying to move, to straighten my body, to turn my head, but nothing seems to work; I can't seem to find myself, my whole self. I don't know where my arms are, or how to move my legs. My helmet and goggles are gone. I am packed inside my head, my whole being concentrated inside my brain. I have retreated there, have abandoned everything I can't feel. There is no other part of me that I can identify. I am alive, I can see, but I am hiding deep inside my brain. Nothing else works. And then the stars blink out.

The right side of my face is so hot that I want to scream, but I can't get my mouth open. I think I am on fire, that all of me is burning, but then I realize that I can't feel all of me, that I can feel only my face. I open my eyes. My head is still twisted to the left and I stare with blurry vision along the sand between two small rocks the size of softballs that were only inches from my face. The sun is up and into the *arroyo*, searing the side of my face, slowly turning it into something I won't be able to recognize.

I try to roll my head to the right but I can't make it move. All I can do is open and close my eyes and stare in front of me at the two small rocks. I blink several times trying to clear my vision, and between blinks I think I see something move. I stare hard, but the movement, if it has ever been there, is gone.

There is stillness, and silence, an absence of sound that I have only experienced inside a cave, where the darkness and silence were so loud that my ears rang from the effort of trying to hear. But my ears don't ring now. And I think maybe I am deaf.

I used to wonder how I would die. I thought maybe Chaser and I would ride off a bridge somewhere, probably in West Virginia, maybe into the Gauley. We wouldn't mean to do it. We just wouldn't make the curve coming into the bridge, would hit the guard rail, flip both the bikes through the girders and watch the world spin, dropping. It was kind of exciting. A bridge was romantic, somehow. They would talk about us for years.

But I am going to die in a nameless, mean little canyon just beyond the far side of a fucking little ditch, carefully dug by some cretin with the IQ of a maggot. There is nothing romantic or exciting about it, just lying there, trapped inside my skull, my ears dead, my eyes blurred, waiting.

I don't know what else is broken. I didn't know if I would ever find out.

Once, lying on a rock ledge high on a canyon wall in Arizona, I heard a beetle walk. I had never thought about that before, whether or not you could hear a beetle walk. Wendell Klah, a crazy Navajo, used to ask me things like that, trying to educate me. Everything that moved in the wilderness, he said, made its own noise. Could I hear a beetle walk? Could I hear the sound of sunrise? Could I hear the blink of an eagle's eye?

I had crawled onto the ledge to get out of the sun, to sleep away those boiling hours when no intelligent being walks in the desert. I awoke without opening my eyes, listening to the smallest sounds I had ever heard. The sounds scurried into the distance, then came back, then stopped. I opened my eyes. A few inches in front of my face, close enough that I had trouble focusing on it, was a small, black beetle, pointed directly at me. We were motionless for some long seconds, and then he turned and walked away. I heard him.

And that's how I know I have my hearing back. Lying there, with my eyes closed, I hear a beetle walk. I pry open my eyes, try to look for him. I know he is there, walking, scurrying back and forth, making his sounds into the world. I revel in the tiny sounds. I can hear. I can hear.

And I am beginning to see better, to focus. The rocks out in front of my face gradually grow sharper as my eyes respond, and I can feel the tiny needles of pain from the sun drilling through my eyes and into the back of my skull. I blink, and then again and again, trying to get the moisture working there. Blinking my eyes is more work than I have ever done before. I almost faint. But the moisture comes and the sharp little pains subside and after a while I can see clearly.

And there he is.

His little feet scurry across the hot sand making their tiny noises. I can't see his eyes in the front of his shell but I know they are there, those hot little eyes, that there is not much in the way of a brain behind them, that he was born pissed off, that nothing he ever does makes him feel any better, and there is nothing whatever I can do about it. And I wish I had never heard him walk.

That scorpion.

He comes toward me. I can't move my head to follow him and he disappears into the void beneath my chin. I know that he is crawling on me. He has come up on my shirt and is exploring, moving toward my neck, looking for a fight.

Well, fuck you, I think.

I have never been so powerless. I can blink my eyes, I can breathe. I think I can lick my lips. But I can move nothing else. I have a scorpion crawling somewhere below my chin, and I don't know where he is. And for some reason, that makes me intensely angry.

I am lying in the sun and I am going to die. It is just a matter of time. I am not going to die from the scorpion—fuck him, he is just an insect.

I am going to die from the sun and from dehydration and from not being able to crawl away from here and from the ditch and the son of a bitch who dug it and from the wreck and from my not being aware enough on the bike to avoid the whole damned mess in the first place. I don't know what is wrong with the rest of my body. Maybe there is some stuff broken. Maybe I am bleeding. I don't want to die quietly, but I don't know how to fight.

It becomes a matter of will. I *will* move my head. I *will* look around, maybe for the last time, but I will look around. I *will* see the place that kills me. I begin to concentrate, to try to put my mind and whatever energy I have left into the dead area below my chin, my neck, into some sort of massed effort that will cause my head to move.

I concentrate. I strain. I feel sweat run across my forehead, a tiny pool of it gathering in the corner of my right eye, stinging. Minutes go by. Seems like hours.

My head moves. It is tiny at first, but I feel the movement. My vision shifts slightly and there is a tingling sensation somewhere in my body. I rest for a moment and then try it again. It is better now. My head moves at least a half inch. In a gasping spate of concentration I try once more, and my head rolls almost upright, my chin dropping toward my chest.

I catch the scorpion between my chin and my chest, and the tiny, angry, little bastard stings me. And I hate him for that. I press hard with my chin and I think I feel him hit me again, but I can't be sure. His first hit is sending waves of stinging sensation into my chin and up into my head. I know he might hit me several times and I will never feel any of them beyond the first one. I try to remember if a scorpion can sting more than once, and I think maybe he can. And I hate him even more.

I can feel him moving, trapped under my chin. I press harder, gradually, slowly, grinding my chin back and forth, back and forth. I can feel him struggling, fighting my weight. Die, you little prick, I think. Die with me. And then he stops moving. So do I.

I must be getting well. I can kill a bug.

I am dizzy, heavy with the venom of the scorpion working in my brain. I try to move my head again, but I cannot. The scorpion, if he is still under my chin, is dead, and my anger towards him is gone. And I need anger to move my head. My head is tilted slightly to the left and I can see my legs out of the corner of my eye. They are close enough to touch, but I can't raise my arm to touch them. I try to make some sound, to talk, but that doesn't work either.

The sun has been gone for a long time and the darkness pools in front of my face. Clouds began to form in my mind and I know it is only a matter of time until I pass out. When I see the moonlight for the first time, I realize that my eyes have been closed. And then the moon goes out and I am covered again.

When I hear that sound, that slight catching of breath, that gasping sound that we all make when we've just seen something that we never want to see again . . . when I hear that sound I know I am still alive.

And then there is the pain.

There is a type of pain so deep, so intense, that your mind simply removes itself from it. You feel the pain from a distance, looking back at it, or down at it, from some other place, through a mist that filters out the reality of the agony. I have felt that type of pain before and if I ever really prayed in my life the only thing I prayed for was never to feel that pain again. But somehow it always comes to me.

And here it is.

And then I hear the sound again, the catching of breath.

My tongue seems to work and I move it around and find that my mouth is moist, smooth. Someone has poured water in there, sometime.

Gradually, my head regains some movement. I can roll it gently back and forth, and when she brings me water I can tilt my head to one side to drink as she pours it, cool and sweet, over my lips.

"You do not ride so very well," the priest says. I try to see him but he is standing with his back to the sun, shading my face. "And your face is very red. Are you embarrassed by your lack of riding skills?" I can hear the soft chuckle in his voice.

"Ditch . . . ditch," I mumble, glad that I can make a noise from my throat.

"Ah, yes, the ditch. We will have to talk about the ditch."

I feel hands under my arms—I can *feel* the hands—and I am being pulled backward and loaded on a crude travois. Narrow straps and uneven pieces of rawhide are strung between the poles and I am dragged over them until most of my body is held in the crude cradle. The priest and the woman pick up the ends of the long poles and begin to drag me down the canyon. Their gait is uneven. The poles ride over rocks and thud into depressions in the canyon floor. I am being rescued, but it is a rescue from hell.

When I hit the ditch, I could have broken half the bones in my body, could have broken my back, could have broken . . .

But the priest and the woman do not check my body. They simply load me onto the travois and start away down the canyon. I feel no pieces of bones grating against one another; I feel no specific pain. I simply feel the pain of the universe.

I hear the woman talking softly. She is explaining why she dug the ditch. I do not hear all the words, only hearing that she dug the ditch.

She dug the ditch.

I clamp my mouth shut. I will wait until I can stand, until I can use my legs and arms.

This is not over.

1986

Dream World

I live in a dream world.

I emerge now and then to spend enough time in the real world to appear normal, to appear sane. Or almost sane. But I'm never fully in the real world. I'm always just a single step from the dreams, from the fantasies. A single step, a blink of an eye, from being somewhere else, if only in my mind.

But the dreams are slowly dying. Each year, each month, each week it is harder to find the dreams. Each day, each hour. Each second. Sometimes I hear them passing, the dreams, tiny zephyr sounds somewhere in my mind. But mostly they slip by without my knowing.

For all my life there have been the dreams. Every day, dreams. Other places, other things. I remember Willi telling me about Everest, telling me that I could do it. It became a dream. And then on this one bright morning I awake and I am old. And the dream is dead.

And when all the other dreams are gone, I, too, will be gone.

1987

Helen 2

I was supposed to have been gone for 90 days.

I have been gone for 13 months.

I don't know when it will end.

I don't know when I will get back there.

Being without her is like being without my heart.

1988

Morning Prayer

She loves graceful things of movement and power, things that paint with motion.

Ballet dancers

Ice skaters

Horses

Her daughter's fluid movements as she runs with her children

Her son's skiing

And she married a man who can't even dance.

I am not a prayerful man.

But every morning when I awaken and she is still there beside me, a small and silent prayer comes up from my thankful heart and escapes me and I cannot catch it nor do I try.

And I love her for keeping me alive, even though I do not want to be.

1989

A Mark on the Wind

I am a writer.

Writing is what I do, no matter what else I am doing, have done, will ever do.

I write words each day. Most of the words I discard as useless. They tell me nothing. I try to make some sense of the words that remain. It doesn't always work.

But I keep on writing.

A large check. Larger than has ever been mine.

I hold it in my hand, stare at it, afraid it will vaporize in some cosmic magician's trick.

Is it really mine? Is this a fluke? Haven't they discovered that I do not know how to do this? Will they take the money back?

I hold the check for a while, and then I give it to my wife.

My book is published.

I have left a mark on the wind.

1990

The Button

I get off the airplane and rush through wet, gray winter to the hospital and now I sit by my mother's bed in the big white room. Her gray hair is neatly combed. Her eyes are closed, but now and then I see a tiny movement there, as though secret things are going on in her mind. I watch her breathe softly, thinly. I wonder if my mother knows I am here. I wonder if my mother knows I am her son.

There is much to say, and no one to say it to. I have waited far too long. And so I wait, again.

Her shoulder twitches and I take her hand, press my face against her arm, breathe in the scent that says, even after all these years, that she is my mother. In my hand, I feel her fingers move.

I reach under the front of my parka and touch the old, flat brown button that is sewn on the inside, just above my heart. The button has been sewn inside every parka I have ever owned. I can see the day I got the button, as though it were yesterday. But it is far into all the yesterdays of my life.

In the thousand times of my life when I have wanted to run away *from*, I have felt the button. And I have changed my direction.

I squeeze the button, and I know what treasure is.

1991

Boy on a River

I can already see the man in him.

His name is Tristan and he is seven years old and he has never been on the river before and now there is a rapid in front of him making a noise unlike anything he has ever heard. It is a noise not of this world, and not of any seven-year-old's world. It is a noise to end all knowing. For the boy, there will only be the waiting to be in the center of the noise.

He crouches in the front of the raft and grips a safety line that is tied there, his small fingers knuckling white and his lips pressed together until all his blood seems concentrated deep within his body. He looks back at his uncle, at the back of the raft, perched on a metal rowing frame and staring down the river in a concentration of art and skill and survival.

His uncle is a man I know, Toran, a man more skilled than any I have ever known. There is nothing in the outdoors he cannot do. Muscles play in his uncle's shoulders and run in cables down darkly tanned arms to his hands, fingers wrapped in a life grip around the handles of the oars. The hands move the oars into the water only where necessary and without a wasted motion, making careful adjustments of the heavy raft on the bright brown river. The uncle spins the raft easily, the big boat dancing in a tight circle and then straightening to enter the rapid nose first with the boy in the bow, fingers tight around the safety line, spray flying over his head, eyes wide in awe and excitement. The raft tilts forward into a hole and the floor seems to drop away from his feet, but before he can follow the floor it comes up at him again and presses him, rising, into the foam and noise that come in immeasurable amounts over the tubes of the raft. The water pounds him and he is in the center of the noise and it seems to him in his young life that it is a place where he always wants to be. Nothing exists outside the raft and the water and the noise. The world is not there. I am in the front of the boat with him and the boy grips the line and in the middle of the rapid steals a look at me. I am smiling at him and then we are out of the heavy part of the rapid and into the rolling water below, the boat dancing across the tops of the standing waves.

The uncle is leaning on his oars now, watching the boy. The boy has done well.

Grace under pressure, his uncle has told him. Get excited inside, but stay calm outside. Move when you should and only because you have thought it through. Then move decisively. But don't waste anything. That is the test of the river.

The uncle is right and I love him and I love the boy. And the boy understands.

Maybe we will never do this again. But we have done it once. We will remember it.

Such things are possible when you are young, and still young, and then

not so young.

1992

Arrow in the Light

There is an arrow in the light.

It is a flickering shaft that dances through the golden glow of late afternoon in the far mountains, cutting a graceful arc toward a target that it never hits. It snaps past the deer and disappears, lost in the depths of the shadows and the forest floor.

The deer raises its head, curious at the strange sound, the muffled hissing that an arrow makes as it drags its fletching through the air. But the deer never sees the arrow. And it never sees me. And I do not shoot again.

I stand quietly behind some brush and watch the deer as it searches for food at the edge of a stand of timber. I blink my eyes, and at the end of the blink the deer is gone, instantly, quietly. I never see it again.

I don't know why I never hit the deer. I can hit other targets with my arrows—old paper cups, bits of dead wood, clumps of grass—but I never hit the deer. Chaser tried to explain it to me. If you kill the deer, he said, the hunt is over. And for you the game is in the hunt, in the process, in the journey, in the stalk, in your mind. You don't *want* it to be over. It is important to you that things stay in balance, that the deer stay in the forest, that the arrow stay in the air. *You are most alive when the arrow is in the light.* Oh, you wouldn't mind too much if you actually killed the deer. You are, after all, a hunter. But you won't kill the deer.

For years, I do not believe that. I am, after all, a hunter. When autumn comes to the mountains of West Virginia and the air turns to a pure, cool liquid that flows across my face and into my chest; when the turning leaves paint the high ridges with color that caresses my eyes; when the fragrance of the moist forest floor drifts magically through my mind and stays there, to be renewed year after year with the coming of another autumn . . .

When autumn comes, I become a hunter.

It starts early for me. As a child I live with my family in a small cabin at the edge of a tiny clearing, deep in the woods of West Virginia. My father hunts—not for sport, but to put meat on the table. I follow him, thrilled that he will take me, terrified of the sound the old shotgun will make when he snaps it to his shoulder.

After a while, I do not fear the sound. It is just a part of living, of finding food.

I grow. Too large, some say. But I grow and I follow my father, my hair shoved up under an old wool hunting cap, hands hidden in mittens that one of my uncles had left at the cabin years before.

And then one day he leans the shotgun against a tree as we stand silently at the edge of a clearing, just watching and waiting, for turkey, maybe. My father looks at me and I realize that he has to look up. Up. Somewhere in there, some time, I have grown taller than he. Taller, I say in my mind. And he hears me. He takes up the shotgun and places it in my hands, so carefully, so quietly, and steps slightly to the side, out of the way.

I am the hunter now.

I never get over that.

And I never get over West Virginia.

For years, when autumn comes I get on a motorcycle and head east, riding deliberately, dropping from the Rocky Mountains down onto the high plains and onto the Great Plains and then across the rivers and through the stands of hardwoods that began to appear, and coming, eventually, to West Virginia, and to Chaser's old house at the upper end of a small valley where the greenbriers grow thick enough to make fences, and the black walnuts are there for the gathering.

I have hunted in other places, but it is never the same. For years, when autumn comes, I can think only of West Virginia. And, besides, Chaser's crumbling old farm is one of the few places I've ever ridden where being there is as good as getting there.

I wander through the bright woods, carrying one of Chaser's longbows, spending days walking the hollows and the ridges, spending hours looking for "sign," spending tense minutes stalking the ghostly image of a deer that usually is not there.

And sometimes the deer *is* there, within my range, and I spend tightly compressed seconds of great tension and excitement, calming my heartbeat and drawing the bow. I release the string.

And then there is an arrow in the light.

But I never hit the deer.

And that's how I grow to love to hunt on another farm—Jory's. I know there will never be a deer to hit.

I never knew Jory to hunt. I suppose he did, sometime in his past, but as he grew older he just gave it up, content to work his secluded, green, ridge-top farm high in the mountains of central West Virginia, content to walk his woods and care for his cattle, content to grow old with a peace and dignity few of us will ever find.

I never really know his age, but he must be eighty, maybe older, when finally Chaser takes me to meet him. He was born in the Alps, high among the crags of some far and secluded place in Europe, and when he came to the mountains of West Virginia as a young boy he knew deeply that he was home, that he had found the old mountains of a new country and that he would live there, always. And he brought his philosophy with him.

Jory's farm and the surrounding woods hold more deer, Chaser says, than any place in West Virginia. And Jory's sister, Greta, a widow, lives with Jory and is the best cook in the mountains. To stay with Jory, to talk with Jory, to hunt Jory's deer, to walk Jory's farm, to eat Greta's cooking—these are things that most hunters only dream about.

The farm is secluded, straddling a high ridge and running across open ground and then into the woods. There are no close neighbors and Jory can walk long distances across open meadows and through thick woods without seeing another house, or barn, or road. He will see only his mountains, rolling away into the distance.

Jory's house sits in a low, open saddle in the center of the ridge. To the north, a meadow stretches away until, at the far end, it is closed in by trees standing limb to limb, forming a forest wall of dense protection for the field and for Jory's cattle.

To the south, the land rises slightly to his barn, a solid, heavy building built to withstand any storm that might come thundering over the mountains to hammer into Jory's ridge. Only a short distance beyond the barn the land climbs steeply to a small, green, treeless knoll. The knoll is a special place for Jory. It is his church. It is the place he goes to give his thanks to his God for his life and his house and his barn and his animals there in the heart of West Virginia. From his front porch, Jory can see the top of the knoll beyond the barn. He can watch the warm deep light of the setting sun flow across the mountains and then touch the very tips of the high grass on the knoll. When the last light of day is there, on the grass, so is Jory.

And the top of the knoll is the very first thing Jory seeks at the beginning of each new day. On the quiet mornings of his life, he rises just before dawn and walks past the barn and up the rise. He stands in the thin silver light and looks down on his barn and his house. He looks farther to the north, at his small herd of cattle and the trees beyond. He turns his eyes to the west and looks above the forest, looks into the distance where he has never been, far beyond the farm, beyond the trees, beyond the mountains. But he has no need to go to those far places. He has no need to leave his mountains.

Jory built his house in the saddle of the ridge, nestled it off to the side slightly so that it doesn't dominate the countryside. The house belongs in its surroundings; it is white, two-story, squarish, solid and homely. And it is home. There is a screened-in front porch that opens directly onto the thick grass; his cattle can graze right up to the front door. At the back, the house and its foundation are part of the rising ridge, extending the line of the land straight up to the top of the brick chimney.

The house is a lot like Jory; it is solid, there is no pretense about it, and it has come to the ridge to stay. It is a house for a simple, good life. It is furnished, too, like Jory; no decorations, uncomplicated, and everything you see is real. The only utility in the house is electricity, but Jory doesn't use it much. He prefers the soft light of lanterns, or the glow from the wood stove in the kitchen. If you want water, you work the hand pump at the large, shallow kitchen sink. And the outhouse is only a short walk down the ridge.

Jory and Greta live downstairs, and visiting hunters—those few Jory allows to hunt there—stay upstairs. Each upstairs bedroom holds a bed, a chair, and a small table. There is no heat. The only light is provided by a bare bulb that hangs from its own wire, dangling from the center of the ceiling. There are no curtains on the upstairs windows. If you are in the upstairs rooms before dark, you can look out the windows and see across the fields and into the forests and understand, just a little, what Jory understands fully.

The first time I go to Jory's farm, Chaser and I get there in late afternoon. Jory is coming in from the north field. He is a small man, and looks even smaller in the flapping bib overalls he is wearing. He shakes hands and invites us in. But before we go inside, Jory has to look at the motorcycles, at Chaser's vintage Harley and at the patched-together BMW that has carried me from New Mexico. He laughs at the bow carrier Chaser has hand-built and attached to the side of the Harley. Jory loves the bikes. We know he wants to go for a ride, and I know that Chaser, tomorrow, will take him and then Greta flashing down the dirt road that drops, curving, away from the house, out to the highway, on a roaring, fleeting charge that Jory will talk about all winter.

Greta has the wood-burning kitchen range glowing. Supper is almost ready, to be served in the soft, last light of late day before the chill of full darkness.

We eat Greta's supper of fried chicken, baked yams, fresh green beans and hot, homemade bread. And butter that Greta has churned only that morning. For dessert we eat apple pie served from a dish that must have been four inches deep, still steaming from the massive oven in the old wood range. The pie is piled with vanilla ice cream—Jory's one great weakness. The ice cream is stored in a huge chest-type freezer that sits in *the* place of honor—on the front porch. The freezer is Jory's only concession to modern living; it is his one truly modern appliance.

After supper we sit in the small, spare parlor and talk until the Appalachian evening thickens into darkness, and beyond. We talk of what it means to live in these mountains. We talk of hunting, of the deer, of the farm, of the forests and the fields, of motorcycles and good whiskey and a Europe Chaser and I would never know and an America that Jory has only dreamed about.

And we talk of the ghosts and spirits that are supposed to walk the highlands on cold, moonless nights. I have heard these stories before, tales of ghosts that are supposed to roam the Appalachian Mountains, yarns about the spirits, the "haints," the softly glowing lights floating through the distant woods. But I don't believe these stories.

The late-autumn night chills the house, and the soft heat from the parlor's small wood-burning stove keeps us gathered tightly within its reaches. My head begins to nod and I struggle to stay awake, to listen to Chaser and Jory, to enjoy. Greta has long since gone to her bedroom; her day will start before we were out of bed, when she will arise in the crisp darkness and fill the house with the aroma of coffee, biscuits and ham, all cooking on the kitchen range that always seems to glow and always gives off the faint perfume of wood smoke.

Chaser has a box of cheap cigars in his pack. Chaser doesn't smoke; he has brought them for Jory. Jory loves cigars, the cheaper the better; a man should have a smoke, Jory reasons, but he shouldn't smoke up all his money. Chaser brings out the cigars and gives them to Jory and Jory gives one to me and we sit for a while longer, Jory's cigar glowing in the dim light and my head spinning from inhaling a cigar that should have been thrown out of a truck window along some lost sandy road in Florida. I don't remember when we go upstairs to bed. It seems late, but I don't believe it is. In Appalachia, it always seems later than it really is.

My room is stark, chilled with lack of use. I undress and drape my clothes across the back of the chair. I dig some long underwear out of my pack and put it on, then climb into the bed and burrow beneath the layers of quilts. Jory's stories sing in my mind, and the music of their words is with me when I fall asleep.

And so the routine begins, the daily ritual of hunting in Jory's mountains. Chaser and I rise long before daylight, eat the huge breakfast that Greta, magically, always has ready at exactly the right time, and walk quietly away from the house and into the black, silent woods. We separate, each finding his special hidden place. We hold our bows the way Merlin must have held his magic staff. And we wait for the deer.

The deer never come.

When, each day, we realize that the deer are not coming, we move and find other places where we will take up the stand the next day. We read the woods, which are thick with deer sign. We follow trails. We are alive with the hunt.

But there are no deer.

In the evenings we return to the house to find a huge pot of black coffee near-boiling on the stove, and thick slices of warm bread stacked next to a bowl of hot, homemade applesauce. After that, there is supper. After supper, the stories begin again, lasting until the cigar smoke flows gently out of the parlor door and pools in the kitchen, causing Greta, with great commotion, to fling open the back door. And then someone makes the first move toward the narrow stairs, and to bed.

It is a wonderful routine. And it lasts for days.

And the deer never come.

I awaken with an image in my mind that I cannot shake and cannot identify. There is something moving in my mind; moving in the crisp snap of the blackest hour of night; moving through the plain, almost barren room where I have been sleeping; moving through time.

In the fraction of a second that it takes to open my eyes, I know several things: I know I should not be awake, that it is not time to get up; but I know I am awake and alert, as awake as I have ever been in my life. And I know that I am not alone.

In the blackness of the room I can barely see the outline of the window. I slip out of bed on the side away from the door, half expecting to find someone standing there, outlined in the darkened doorway. There is no one.

My back is to the window, but it doesn't matter. There is no light outside, not of any kind. The night is of a blackness that can only be experienced on a moonless night in the mountains, a denseness that seems able to be touched. But when you put your hand out to the darkness it seems to move away, just beyond your reach.

I am not alone, that much I am sure of. Somewhere there is another . . . something . . . that is awake, just like I am. I ease to the doorway and squat, carefully keeping my balance. I roll my shoulders forward so that I can see into the hallway, but still kept my legs bunched under me; if there is something out there, I don't want it to come straight into my face. It is a move I have used many times to good advantage, but now I just feel foolish. There is nothing in the hallway, at least not that I can see.

I wonder about Chaser, asleep in a room down the hall. I should awaken him and tell him.

Chaser, I will say, we aren't alone.

Brilliant, he will say. And if he doesn't whack me with his bow, I'll be lucky.

I turn to go back to the bed, feeling foolish, but still uneasy. And I face the window.

Through the window, across the north field and almost to the woods, I can see a light. It is moving, bobbing, blinking, dancing in the darkness. It is a soft light, glowing with a tenderness that makes it seem to fit, somehow, there in the field near the woods. It belongs. It moves almost constantly, first to the edge of the woods, then into them, then back out again at some distant point. Once, it darts down the field and over the rim of the hill, only to reappear at the upper edge of the field and dance across the darkness to disappear again into the forest.

I am drawn to the window, fixed in place. I hear someone breathing and I turn quickly, glad that Chaser has come to see what I have seen.

Chaser isn't there. The breathing I hear is my own.

I think I will get Chaser and Jory and stalk the field. If there are three of us, maybe we can trap it between us. But I don't awaken them, don't even go to their rooms. I know, I just *know*, that if I take the time to wake them up the light will be gone. And how will I explain what I have seen? And why would they believe me? "Haints," after all, are only stories in the night.

I will do it myself. I quickly dig out my favorite hunting hat, a soft wool beret. I pull it on, then strap on my hunting knife. I pick up my bow. I don't use a quiver—just carry a couple of arrows in my bow hand. Last, I pick up my boots. I will put them on outside, after tiptoeing down the stairs and through the house.

Outside, the cold hits me instantly. I get into the boots quickly. I must be something to see: a hunter carrying his bow in the black of night, wearing only a beret, his boots, and a full set of dark-colored long underwear. But how I look does not bother me. What bothers me is the light, which I still can see dancing at the far end of the field.

I decide to gamble. Rather than take the time to stalk straight in on the light, I decide to drop off the edge of the ridge, get into the brush and high grass just out of sight, and then rush the light, coming back into view of it and going back into a stalk only when I am approaching bow range. I don't actually plan to shoot at the light; I only want to see what it is. Or so I say to myself.

In a few seconds I am down off the ridge and running north along the edge of the trees, out of sight of the field. The grass is soft from the cold and dampness of the night and I make no noise. When I think I have gone far enough, I stop, catch my breath, and carefully nock an arrow on the bowstring. I am, after all, a hunter. I ease up the hill to the field, then began a stalk that takes me to the edge of the woods.

The light is gone.

I have to struggle to keep the cold from shaking me like a dead leaf in a winter breeze . . . and then the light appears in front of my face. It pops out of the woods just to my right and flashes across in front of me, then turns into the field and floats away, down and into the far woods. It disappears. For an instant I freeze, then realize that the light has not seen me, has no idea I am there. I start carefully after it, but then, in some sort of wild and unreasoned excitement, I break into a full run.

I am almost on top of it before I see it again. It is only a few yards from me and I think of just dropping the bow and plowing into it, tackling it, grabbing it. But I don't know what *it* is, and fear of the unknown calms me down. I move closer, an inch at a time. The light has stopped moving.

If we are lucky, there are a few times in our lives when we have a revelation, an understanding, a sudden rush of knowing, of awareness, of *being*. If we are lucky. That night, in the thickness of the cold air and the silence of mountains in darkness, I am very lucky.

The light is a kerosene lantern. It is being carried by Jory.

It takes me a long time to get back to the house. I ease away from the light, back across the field and into the fringe of the woods on the far side. I have been cold from the moment I left the house, but no longer. I am comfortable, walking there in the woods in my long underwear, carrying my bow, feeling the weight of my knife pulling against my belt. I can stay out here forever, I think. I go past the house and around the barn, up and over the knoll beyond, and down into new woods. After a while, I curl around to the north and back to the house. I don't know whether I get back there before Jory, but it doesn't matter. I know he has not seen me.

And that's how I learn why the deer never come. It is because they come in the dark, to move into the field and bed down with Jory's cattle, to browse at the edge of the woods in sight of the house, to know they are next to a human who only loves them. And deep in the night, when the hunters are drugged with full stomachs and heavy sleep and the house is silent, Jory takes his lantern and goes into the fields.

He swings the lantern, he dances, he runs, he hops. He creates a ballet of safety, of warning, of pure joy. He ranges the meadows and the edges of the woods, running, spinning, swooping. He makes sure the deer are up and running—I hear them crashing through the woods in full flight. And he spooks the deer into the next county.

Jory. He loves to have the hunters visit. He loves the *idea* of the hunting, of the storytelling, of the eating of good food and the smoking of cheap cigars. But he also loves the deer. And he has found a way to have it all.

And so, in the years after that, at Jory's, I become a different sort of hunter. I still stalk the woods and I still carry the bow, but I don't get up particularly early in the morning; I don't stumble through the tangled forest darkness trying to get there, somewhere, before dawn. I spend more time thinking than walking, more time looking than hunting. I enjoy. I am aware. I am in process. I *become*.

Usually, I let the others rise early, eat, and leave, and then I wander downstairs and into the warm kitchen where Greta rounds up a breakfast that would stun a bear. I eat, then wander off into the woods in no particular hurry. I don't go very far. I find a protected opening in the undergrowth, or a sunny patch of grass, and I just lie down and go to sleep in the warm autumn sunlight. My hunting gear begins to include items that keep me comfortable; I may be the only bowhunter in West Virginia to carry a small, down-filled pillow. And books. And a notebook.

The other hunters never come back to the house for lunch. They stay out all day, usually moving far into the woods and only returning in time for supper. I *always* come back for lunch. I just drift in, and Greta always knows I am coming. I think she knows everything. She has been baking, and fresh bread will be cooling on the sideboard. She gathers apples every day and makes every conceivable dish out of them. My favorite is the hot, homemade applesauce, which I spread thickly over the warm bread. A pot of coffee will disappear in the process.

And then, back to the "hunt." And another nap. Hours spent scribbling in my notebook.

I never tell Jory that I know. It would have been so very wrong to do that.

Chaser knows. He must have known for years, and still he comes to Jory's farm. As I do.

There are moments, in our lives, when we do some things for the last time—we will never do them again. But we never really know when those moments happen, never really know, in our lives, when those moments come. And go. We see the face and grip the warm hand of a friend for the last time, but we seldom know.

And so it is with me, and with Jory. One cold October morning I ride away. For the last time.

We are nothing more than our memories. If we do not remember, we have no past, and no path to the future. When I realize I have ridden away from Jory's for the last time, I give up hunting. But I still remember Jory for his love of his land and the animals with which he shared it. And I remember him for giving me that sudden rush of knowing, deep within a place that I only suspected was there.

I will have the memory when I die.

I never hit the deer. I didn't *want* to hit the deer, it seems. I wanted the process, but not the end. I wanted only the journey. And so did Jory.

An arrow in the light.

A lantern in the night.

Somehow, with Jory, it all balanced out.

Finally, I understand.

1993

Lowenstein 2

I'm still here, Lowenstein, you son of a bitch.

The music ends and the applause dies and my wife and I move to the lobby in the soft flow of people that always follows a classical performance.

Wine is being served and as I pick up the glasses I see Lowenstein across the room. I have not seen him for ten years. He is sipping from a glass and talking to a woman who stands in front of him, her back to me. As he talks, his eyes rise across her shoulder and he sees me. He flinches, and I know he has spilled some wine. I wait for him to look away, but he cannot. I hold his eyes for some awful length of time and then walk toward him. He takes an involuntary step backward. I stop beside him.

"I'm still here, Lowenstein, you son of a bitch."

I do not look at the woman.

I walk away.

1994

Peyote

Yeah, I am still here, and I wonder what it all means.

I think about the Indian and the Mexican. I know the Indian is alive, and I know where he is. In my heart, I think that the Mexican is dead, but I do not know why I think that. I do not want him to be dead; there are so few of us left.

I wander around in the desert for a few days, not going anywhere. I down-climb into a canyon and sit beside a tiny stream, a rivulet, no wider than my hand. I sip the water. I sit there for two days, but I cannot clear my mind. I am full of clutter, a sloping mound of trash leaning against the back wall of my mind. I cannot get rid of it.

I leave to go find the Indian.

I sit with Wendell Klah on the edge of a high mesa in the reservation country where he was born. In his pocket he has some hard, bitter buttons that he has gotten from some Utes. Damn Utes, he says. Wish they'd keep this shit to themselves. But he has a pocketful of the buttons.

You have to do this, he says. All the answers are in here. And a cleansing.

He puts one of the buttons in his mouth, and hands one to me. I put it in my mouth.

For a long while, nothing happens. We just sit there, chewing, feeling the bitter taste running through us.

And then we puke.

The puking is so violent that I think maybe I pass out for a while, falling over onto the hard clay, the meager juices that are left in me dribbling down my chin.

Wendell has brought water and we drink until we can drink no more, and then we puke again.

When the puking is over, we lie exhausted on the earth, trying to recover, trying to sit up without the world spinning out of control.

We chew again, staring into the late evening sun. The sun is red, and then blue, and then some colors I have never seen before, have not seen since. My eyes blur and the colors run together, washing over each other and over me, blending and yet crisp, clear and individual. I can see each color separately and distinctly, and yet I can see the whole, flowing out over the mesa and covering the red land with a warmth that I have never seen before, never felt before.

And I see the Mexican. And Ruker. And my father. Giant hornets fly in front of me.

The warmth lasts three days. We sit, stare into the horizon, nod off, fall over on our sides, sit up again.

When it is over, I see no one.

My head feels strangely empty, clean, uncluttered. It is uncluttered because, after all, I still have no answers. But at least the questions are gone.

And I am more hungry than I have ever been in my life. But I am not sure that I am hungry for food.

I know that I have been very fucked up, here on the mesa, maybe more than at any time in my life. I think maybe I never want to do this shit again.

But, what the hell, I think, maybe those Ute guys aren't so bad, after all.

1995

Belonging

I don't belong anywhere.

I have never belonged anywhere. Of all the times and all the places, I was just a visitor, a tourist, sometimes even an explorer. But I didn't *belong*. Once I saw the world I was in, I wanted to see the next world, wanted to go on, wanted to see.

I love this place, here, where I live. But throughout the fast years of living here I always feel like a visitor, a traveler just passing through on the way to somewhere else. I don't belong here. I know that.

"When all the goodbyes are said," I once wrote, "I want to be the one who is leaving." But I am beyond leaving, now. I am finally rooted in place.

I have no will to leave.

And then another book is published.

1996

Lujan's Place

There is a small metal cup that sits on a stack of books resting on an old table in the corner of the room, a place that is touched by the early sun through an old windowpane, the cup warming quickly in the soft light.

The cup has been there for years. Or something longer than years.

The cup is Mexican enamelware, a soft blue color with white flecks, one of those nondescript things that finds its way across the border and ultimately ends up as a tiny flowerpot on an adobe windowsill. But not on my windowsill. My cup sits with some of my favorite books, and now and then I drink from it. It is one of my cherished things.

When I bought it, in Mr. Lujan's Place, it cost a dollar and ninety-eight cents.

How long has it been now? A decade? More?

Lujan's Place, he called it. He didn't even call it a store. For, in truth, it wasn't. He sold things, yes, but the things were just an excuse, a reason, a peg on which to hang the essence of his being there. And that was the heart of it. His being there.

I bought things I didn't need, just to go inside. The place was smaller than some people's living rooms and the chest-high racks of Mexican enamelware and thick, heavy pottery made it even smaller. But in spite of its size, it was the largest store I have ever known. There was an eternity to be seen there, an infinite number of things to learn.

His hands shook but his mind was steady and the warm flickering of his eyes lit up the tiny store. He moved slowly and, toward the end, with a shuffle that was at once ancient and dignified, feet sliding toward some unknown destination that he saw more clearly than I.

I never knew anything about him, about Mr. Lujan. Not really. I didn't know what made him laugh or what made him cry. I didn't know if he liked the smell of chile roasting in the autumn or if he wanted strong coffee in the morning to start the day. I didn't know whom he loved, or who loved him. All I knew was . . . he knew things.

He knew things. He knew about herbs and lanterns and the oil on the leather of the headstalls that hung, almost unnoticed, at the back of the store. He knew the texture of the grind of delicate green leaves and the weight of brown powders and he taught me to pronounce *epazote* without my face getting red.

He knew about the soul of Santa Fe, about the denseness of the history that rose from Galisteo Street like heat waves from a desert floor in summer.

His Place was a link with the past. His Place was a cup inside of which lay wisdom.

I always wanted to touch the walls. The coats of paint there, like the rings of a tree, read out his clear and silent history, layers of light and darkness in the years of Santa Fe and one man's bright and warm place within it.

Somewhere under there, a layer was put on years ago when I came to Santa Fe and I wondered what his hands looked like back then, when he painted it.

And then Mr. Lujan's Place is gone.

Suddenly, I feel old.

For a while, each time I walk by, the windows are dark, empty, like the eyes of a body with no heart. Dust gathers on the glass and filters the light that creeps into the little room, dappling across the cold floor and into a far corner where an ancient, toothless push broom stands final guard.

Everything else is gone.

I stand in front of the glass and stare inward—inward into the empty Place and inward into myself. I think that, surely, I will see him in there if I look hard enough, want hard enough to see him, silently waiting in the back, near the headstalls, by the push broom.

But he is not there.

Another store takes Mr. Lujan's Place and when I walk by for the first time something switches off in my mind and a small space closes off back in there, locked, and I know that I have captured Mr. Lujan for the rest of my lifetime. Captured him as he was, as I want him to be.

Mr. Lujan's Place is gone.

They sell t-shirts there now.

And then I read that Mr. Lujan, too, is gone. And suddenly I feel even older.

Things change.

How long has it been now? A decade? More?

Who will remember Mr. Lujan?

Who will know that he was here?

I.

1997

Dinner with Carmen

I can feel the gentle nudging of soft pain in my shoulders and I know there will be days when I will not want to lift the boat, will not want to paddle. And so I decide to go back while I still can.

Things have changed, as I knew they would. Large hotels, tennis courts, bars playing American music.

It is late, and I park the truck in a paved lot where I once slept on the sand under a *palapa*. There is no *palapa* now, only a security guard whom I pay to let me sleep there, and to watch the truck while I am gone.

At first light, in minutes, I have unloaded the boat and have it at the edge of the tiny waves, my gear and supplies tucked and taped inside. It is already so hot that I am sweating when I move the boat out on the water and climb in, pulling the spray skirt tight around me.

Things have changed, yes. But here, on the edge of the Sea of Cortez, and out there, on the near horizon, on Carmen Island, it is still Baja. The old Baja.

I am stiff from lack of paddling, my back aches, my eyes squint from the sun glittering across the water as though reflecting from shards of broken glass. But the beach is now only yards away, the light surf moving gently against the sand. It has taken me more than five hours to reach the island.

But I am not where I want to be. I am too far south. I turn the boat and paddle north along the shore, just outside the surf. In less than a half-hour I see the rocks that guard the entrance to the tiny, circular bay. When I paddle through, it is like being on a pond in the center of nothing. There is no breeze, no surf; the water does not move. The boat leaves small ripples behind it, the water so flat that the ripples, I think, will actually reach the shore.

I try to remember where I was, all those years ago.

There, just behind the rocks at the entrance.

I paddle over there and land the boat, then drag it far out of the water and lash it to a thick stand of brush.

I get out a water bottle and sit on the rocks, waiting for some feeling, some stir of emotions. But nothing comes.

The island has not changed, at least not that I can see. It is timeless, a rise of desert, holding off the ocean with dry will and reserve, cacti and spiny-limbed brush standing like desiccated watchmen, guarding rocks, gravel and sand. The island is brown, the ocean is blue, maybe green, and I wonder if there have ever been any other colors on this land.

I scan the beach in front of me. Somewhere here, somewhere within a few paces, is the spot where the paddle lay, gently bobbing in the water, waiting. But I do not remember the precise spot. I have another paddle, now, and another boat, and they are safe on the beach behind me.

I have eaten little on the way across from the mainland and I am hungry. I go back to the boat and reach inside for the dry-bag with the food

I have brought. The food is basic, nothing more than trail mix, a couple of oranges and some energy bars.

I hear what seems to be a low moan and I look around but see nothing. Then, I glace out to sea, toward the mainland in the distance. The water has changed, far out there, angry now, white foam flying from the tops of waves like gray hair blowing in a hard wind—and I hear the moaning of the wind and I remember the speed with which a Baja storm can attack.

I know I have about fifteen minutes, maybe twenty, before the storm hits the beach. My beach.

I forget about the food and, instead, I break out a light mountaineering tarp that I always carry, whether or not in the mountains. I spread the spray skirt over the cockpit and pull it tight, then lash both ends of the boat—and the paddle—to the brush. I look quickly around at the low hills that come down to the inlet, looking for shelter, but see nothing that is an improvement over where I am. I tuck myself into the brush beside the boat and wrap myself in the tarp. I wiggle until I have made depressions in the sand for my shoulders and hips, and I relax. And wait. In minutes, I hear the first drops of rain against the tarp. Before the storm hits fully, I am asleep.

Baja storms come quickly, explosive in their energy, and then can be gone in a matter of minutes. Or hours. This one stays all afternoon. When I know the rain has stopped and the wind has died, I crawl slowly out of my tarp and stretch my stiff body until the aches have given way to a stiffness that does not seem to hurt. Much. I inspect the boat and paddle. They are as I left them.

Thick, low clouds still following in the wake of the storm give the light a heavy, forbidding cast and I know part of the light is not there—it will be full dark in minutes. It is far too late to make the crossing back to the mainland; I have no stomach for paddling in the dark on the Sea of Cortez.

Again, I break out the food bag, but do not even open it. Although I slept through most of it, the storm seems to have sapped my energy. I think about crawling back inside the tarp and waiting for morning.

But I know I have to eat. I take out a couple of energy bars, a fistful of trail mix and an orange. I go and sit on the rock and look out over an ocean that is becoming black with a speed that is frightening. The water is black. The beach is black. There is no moon behind the heavy clouds, and the air is black.

I don't know why I came back here. I did not have to come. I have nothing to prove.

I do not actually see the first, tiny flash of light from far down the beach. It hits my eye from the side, one of those things that you think might be there, but are gone before you are sure. I stare down the beach, peering into the darkness, but see nothing for a few minutes. And then there it is again, a tiny flicker of yellow light.

A flame.

I am still carrying my meager food supply and my water bottle when I walk up on the fire. There is no one there.

There is fresh wood in the flames and, to the side, a large, heavy iron skillet rests on a flat rock. A long, low wooden boat is pulled up on the beach, its oars shipped, a heavy rope running from the bow across the beach and secured to a rock the size of a small car.

I look around, but can see nothing outside the ring of firelight.

"Hello," I say softly.

There is only silence.

"Hola," I say again, not raising my voice.

I know there is someone there, and I know I am being watched. I begin to realize that I have walked into the light of the unknown. I know better than to do that. I begin backing away, wanting to melt into the darkness.

"*Señor*, you seem to be a man of no evil intent."

I stop. The voice comes out of the darkness, not very far away.

"I mean you no harm, *maestro*," I say, as easily as I can manage. "I have only some food and a little water." I am still within the light of the fire. I put down my food, lift the bottom of my light jacket, holding the jacket open. I turn slowly. I am wearing only a light shirt, shorts, and the jacket. I am concealing nothing.

"I want nothing. I only came to your fire . . . a moth to the flame." I try to put a grin in my voice. "But that is not a good explanation," I say. "Moths are burned by the flame. I do not wish to be burned, *maestro*."

I hear nothing for long seconds.

"Then, *por favor, señor*, share my fire, and share my food."

He walks slowly out of the darkness, barefoot, long black hair flowing around an angular face, his shirt hanging down below his hips.

A machete dangling from his right hand. Even in the flickering firelight I can see the polished edge, the sharpness. He sees me looking.

"I apologize, *señor*. The knife is for evil, and for cutting fish."

He grins, and walks farther into the firelight.

I lift my hand and reach out to him. I tell him my name.

He shifts the machete to his left hand, a casual, practiced movement. He takes my hand, lightly.

"I am Mateo," he says, with a slight nod of his head.

We stand that way for a few moments.

"*Maestro*," I say, "I think I should go back to my little boat. I think I am intruding on a man and his fire, and his time alone . . . "

He reaches down, picks up the skillet and hands it to me.

"*Señor,*" he says, "there is a small bottle in that box. There is good cooking oil in it. *Por favor,* wipe oil on the skillet and put it on the coals."

I take the skillet and look around for the box. It is on the edge of the firelight.

"And, *señor,* I hope you are hungry."

I wipe down the skillet, trying to follow his movements as he goes to the boat. I think he climbs inside, and then out again. When he comes back to the fire he is still carrying the machete, and a yellowtail that must weigh twenty pounds.

"I caught this one an hour before the storm. It should make a fine dinner," he says. There are some pieces of sun-bleached planking, still wet from the storm, on the sand where the skillet was and he puts the fish on one of the larger ones. In only a few seconds, with only a few strokes of the machete, he opens the fish and has enormous fillets laid out on the plank.

"A machete?" I ask.

"Once," he says, "I had a proper knife for the fish. But it was broken when one of the oars fell across it. *Pero,* I gave it to my son. It is good to be able to give something to a son. No matter what."

For a moment he stares across the fire and out into the blackness above the water. He seems lost in some vision, but his expression hardly changes.

From the wooden box he takes some onions, heads of garlic and tortillas wrapped in a soft cloth. Using the machete, he cuts up the onions and garlic and drops them into the hot pan. I hear the sizzle and inhale the scent of pungent aromas and suddenly I am hungrier than I have ever been in my life.

With a stick, he stirs the onions and garlic, adds some salt, then squeezes a fresh lime into the pan. And then he drops in large chunks of yellowtail.

He does not leave the pan on the coals for very long, just long enough for the yellowtail to begin to flake.

He takes the pan from the fire and I realize that he has no plates, no utensils, only the stick he uses for stirring.

I get two of the pieces of planking and hand one to him. He grins, and scrapes large helpings of the fish out of the skillet and onto the wood. We settle back onto the sand, using our fingers to eat the hot food. He opens the package of tortillas. I take one and put a piece in my mouth. The tortilla is soft, light, almost delicate. I can think of nothing better to go with the fish.

"My wife made them last night," he says. "She knows that if I have tortillas and my boat, I will not be without food." He chuckles, looking back through the night toward the town of Loreto, miles across the water.

We eat what he has cooked, and, while we are eating, he cooks again, as before, another huge pan of fish, onions and garlic. And tortillas.

And we eat that, also.

We sit in the night, our butts dug into the sand until it would be difficult for us to fall over, the fire dying, the stars beginning to make their way through the overcast. A few minutes ago, he took a large Coca-Cola bottle—maybe a one-liter size—out of the box. The bottle had a cork in it and he pulled it loose, leaving it resting in the mouth of the bottle. He set the bottle upright at the edge of the coals. Now, he reaches down and turns it slightly, letting each side of the bottle feel the heat from the coals that are remaining. He has two tiny glass jars, perhaps empty jelly jars, something his wife may have brought home from the store, or perhaps picked up along the street. The jars sparkle with the reflection of the coals. Using his shirt as a pad, he picks up the Coke bottle and carefully pours into one of the jars. And hands it to me. I sip it. He watches.

Coffee. Thick, rich, with nothing in it to cut the full flavor, perhaps the strongest coffee I have ever had. It is like nectar with an edge, iron ambrosia.

We drink all the coffee.

The storm is gone, and even in the earliest daylight, the heat of Baja begins to return. I roll out of my tarp, drink some water, and look out at the water. Another "Baja day," one of those days when the entire surface of the Sea of Cortez appears to be a giant mirror, without a ripple, without a single disturbance. About three miles out I see a tiny break in the surface and I know that there is a whale out there, resting, enjoying the idea that the ocean is his, truly his.

I put the kayak back into the water and start slowly toward the far shore.

I look back over my shoulder at Carmen Island, Carmen, lying there, waiting.

And I know I probably will never be back.

I look south and see the wooden boat, just putting to sea. Without thinking about it, I turn the kayak and kick up the paddling cadence. I close on the boat quickly.

Mateo holds his boat steady, watching me come. I pull alongside. I raise my paddle in both hands. A salute. Mateo grins and raises his hand.

I reach beneath the spray cover and pull out the knife, a custom fillet knife in a custom sheath, a knife that I have had for years, have hardly used, but always seem to have with me when I am near the water.

I toss the knife into Mateo's boat.

"*Señor,*" I say, "this is not in payment for the dinner. It is not payment for anything. It is just time for this knife to have a new owner."

Mateo says nothing, his eyes fastened on the knife in the bottom of his boat.

I paddle away.

"Maybe one day, a knife for your son," I call over my shoulder.

I have never felt so good in my life.

Even the water is expensive.

We sit at a table in a restaurant in San Francisco. I am with a couple, old and good friends, and this is a night of reunion. The food is incredibly good, the wine is beyond imagining, the company is warm and gracious, the conversation easy and flowing. My friends know the owner of the restaurant and he comes to our table, does all the proper things, all the time scouting the room for anything that might need his attention, his correction. His restaurant is impeccable. He is impeccable.

He looks at me.

"Is this not the best meal of your life?" His question is only half in jest. Before I can answer, he suddenly leaves our table, some tiny problem requiring his attention.

I watch him walk away.

"No," I say quietly. "Not even close. Maybe third place."

My friends do not understand.

I do not explain it to them.

1998

A Finding in the Sky

The Earth is above me, and it isn't supposed to be.

I grip the handhold on the instrument panel, push my head back against the seat and look up, and there it is, the Earth, swirling over my head. I have never been upside-down in an airplane before, but it is the only way I can ditch the kid flying the other plane.

I am flying as well as I know how, trying to roll the Marchetti airplane up and over, reversing direction in a vain attempt to lose the kid, to reverse the situation, to get him in my sights, to win the dogfight.

It doesn't work.

I bring the plane around and level it out. The other plane is nowhere in sight. "Lose sight, lose the fight," the briefing pilot had said.

And then I know where he is, the other pilot . . . the "kid" . . . my son, Toran. I can't see him, but I know. He is circling behind and above me, not at all impressed with my weak evasive maneuver. He will circle high, then, to pick up speed, he will dive his own Marchetti toward me, a metal bird of prey stooping at incredible speed. He will roar below my line of flight and then rise sharply—the fighter pilots call it a "yo-yo"—

using the burst of speed to catch me and to bring his "guns" to bear anytime he wants. Getting me in his electronic sights. Pressing the trigger. Trying his damnedest to "shoot" my aging ass out of the air. It will take him less than a minute.

"Tracking, tracking, tracking!" It is Tor, on the radio. And I know this aerial dogfight is over.

"Die like a man," I hear on the radio, the voice chuckling.

But I don't want to die like a man. I want to *live* like a man.

Too late. I have been tracked. And shot. My plane trails smoke. I have lost.

"Knock it off!" It is the radio again—the code phrase that means the fight is over.

Okay, kid, you win this time. Now, let's do it again.

In the beginning, when he was very young, there was a time when he wanted to do everything I did. *Everything.*

Even mountaineering. He was too young, I knew, but now and then I let him tag along, stumbling and grumbling, lagging behind my friends and me as we climbed at high altitude.

Once . . . it was still early morning when we broke out of tree line and could see the hard naked mass of the mountain stretching away to the summit and the sky. The sour look on his face changed to one of awe. He knew, for the first time, that he was on a real mountain. The grumbling stopped—and he stepped to the front and charged the rock. For the rest of the climb—to more than 14,000 feet—he led the way.

On the narrow ledge that was the summit, he stood in the cold light and stared out into forever. I could hear the snap in his eyes.

He had done what I did and we were there, on the summit, a man and a boy. What would we be, I wondered, when we were both men?

He was only ten.

But time passed. And things changed.

Tor and I are circling high above the desert in a cool, crystal, September sky. We are flying real fighter planes in simulated air combat, trying to "shoot" each other out of the sky. Each of us is piloting a SIAI Marchetti, an Italian-built, propeller driven, incredibly powerful, 270-mph fighter-trainer attack airplane, capable of unlimited aerobatics—one of the meanest, fastest and most nimble aircraft of its kind. Used by a dozen air forces around the world, Marchettis are considered one of the finest aircraft for training pilots in air combat.

The Marchettis we are flying are equipped with electronic tracking systems, including electronic "guns," sending out beams and signals rather than bullets. But no matter that the guns are electronic . . . it is all very real to me.

Aerial combat. Dogfighting, the pilots call it.

We set up the next dogfight. By rules, the planes are supposed to start the fight "even," passing left-side to left-side at high speed, 500 yards apart. As we rocket past each other I stand the airplane on its left wing, whipping around like the cracking of a whip, intending to snap into his trail, right behind him. It is the sharpest turn I have ever done in a plane. I can feel the g-forces in my stomach and in my mind, trying to smash my body through the bottom of the aircraft.

I have him now, I think.

But he is gone again.

I look up, directly into the sun. Tor has taken refuge in the fireball, a World War I tactic that still works today. There is no hope of my finding him in all that flame and light. He, on the other hand, will have me clearly in his vision—and soon have me in his sights, a brightly illuminated sitting duck. He will make one snap turn, dive on my aircraft, and fix me calmly in his sights. And that's what he does.

"Tracking . . . " I am getting damned tired of hearing him say that.

I have lost again.

He is young and I am young and I don't have the seasoning to be a father. When something goes wrong, I underreact, or overreact, or have no reaction at all. I never seem to get it right.

When I run out of the wisdom of fathers, of which I have little, I retreat into just trying to live some sort of life that says I am, simply, a man, hoping that will be enough.

But it isn't.

For some years I work for Outward Bound and somewhere in there he becomes, inexplicably, a teenager. Now, he *never* wants to do what I do. This Outward Bound stuff is for outdoor geeks; he's tried it and it isn't much, he says. Who, in his right mind, wants to hike in a cold, slanting rain; climb unfeeling mountains; sleep on unyielding ground; run rapids so violent that all you can hear is the noise of them in your mind long after you have left the canyon. Who, indeed? Not him.

Some time slipped by, and things changed again.

We are setting up the next fight. Just above the far horizon I can see the glistening speck of Tor's Marchetti coming toward me and I know he will have the throttle to the wall and that we will be passing each other at a combined air speed of more than 400 miles an hour.

Okay, pal, this one's mine.

As we flash past each other in the start-the-fight formation I again whip the plane hard to the left, this time sliding below his line of flight. I hold the hard turn, watching as his plane claws up into a steep climb, and I know he is looking over his shoulder, trying to find me. As he climbs, I level out and close the gap. He turns again, but it is too late. I am on him now, coming up fast. And then, there he is, sitting in the tiny inner ring of my sights.

"Tracking . . . " It was my turn to say it.

I have him now. All I have to do is press the trigger.

But I don't.

When he is fifteen, he changes his mind again. He goes to Outward Bound—that bastion of outdoor geeks—and becomes, at the time, one of the youngest to complete an Outward Bound standard program. When he comes back, he is different. He is made of the same material, the same spring steel, but it is tempered, somehow. It has a form, a shape that takes a while for me to recognize. It is, in fact, the shape of a man.

He grows, and suddenly—I don't remember the week, month, the year, but it is *suddenly*—he is back again to doing *everything* I do. Except he does it *better.*

Running rapids is something *I* am good at. *He* rows a tiny 12-foot raft through the Grand Canyon, solo. He is better.

I climb, addicted to the mountains. *He* climbs as though gravity does not exist. He is better.

I learn to ski late, but enjoy it and manage to progress. I am barely competent. *He* is raised on the mountain, skis with a careless grace. As a preteen, he is considered Olympic potential. He blows it off: running gates day after day is far too boring. He skis the wilderness. He works for years as a professional ski patrolman.

There are countless other examples, but why bother.

And so we create "findings" together.

To feel alive, we have to find the challenges—not virtual challenges, not the challenges of games, but the real thing, with real blood and the heaving of lungs and the grinding of bones and sweat running down our faces until our vision is blurred.

"Sometimes," he says, "*finding* the thing is better than the thing itself."

Findings—those joyful points in life where the gathering of time and place and people and experience flow together to stamp an image in the mind that will never fade. Some call it making a memory. I call it making a life.

I don't remember pressing the trigger. Maybe the plane's electronics are designed to cause a trail of smoke when the system realizes it has been tracked. I watch the gray smoke trail stream from Tor's plane. I have won a single dogfight. Not bad for an old guy.

The dogfights are over.

The mock-combat wasn't my idea. It had been the idea of Tor and his wife, Sarah. When I hear about it, I immediately want to do it.

And then it hits me. *Now, I want to do what he does.*

Somewhere along the way, we have changed places.

We are headed back to the airfield, practicing the way real combat pilots fly in formation. I am concentrating on the wingtip of Tor's plane, flying in concert with the heartbeat of my son, *less than thirty feet away.* I can clearly see the rivets in the skin of his plane—small, hard little pins that hold the plane together. I stare at them, knowing that each rivet, individually, is really nothing. It is only when they are all there together that there is a machine that can fly.

I think of the tiny shared experiences, the rivets, in our lives, Tor's and mine. We are father and son, but even more than that. We were two hearts pumping the same blood, two minds playing out the same scenes. During the dogfights, I knew where his airplane was, even when

I could not see it. I knew when he moved the stick. I could feel him breathing.

Now, flying in tight formation, I can see easily into the other cockpit. I can see my son. He turns his head and looks directly at me. I can see his smile. He raises his hand and sticks his thumb high in the air.

We have found each other again.

A finding in the sky.

We are a machine that can fly.

1999

Arctic Circle

Any minute now, I will awaken, and the ride will be over.

It has never felt real.

Somewhere out there, up there, away from here, is the Arctic Circle. That is where we are headed, Denali and I. In late September. On motorcycles. In freezing temperatures. If we make it, maybe, then, it might seem real. Maybe.

Denali rides ahead, all 6'3" of him settled into his bike like he was born to it. I watch him lean into the curves, thankful that I have a friend like Denali. I think of other guys I had gone venturing with, guys who were sometimes fun and sometimes not, guys I could sometimes trust, and sometimes not.

You can be a male, and not be a man.

Denali is a man.

Denali and I have some coffee, saddle up, and leave town, heading west. Five miles out of town the rain comes again and stays, a hard, driving, steady opening of the heavens. We bore through it, heading for the next little town, not even on the map. We blow through the town, through the one intersection, rain flashing from the passage of our tires. Outside of town, we shoot instantly into spare and desolate country. The road goes west but we want to go north so Denali turns onto a raw dirt track—a raw *mud* track—that drops off into a flat and disappears into a cut canyon so narrow that, if I crash in the mud, I'll probably smack off both walls before I hit the road.

I see Denali's taillight grow quickly smaller through the rain and I drive faster. We disappear into the canyon, watching the walls close in against the sides of the bikes. We are doing 50 mph over mud and gravel and through standing water, bits of stone flying out from the sides of the tires and pinging against boulders at the side of the track, mud sticking to everything that moves. If a truck comes from the other direction, I doubt that I will see it in time to get the hell out of the way.

And the rain keeps coming. It can't get any worse than this.

We break out of the canyon and see flat riding ahead. We keep our speed, mud flying from the bikes like motorboats on a flat lake. Denali's rear tire is throwing a rooster tail of mud fifteen feet in the air and I have to drop back about thirty yards to avoid the downfall.

Denali plows his bike off the road onto a turnout, nothing more than a flat area of thick mud. I follow. We turn off the engines and just sit there looking at each other, the rain still drizzling on our helmets. We are wet, cold, tired, hungry, almost too stiff to get off the bikes. But we do. Denali is taller; other than that, no one could tell us apart, two mud-covered men standing by mud-covered bikes in the middle of mud-covered nowhere. Somehow, water has pooled in Denali's jacket, then has burst inward and sloshed down inside his pants, soaking him from the crotch down. We stand in the rain, just looking at each other. Then our hands come up and we both raise our face shields. We are both laughing. And then screaming.

It can't get any better than this.

Days later. Many days.

The wind blows all night, is still blowing when we rise early in the cold morning.

We talk it over at breakfast, both of us a little tense. It isn't the weather. It is where we are, and where we are going. By noon we will be in Fairbanks, about a hundred miles away, and early the next day we will ride due north, leave the paved road, jump onto the Dalton Highway and officially be on our way to the Arctic Circle. Maybe spend the night somewhere near the Yukon River. The morning after that . . .

The Arctic Circle.

Two days away.

Neither of us can relax.

We have no idea that this day will be a day that we will remember vividly for the rest of our lives.

We ride out of Delta Junction with the wind at our backs, blowing so hard that I think we could stay upright and moving, even if we turned off the engines. The wind catches our jackets and finds every tiny wrinkle and pocket, fills them, and drives us forward. The wind speed, from directly behind us, and the road speed of the bikes matches and it is as though there is no wind at all. I can hear the engine clearly, every little tick and groan of it, hear the tires on the pavement, hear everything. We are riding at sixty miles per hour. I know that if we stopped the wind would blow us over.

Twenty miles out of town the wind stops.

When we get to Fairbanks it is still early in the day and the weather has turned, spilling warm sunshine into a landscape that lies gentle and inviting. We pull into a supermarket parking lot, go inside, have some coffee and check the maps.

Hell, this is where we will turn north, *really* north, dead on for a run to the Circle.

It is still early and it isn't hard to make the decision. We will top off our tanks, grab some food, ride a little farther north, maybe to a little place called Livengood. Maybe stay overnight there, make a run for the Circle tomorrow . . .

Cut a day off our time to the Circle.

The weather is holding. The sun bakes our backs and the air is tender and sweet and we know this is the warmest day's riding we have had in more than two weeks.

The highway north out of Fairbanks is four lanes, then two lanes, then two lanes that get very narrow, and then two lanes that go off into the wilderness with no good reason, or so it seems.

When we get to Livengood, there is nothing here. No houses, no store, no fuel . . . nothing. It is only a name on a map.

We could camp here, of course; we have everything we need. But why camp here? There is lots of daylight left, and the Yukon River is only . . . somewhere to the north. We keep riding.

From the beginning, the weather has tested us. But now, north of Fairbanks, with our ultimate goal a hundred miles farther north, the weather gives it up. It is almost as though we are being rewarded for having kept at it, for having kept on riding when riding was insane, for being wet and cold and muddy and driven by the wind. Now, there is no wind. The road is dry. The sun bores down into the gentle valleys and the low ridges with a bright, gentle light that paints everything we see in colors our eyes have trouble believing. We cross low, rolling hills that give a view north for miles on end and we can see the Dalton Highway snaking over the far horizon, tracking the oil pipeline that is always beside us, sometimes out of sight, but never far away.

There are hundreds, thousands, of places we can stop and camp. But we just keep riding.

And then, there is the Yukon River.

I had thought about the Yukon. Seen pictures. But the pictures were deceptive. I think of the river as a picturesque stream running gently toward the sea, a stream where we can spend some time, just listening to the babbling of the water, resting . . .

What the hell was I thinking? The Yukon is a freshwater ocean, the water barely above freezing, and storming toward the sea at eight knots.

Somewhere just north of the Yukon, we know, is a tiny rest stop called The Hot Spot. We have been told there is food there, and gas, and even a room for the night.

And five miles north of the river, we find it.

The Hot Spot is a collection of portable buildings and miscellaneous huts down a short dirt road off the highway, cobbled together at the edge of a parking area wide enough to turn a semi-trailer rig. If you drove past The Hot Spot in any other place, you wouldn't stop there. But this isn't any other place; this is five miles north of the Yukon River and less than an hour's ride from the Arctic Circle.

We stop at The Hot Spot, rent one of the three rooms they use as motel rooms, unsaddle the KLRs, and have two of the best hamburgers we had ever had. With little more than an hour of daylight left, Denali and I sit at an outdoor table and drink steaming coffee, content to wait for the northern sun to go down. We pull our riding jackets tighter against the coming chill of an Arctic night and dream, and talk, about tomorrow.

Tomorrow, we will ride to the Arctic Circle.

This is the best—the best day, the best weather, the best riding, the best evening, the best place.

Until the trucker pulls in for coffee.

We are just making polite conversation, three guys in a sort-of inn where no inn should ever be. The trucker asks us what we were doing there, and we tell him.

"Going to ride up to the Arctic Circle, tomorrow."

"Why?"

"No particular reason. Just to say we've done it, I suppose."

He looks at us, a quirky little smile on his face.

"You ain't gonna get there," he says. "There's a bridge about a quarter-mile south of the Circle. Construction people have it closed. Ain't gonna open it for days." The driver smirks and sips his coffee. "I just come from there."

Denali and I can't believe what we were hearing. We have ridden thousands of miles to get here, and now we are going to be stopped, 40 miles short of our target.

"How long is the bridge?" I ask.

"Not long. Maybe a couple hundred feet."

"Is it a steep canyon?"

"Nah, don't think so. Never really looked too close at it, but it don't look all that steep."

The driver finishes his coffee and, still smirking, goes back to his truck.

Denali and I talk it over. We have come all this way. We are *not* going to turn around now, bridge or no bridge. Tomorrow, we will ride up there. If we can't get across the bridge, we will take the KLRs off the road, down into the canyon, and try to ride across. If that doesn't work, we will stash the bikes in the brush, wade across the river and hike to the Arctic Circle. By damn, we *will* get to the Circle. That is the plan. And it is a good plan. But a little of the glow has gone out of our evening.

And then another trucker drives in.

Introductions. Chit chat. And he asks us what we are doing up here. We tell him the whole story, including the part about the other trucker—about the closed bridge.

"Hell, the bridge is open *now*, but they are going to close it at dark, tonight. That other guy was bullshitting you. I just came from there, drove across the bridge. I'm heading south. How do you think I got here? But the guy was right about one thing—when they close that bridge, it'll be closed for days."

Denali and I look at each other, not saying a word. We have less than hour of daylight. The bridge, and the Circle, are 40 miles away.

It is worth a try.

We leave our coffee cups sitting on the table, run to our room and grab the rest of our riding clothes, dressing as we head for the bikes. In less than five minutes from the time the trucker tells us the bridge is open, Denali and I are riding north over the Dalton Highway.

We have to get to the bridge before nightfall. We start at forty miles per hour, then fifty, gravel flying. Gradually, the gravel gets smaller and patches of hard dirt show through. Sixty miles per hour, the bikes doing little dances on the uneven road. Seventy miles per hour.

The country breaks open. The trees fall away into low shrub and clumps of grasses, lit from the south by a sun that is retreating as fast as we are riding north. I top a low ridge and there is nothing in front of me but the Arctic, stretching away to the Brooks Range in the distance, the snow-covered peaks glowing in the sun. I try to concentrate on the road, on the ruts and patches of gravel, but I can't help looking at the terrain, a country so beautiful that, for a brief moment, I think about slowing down, just letting the damned bridge close in front of me, just enjoy a piece of the Earth I have never seen before.

Thirty miles north of The Hot Spot we hit *pavement.*

Then we are doing eighty, maybe a little more.

I am checking the odometer. We are almost there.

We scream over a small rise and can see the bridge

. . . and the trucks that are stopped on the road.

The bridge is closed. No one is going anywhere.

We ride slowly to the end of the line of trucks, then ease around them to where we can see the bridge. Barricades stretch across the road and a construction crew truck is parked at an angle behind the barricades, a further message that the road is closed.

We get off the bikes—and realize that the truckers have turned off their engines. Truckers only do that when they know they aren't going anywhere for a *long* time. Some of the drivers walk around in the fading light, smoking, swapping stories.

Everybody looks at us. You can see it in their faces: "What the hell are those bikers doing here at this time of year?"

We can see someone in a hard hat standing by the barricades. Denali just looks at me. Hell, it's worth a try.

He ambles up to the hard hat. I stay with the bikes.

In less than five minutes, Denali motions to me. I walk up to Denali and the construction boss—a woman.

"There's nothing wrong with the bridge," Denali says. "They have traffic stopped here because of some work farther up the road. The boss here is going to let us cross," Denali says, nodding at the woman. "But then they're going to barricade this bridge. We've got 15 minutes to get over there, and get back."

We hustle back to the bikes, fire them up, the truckers standing mute, watching us. We ride around the barricade, accelerate across the bridge until all you can hear in the Arctic is the heavy thumping of single-cylinder engines at very high rpm. We head up a shallow rise, turn off to the right onto a short side road, into a graveled parking area, and pull up in front of a sign.

The sign reads: *Latitude 66° 33'.*

We were sitting on the Arctic Circle.

With less than 20 minutes of daylight left.

We stand at the Circle, almost in awe. It isn't as though this ride has never been done before; lots of riders have done it. But it has never been done by *us*. Until now.

I look at my odometer. I have ridden exactly 4,400 miles from where I got on the bike in New Mexico.

We get off the bikes and clap each other on the back, laughing, yelling, almost as though we have conquered something, made something, have done something. And we have.

We spend our 15 minutes looking at the countryside, breathing the air, wondering, dreaming. The only thing man-made at the Arctic Circle is a wooden sign saying that we are, indeed, at the Circle. But *we are* here and, below us, to the south, almost the entire planet. We love it.

We are out of time, and we are rapidly running out of daylight.

I have never before been so aware of what "south" means.

We turn our backs to the Arctic Circle, sit on the bikes and stare into a distant sun that hangs low, soft and cool in that far and mystical place where we were going.

South.

We ride slowly back across the bridge, wave at the woman in the hard hat, and keep going south. Only, this time, there is no hurry, no rush. We have done what we came to do. We take our time.

It gets darker, colder, but both of us are so high from the experience of getting to the Circle that the darkness and the cold does not bother us. We just ride. And we could have kept riding until the bikes gave it up. For days, for thousands of miles, we have driven toward one point on the earth. And we make it. We have been there. Now, there is only the riding south.

The whole thing is a mystical experience. I don't know how else to describe it. Riding across low tundra-covered ridges in the silver arctic light and seeing the Brooks Range in the distance behind us produces a sensory overload from which I may never recover. It is as though we are riding on the roof of the world, and if we keep going we will simply ride off the edge of the planet and into some state of being where there is only more of everything in front of us, nothing behind us, and the low, sweet singing of the engines is the only music we will ever hear, or ever need to hear, or ever want to hear.

In the early morning light of this day, , all we had wanted to do was get the hell out of Delta Junction. Maybe lay over in Fairbanks. It didn't turn out that way. Instead, we have ridden to the Arctic Circle. Now we will ride back south to within five miles of the Yukon River. On the same day.

By the time we get back to The Hot Spot it is pitch black and the temperature is dropping like a stone through clear water. But we are wired, too hyper to even think about going to bed. The lady who does the cooking is still in the kitchen. We sit at one of the outside tables, wearing every piece of clothing we have, drinking coffee. We say very little. There is nothing, really, to be said. What we have experienced this day, the images that have blown through our minds—sometimes, it's better not to try to put all that into words.

We finally force ourselves into bed in our tiny room. Fifteen minutes later, the northern lights come out and play in the sky. We get up and go back outside.

2000

Fantasy World

Every place I have ever been, everything I have ever done, has been nothing more than a way station, a brief stop on my way to something else.

I have never known the inside of anything.

I have never been on the inside of anything. Always on the outside but never looking in. Always looking . . . away.

Perhaps because away is always where I want to be.

The here and the now are not where I live. My mind is always elsewhere. I search for a fantasy world that is more real to me than anything I have ever known.

No matter what I have, or where I have it, I'm always looking to the next thing. I cannot stand in any one place without looking at some other place. I cannot do any one thing without wondering about some other thing. No matter where I am, or when I get there, I'm always looking over the next hill, into the next canyon, peering at the next summit, studying the horizon. There is always a fantasy world, a fantasy place that, I am sure, must be better than the one I'm in, must be new, must provide another experience.

All things, to me, are steps in a journey. I am never truly happy unless I am moving, working the journey.

Stopping in a new place is happiness—for a short time. And then I am moving again.

Through mountains, through canyons, through forests, through the pages of my life—but always *through*, always moving.

It is a constant uneasiness. Something drives me. It isn't about money. Certainly, I like money as well as the next man, but it is seldom money that motivates me. It is always something else, some drive not to be left behind, some vacant wish to be somewhere else.

And those other places become dreams. Fantasies.

The problem is, I don't know where they are.

The years slip by like otters sliding down a mud chute into the ocean, and with as little noise. I try to count them but I lose track and then I realize that counting is not the point of the thing. Whether I count them or not, they are still gone.

The fantasies, the dreams, die, one by one, killed by time.

And I think I am free.

But other dreams take their place, one by one.

Freedom from the dreams is what I dream about.

Freedom from the dreams will not happen to me.

Ever.

2001

Friendship

I feel good, and satisfied, but vaguely down, as though something grand has come to an end.

And it has.

Tomorrow, for the first time in a month, Denali and I will travel without the motorcycles.

There is something about making a turn in a road that has no known end. On the map, of course, the road ends. And that's where we have been riding, on a map. But not in our minds. In our minds, we ride on a single-track dirt path that seems to fade into the rain and mist, as though we can ride into some other dimension where all the curves are sweeping and long and the air is warm and sweet with sunshine.

That's what we dream. That's what we do.

We scream over roads never meant to be screamed over, rip past scenery that, at any other time, would have stopped us cold. Everything in Western Canada and Alaska is beyond our imaginations. For every river and lake we have ever ridden by in past years, now there are a hundred rivers and lakes. For every mountain, there are a hundred mountains, sheer walls, the fingers of glaciers probing the lower reaches, phalanxes of trees coming to an abrupt halt at a line beyond which only the most determined can survive.

But this is not about survival. We can easily survive.

This is not a test of endurance. We can easily endure—and have endured many things more stressful than this ride.

In fact, it is not a test at all.

This is about *experience*. A thing to do. A long stream of perceptions that infuse the mind.

This is about the gathering wave. And we ride the crest of it.

This is about friendship.

2002

A Death in the Mountains

It was only a matter of time. We all knew that.

We walk down the wide, worn wooden stairs. No one speaks. There is no sound except the strange drum-like noise of our feet on the hollow steps. His wife grips the old man's hand and he can feel the tremor of her body through her fingers. The lawyer walks in front of us, not looking back. He has done this before and he knows what to do, what not to say.

We go outside and stand in the bright sunlight. Such light has always charged the old man with energy, as though his body were some sort of solar collector that gathers the charge of the light and pumps it into his heart. But not today. He wishes for dark, so others cannot see him. His only want is to hide, to step aside from the systems that trapped him. But he cannot. He is in the sunlight with his humiliation and there is nothing he can do about it.

They have taken everything.

I see his wife's fingers tighten on his hand. Tears run slowly down her face and she turns away from me, not wanting me to see. But I have already seen. She is hurt deeply. More than that, she is lost.

For two hours on that bright morning he sat in a high-ceilinged room in the courthouse, watching and listening as he was told who his friends were, and were not. That his land was gone. That his pride was gone.

The judge stared at him, wondering, perhaps, how such an old man came to be here.

But the judge knew.

We all knew.

And then it was over.

The lawyer shakes our hands and we thank him. I have already paid him; the old man has nothing with which to pay.

I have heard others say they were broke. What they really meant was, they didn't have any cash. For the moment. But they had houses, cars, stocks, other things they could turn into something, if need be.

Not the old man. He has nothing.

They stand there after the lawyer is gone, holding hands in the sunlight, the wife crying softly.

He wishes to be taken from the Earth. But there is no one to take him.

Not yet.

Hard winter comes.

The sun rises on the first day of a new year. It rises as on any other day. There is nothing special about it.

The old man awakens terrified in a bed that is not his, in a cabin that is not his. He watches the light grow outside the window and he longs for the dark. He is less afraid in the dark. In the dark, no one can find him, can see him.

He is old, and he is closer to the day he was born than he has ever been—naked in thin light, weak, and not in control of anything.

He has no job. He is too old for a job.

He has nothing. The coal company has it all.

Strange, he often thinks. He has never been in a mine. And yet the mine has always been in him.

His wife still sleeps beside him. He hears the small noises she makes deep within her throat and he knows that she is dreaming bad things. She trusts him to care for her and he no longer knows where to hold that trust. He only knows what it weighs. He cannot lift it. If she falls ill, he cannot pay for her care. If she is hungry, he cannot give her food. He can give her only of his heart and mind and these are not things to keep her alive.

God, God, he thinks, it isn't supposed to be like this.

Colder. And still.

He watches as his wife moves silently about the cabin, looking for something to do, something that is right. She is wrapped in a thin housecoat, her gray hair hanging limply around her face, her arms wrapped around her waist.

But there is nothing for her to do.

The temperature is one degree below freezing.

His wife cries silently, trying to hide her face from him.

But he knows.

It is only a matter of time. We all know that.

There is really nothing left to do.

And so the time comes.

And so the old man dies.

I knew him.

I am of his clan.

His was a family of hard, flinty men and spare, dark-chiseled women, and he was the last of them, of those mountain people.

He was born out of the smoke and mists that crawled up the hollers like the heavy scent of death, bent men walking underneath it, axes slung heavy over shoulders, mine timbers piled jumbled by rutted, muddy tracks that slashed through stands of doomed timber.

He died, and he was the last of them, the ones born to the hills, the real and true hills, the hills of wraithful spirits and a wrathful God, the hills that aren't mountains but may be the most hardened mountains of all, mountains that loomed in his mind and the grizzled parts of his heart.

In the mountains of West Virginia.

My brother found the photographs, those brittle, faded pictures gathered from the cracked bottoms of cheap, ill-fitting bureau drawers and slipped between the pages of crumbling, yellowed albums. In the old pictures, the man stood straight, a young man then, trying to be taller. And he did not smile, knowing, perhaps, the spare and long life ahead of him.

And so the old man died. On Christmas Eve.

In the old pictures we could not see the cracked bones and raw skin, could not hear a heart born to beat for ninety years without the old man knowing why.

In the old pictures.

In the old pictures he was young and fast and lean. In the old pictures he did not smile.

And so the old man died.

Now, he lies in his box, tight-lipped and stern. At rest, they say.

But I know better. I touch his hand and face, waiting, not believing. He will shake off this box. He has work to do, a wife to care for.

But he does not.

For all but two years he lived his life in the county, never more than a lean handful of miles from where he was born. For those two years he went to a large and foreign city on the coast where he rode dark, growling, smoke-stale buses to work at midnight and came home in daylight to a wife crying at a table with a warped top, pale light reflecting crazily from a cracked window that looked out into a bin where garbage flowed from the tops of fatally dented cans and large rats sat poised, guarding their food.

She cried for the mountains.

It was a foreign city, but it was not the city that was foreign. It was the man, then young. Then falling quickly into old.

In the old pictures he did not smile.

I could not keep up, did not know where he went inside himself. He grew past me, out from me, and I never really knew him although I thought I did. He was there when I arrived and he was always there but he carried a place in him locked and tight that I never reached, a hard and private place buried so deep that no light ever warmed it, a place that hoarded a distant collection of jagged bits and parts that I would never know, never see. And I knew that locked place was there with him in the box. His. Forever. Not mine. Never mine.

And so the old man died.

I stand in the frigid wind on a low ridge, naked trees black and bent against a gray, smothering sky. The box, closed now, rests on crossbars, the raw, cold earth beneath it thrown over with green mats, as though the dirt that will cover the old man should not be seen.

The wind cuts my eyes and creeps into my bones.

There are some words said by men I do not know and I do not hear the words or know why I am standing here, and before the wind can quit this awful place, people are moving back to their cars, the box still on the crossbars. Not for long. I know.

Going away from a grave, people walk slowly, drive slowly, as though trying to slink quietly from the dead before the dead realize where they are, realize what is happening.

And they lay him down here, not more than a handful of miles from where he was born.

In the mountains of West Virginia.

By the time I get to the narrow highway I know the crossbars are gone, the box gone, the covers on the raw earth gone, and I know the black dirt is raining down and he is gone.

His humiliation over.

I am alone in the car. I pull to the side of the road on a gentle curve that looks out over a steep holler. I get out and stand by the guardrail, feeling the knife-thrust of the winter air. I pull it into my lungs.

I want to scream.

But I do not.

Not again.

Not ever.

2003

Where I'm From

All my life, no matter where I am, people know I am not *from* there. Know, perhaps, that I do not belong there. As I know.

I wrote once, long ago . . .

Everything I have ever done,
every place I have ever been,
has seemed no more than a temporary stop
on the way to someplace else.
And something always tries
to hold me back.
Just let me be gone
and be done with it.

I always want to be gone, to be someplace else, to be done with it.

And in that wanting, I never quite know where I'm from, never quite figure out what forms me, hardens me.

And when I think about it, all I get are images . . .

Images . . .

. . . mountains that seem to form us and send us tearing along their sides and down across the ridges to run staring-eyed out into the world like mythical beings charging out of the forests of Valhalla.

. . . hollows, those dark, pungent, quiet places that instill in us a way of moving, a way of seeing, a way of being. Hollows capped with smoke and mist, bottling us up, aging us, keeping us still, our lives clear and silent, like Mason jars of crystal moonshine gathering dust on a wooden shelf in a shed long forgotten on the back side of an abandoned ridge-top farm.

. . . hickory trees and chestnut split-rail fences and walnuts that fall in their soft and bursting black husks, rolling near-silently down the sides of hills.

. . . blackberry brambles woven into masses of thorn-guarded stands too thick to allow my arm inside, and rambling rose tangled so tightly against the leaning fences that, when the fences have long since disappeared, no one notices.

. . . paw-paw bushes.

. . . spike-hard stands of rhododendron.

. . . the smell of the hardwood forests in autumn, a smell so thick and rich that it can flow through your veins like blood—and indeed it is. Blood. Enough blood from the bodies of mountaineers to raise forests from hard desert and then lie in wait for us to come and breathe it in, again. It is not by accident, that color of old maple leaves.

. . . thin, wispy strands of acrid smoke escaping softly from the ends of long guns held by men, and sometimes women, who could hold those long guns for hours, days, years, generations.

. . . creeks, with their slow moving water the color of green eternity, glistening softly in the tiny shards of sunlight that manage to penetrate the overhanging limbs of trees that finger down into the softly moving clouds of dragonflies.

. . . sounds of banjo music played on front porches that have rails just high enough to put your foot on—if you're sitting in a rocking chair. The music . . . hard, ringing notes of pure, clear transcendence that maybe only front porch string pickers can ever really achieve.

. . . "kin," kinfolk, who sometimes, only sometimes, only forever sometimes . . . forgive, but who never, ever, forget. Kin. Old men and older women who lived lives that we will never know, can never be recorded, but lives that have become part of the evolutionary threads of which *our* lives are woven, lives of many colors, spread across the earth.

Images.

They are always with me, no matter where I am.

And when I think about it, I know where I'm from.

There has never really been any question.

There is only one such place.

But what does it matter now, near the end of it all?

2004

The Mountain

I leave the heavy stand of trees long before daylight and am high on the mountain, climbing steadily above tree line with no hint of light showing in the east. The cold night air keeps me energized and it is a long time before I begin to sweat. When the sweat does come, I get more comfortable, my muscles looser, my breathing deeper, my feet feeling every step of the trail through the worn, almost tattered, mountain boots.

The climbing is long but easy and I work at it gently in the dark, my body in low gear and pulling steadily toward the summit high and above me in the darkness.

The black sky presses down against my skull and the stars glitter against my face. When I look up, the stars seem flat against me and I think I can taste the stars but I cannot and in the end I shift my small pack, drink some water and strap the dark sky down over my head and keep going.

I reach the silent summit of the mountain before the light is anywhere and it pleases me to sit there in chilled isolation, breathing the thin black air and waiting for the light. I find a cleft between some boulders and settle myself in there feeling the stones, a stone cradle that holds me, and facing east.

I sit at 12,200 feet, 1,500 feet above tree line, and I know, at that moment, I am probably higher than anyone else in the county. Maybe the state. It is important to me.

Somewhere below me lies Santa Fe. I can see some of its lights, like a cluster of inverted stars, down far and away.

I am alone in the wilderness, but less than twenty miles from sixty thousand people.

I fish my water bottle out of the pack and drink. To sit on a summit waiting on the sun and drinking good water . . . maybe there is no way to improve on that, but I will try.

Stars fade and die. Somewhere out there sunlight is racing across tall prairie grass and I know it will be on me soon.

The black at the edge of the world begins to roll slowly back and then faster and then it is first light, one of my two favorite times of day. I get up from the boulders and find the highest point on the mountain, a bare knob that slopes down and rolls away to the north. Over the years climbers have added stones to the point of the summit and now there is a wide, five-foot-tall cairn. I climb on top of the cairn. There is no wind and in the ringing stillness I think I can hear the day thundering down on me from behind the flare of crystal light to the east.

I came up the evening before, hiking the Windsor Trail until I came to the hard rise that gained the last stand of trees. In the early afternoon I had met a few hikers but later, in the softer light near the trees, I met no one. The hikers in their expensive shoes and designer jackets had moved aside for me to pass, nodding politely. I did not stop to talk with them.

I camp alone in the trees, making no fire. I eat some bannock and drink some water and then sleep, rolled in my old sleeping bag, a foot-thick layer of pine needles cushioning me. Once, I am awakened by an owl making its flat noise and I sit up and wait and try to see it, but I never do. It is a night all men should have, I think.

In the morning I start on up the mountain.

I know that in the first part of my life it was always one of the things I loved most, looking toward a horizon I could not see and watching the light paint its way up and over and flow toward me wherever I was. And I love it now, in this second part of my life. Each time I see the light come I know I have another day, or at least a piece of it, and I am grateful. If the light comes again then anything is possible.

The light comes now.

I take some things from my pack. I have a small mountain stove and I light it, there in the paling air. I pour water from a plastic bottle into a small metal pot and put it on the stove. I turn the hissing stove low, to heat the water very slowly. I have coffee, pure Kona, and I dump the grounds directly into the water. While the coffee is heating, I eat my breakfast, watching the light grow. I eat aged Mimolette cheese and French bread, picked up in town the day before. I eat slowly, in time with the light.

When I finish my breakfast, the coffee has begun to steam and I turn off the stove and pour the dark liquid through a small piece of linen, directly into a strong porcelain cup I have carried to the mountain just to be able to sip coffee properly. I sip slowly.

The light keeps coming.

Some time passes; I don't know how much and I don't care. The Kona is as good as any coffee I have ever tasted and I drink every drop of it, loving the smoothness of it on my tongue and feeling its dark glow inside me.

I sit on the cairn, on the highest point of the mountain, facing east.

And the sun comes, pushing the light in front of it. The sun lights my face before it lights my chest and then flows golden and slowly down me, lighting each inch of me until I am alive with the light and the heat and for some short minutes I am the only thing west of the Pecos River that is in the sunlight. I own it. As I warm, I take off my old parka and then my shirt and then I am sitting half naked on the cairn in the sunlight.

I fish a short tube of thin PVC out of the pack. The tube is only an inch in diameter and six inches long, capped at both ends. I take off one of the caps and tip the tube into my hand and a single Churchill slides out, short, thick, rich, dark brown.

I sit warming in the sun, cigar smoke rising almost directly above me in the still air, the light washing down the mountain now and I know that somewhere down there people are beginning to stir around. I will not stir around. I will smoke the cigar at 12,200 feet and maybe I will pass out and maybe I will not. Either way, I do not care. I will sit here until it is time for me to leave, and only I will decide that.

When the cigar is half gone, I lay it carefully on the rocks. I bring the scuffed pack in front of me and open it, gently take out a small bottle and something wrapped in a soft piece of leather. I unwrap the leather and find a small piece of paper. I hold the paper for a while, up into the sun, gripping it, letting the rising sun warm my face and my hands and the tiny piece of paper.

There are names written on the paper. The names are written in a circle, so there is no name first among them, no name last. Except one, in the center of the circle—*Helen, always Helen.*

I read her name aloud, and then the other names, aloud into the world, one at a time . . .

Toran

Sarah

Darci

Tristan

Korin . . .

I scoot to the side and in the exact center of the cairn I remove several stones and make a small hole. I keep reading, saying the names clearly out into the fresh light on the mountain . . .

Ron

Linda

Ronnie

Tank

Denali

Kelli

Felix

Sandy

Willi

O'Keefe

Virginia

Stuckey

Hutchison

Norm

Din

Chaser

Chetlehe

Caton

Wendell

Nip . . .

Nip's name stops me for a moment, and I am back in the mountains of West Virginia, remembering . . .

And Pops, and Chuck, my other brothers out there.

I keep reading the names, amazed at the number, awed by their presence in my life.

And I know I'm getting ready for the end of it.

Finally, I wrap the piece of paper again in the soft leather.

I unscrew the top of the bottle—cognac, Marcel Ragnaud—and pour the magic into a small glass I have brought just for this.

I carefully set the bottle on the cairn, and stand.

I hold the cognac up into the rising sun, still gripping the leather-wrapped paper.

"Humans," I say. "Friends."

It is all I can think of to say.

And I drink.

I tuck the tiny leather package deep into the hole in the cairn. I replace the rocks, as carefully as I can.

I retrieve the cigar, light it, and pour more cognac into the glass. And a little onto the cairn.

When the sun is directly overhead, I am still sitting on the cairn.

2005

Journal's End

I stand in the pale light of sunset and look into the canyon, a lifetime below, the river so far down and away that it is nothing more than a silver thread, motionless against eons of time. I stand on the edge of eternity. Under my heels there is solid rock. Under my toes, there is 2,000 vertical feet of empty space.

I feel the weight of the old composition notebooks, the journals, in my hands. Dozens of them.

I don't know why I ever decided to keep a journal.

Chetlehe said only white guys were so proud of what they did that they actually had to go and write it down. He said if what I did really mattered, other people would write it down, or tell the stories to their children and grandchildren. I wouldn't have to. Write it down. I thought about that for a long time. It worried the hell out of me. It still does.

Because other people didn't write it down.

Because I am only left with me.

No matter.

I will finish this last entry and then I will not keep a journal anymore.

I stack the journals on the rock beside my feet. I bend and take one of the old notebooks in my hand. I flip it open. South Carolina.

I close the notebook and hold it for a moment, thinking. But I came here to do something, and it will be done. I sail the notebook out into the emptiness of time. For a second or two it sails flat and fast, and then the covers fly open and the notebook flutters like a wounded bird trying to tumble to safety, wings not beating the air but flailing. Useless.

And then the notebook is gone.

The process has started.

I take another notebook and sail it, not even bothering to flip it open to see where . . .

It falls away.

And then another and another.

And I take my foot and shove the small pile over the edge of the canyon.

I lose sight of them long before they ever hit the timeless stones that will keep them.

Lee Maynard was born and raised in the hardscrabble ridges and hard-packed mountains of West Virginia, an upbringing that darkens and shapes much of his writing.

Maynard's novel, *Crum*, was the first original work of fiction published by Washington Square Press, an imprint of Simon & Schuster. In its first month of publication, the novel rose to No. 8 on the Doubleday Best Seller List and was nominated for the Penn Hemingway Award. The novel has been taught in English literature classes in a score of prestigious universities. Sometimes called "the book that wouldn't die," *Crum* was republished by Vandalia Press in the summer of 2001. It was the first book published by Vandalia and within a year became the best selling book in the history of the university.

The National Endowment for the Arts awarded a Literary Fellowship in Fiction to Maynard for Crum's sequel, *Screaming With The Cannibals*, published by Vandalia Press in 2002 and rapidly overtaking *Crum* in sales. A third volume of the Crum series, *The Scummers*, is in progress.

Maynard's short fiction has appeared in such publications such as *Columbia Review of Literature* and *Appalachian Heritage*. His work will soon appear in the literary magazine, *Kestrel*.

As a journalist, Maynard has been an assignment writer for *Reader's Digest* for more than two decades. His journalism and non-fiction work has appeared more than 100 times in publications as diverse as *The Saturday Review*, *Rider* magazine, *Washington Post*, *Country America*, *Dual Sport News* and *Christian Science Monitor*.

Much of Maynard's work is highly controversial. *Crum* was banned in his home state and, even today, stirs deep, conflicting emotions among the people of Appalachia. Nevertheless, Maynard's work has been critically acclaimed. His prose has been held in comparison to Hemingway, Twain, Harris, Faulkner and Salinger.

Specializing in the novel, Maynard has taught at many national and regional workshops, including the Appalachian Writers Workshop, Southwest Writers Workshop, and West Virginia Writers Conference. He has served as Writing Master at Allegheny Echoes.

Maynard has been a management and editorial consultant to newspapers, magazines and small publishing companies. He once served as a college president. An avid outdoorsman, he is a mountaineer, sea kayaker, skier and former professional river runner. He once rode a motorcycle from Santa Fe, New Mexico, to the Arctic Circle. He lives near Santa Fe.